One Knight Only

Realm of Honor

MICHELLE MILES

This is a work of fiction. All characters, organizations and events portrayed in this novel are either products of the author's imagination or used fictitiously.

ONE KNIGHT ONLY

This title was previously published.

Cover Design by Erin Dameron-Hill

Copyright © 2016, Second Edition
Dusty Tome Publishing

ISBN: 978-1-7333887-4-0

Chapter 1

Maggie Chase gripped the steering wheel until her knuckles turned white as she navigated the tiny car through a torrential downpour. The windshield wipers swished back and forth at a speedy rate—which, due to the pouring buckets of rain, turned out to be not so speedy after all. Her bright lights reflected off the sheets of rain and she squinted, as if that would help her see through the dark deluge.

"Please, God," she muttered under her breath. "Get me through this in one piece."

She had resorted to verbal prayer instead of a silent one, hoping that God would hear her even though He hadn't heard a word she'd pled over the last few harrowing hours. So, she drove on, desperate to be off this bumpy, one-lane road. Maggie could feel the tires slipping in the muddy road, causing her to grip the steering wheel tighter. Fear was the only thing keeping her from slamming on the brakes.

"You think you're so smart, Mags," she mumbled, staring hard through the windshield. "Coming out here looking for evidence of a guy who's been dead for over six hundred years."

Oh, sure. Traveling through Scotland sounded like a *grand* idea. A student of medieval literature in grad school, she was completely fascinated with Sir Derron, a fourteenth-century knight and one of Europe's most romantic jousting champions. Seeing the actual site of the tournament would make it easier to unravel the story of his mysterious life and death. She'd found it strange the man seemed to have no surname.

The car jostled violently as Maggie hit a huge, muddy pothole. She cringed, sucked in a sharp breath at the loud crunch. *That can't be good.* There was an immediate *thump-thump, thump-thump* and she quickly found keeping control of the steering wheel was a feat beyond her abilities.

Maggie depressed the brake with as much ease as possible,

slowing the ailing car to a bumpy crawl. Even with the swishing wipers, rivulets of rain streamed down the windshield.

"Figures."

She snatched her cell phone but the battery neared the red mark, desperate for a charge. Not that it mattered. She couldn't even get a call out since she was in a dead zone. Tears blurred her vision as she thought of calling her dad, wanting to hear his friendly voice and whine to him. *"Um, Dad? I've taken a wrong turn somewhere around Dumfries and I'm completely lost. Oh, and by the way, I'm stuck on a deserted road in the driving rain at night, all alone."*

Dad would have sympathy for a few minutes before telling her she should have stayed home. She should have known the trip would be doomed from the start when an Icelandic volcanic eruption interrupted her flight departure. Then her best friend and traveling partner, Beth, came down with the flu the day before they were to leave.

But Maggie was determined to go anyway, even though her father had begged her to stay.

"Don't go, magpie," he said. "It's a sign."

"You always say that." At the time, she'd rolled her eyes at him. Now she wished she'd listened. It *was* a sign. Even the universe was trying to tell her to stay away.

"Maybe I do, but this time I feel it in my bones. Stay here at least until Beth is well enough to travel with you."

"I can't wait, Dad. I have to go. I promise to check in every day. Twice a day," she added for extra emphasis.

He relented but he still didn't like her going alone. She hadn't been immune to the worried crease on his forehead. It felt like Maggie's one and only chance to find out who Sir Derron was and what had happened to him. Now she stared through the foggy glass into the dark night and thumped the wheel in frustration. Maybe she could wait it out.

Ten minutes turned into twenty and twenty into thirty. It didn't appear to be stopping anytime soon.

"May as well get it over with, Mags."

She didn't even have an umbrella.

Heaving a sigh, she switched off the wipers and cut the motor. When she flung open the door, the rain poured in and she grunted, stepping onto the muddy earth. Immediately soaked to the bone, she did a quick survey of the four wheels. Nothing looked out of the ordinary.

Perhaps there was something broken under the car. With a grimace, she squatted, trying hard not to fall into the mud, and peeked underneath. Of course, in the dark with no flashlight, she couldn't see a thing. She stood and kicked the tire as hard as she could.

"I hate you." As if that would make it all better.

Then another thought occurred to her. She grabbed the front wheel and gave it a hard yank. Her hands slipped off the wet rubber and she fell backward in a puddle of mud with a splash.

The last thing Maggie expected to see was her front wheel slanting away from the car at an odd angle. She was no mechanic but she guessed it meant her axle was broken.

"Damn it," she shouted. Even if no one heard her, it sure made her feel better.

The only option she had left was to start walking. But to where, she had no clue.

Maggie lugged her suitcase up the steep incline, her wet hair plastered to her head and dripping in her eyes. She cursed the weight of the thing, but knew she couldn't leave it and her purse in the broken car. Besides, she had dry clothes inside the suitcase. Once she got wherever she was going, she could change.

In the morning, she vowed, she would call the rental company and tell them what happened and hope they wouldn't send her a bill for the damages. Maybe they could send another car out to her. Then she would call Dad to let him know she was still alive and well.

Maggie's arm muscles burned from carrying the suitcase. Over the rocky, muddy terrain, the wheels were no use. She was wet, tired, and hungry, and not even sure she could take one more step.

A streak of lightning split the night sky, outlining a huge castle on the top of the hill. She blinked, confused. She was nearly standing in front of it and she hadn't even *seen* it. She stared at the dark space in front of her, trying to make out the building. She wiped a hand over her wet face, but it didn't help. It wasn't there.

Another bolt and then it was there again. With high turrets and a yawning opening, beckoning her inside. It looked ancient. In the second she saw it she could see crumbling walls. Once the light had faded, though, she couldn't see it anymore. *If only she had a flashlight.*

Maggie slung her purse over her head so the strap crossed her body. She hefted the suitcase in both arms and held it against her chest. She waited, holding her breath, for the next flash of light.

And there it was again. Standing against the inky blackness like a beacon of hope. She bolted into a run, heading directly for it. Once the light faded, she couldn't see it again, as if it had disappeared from the horizon. Still, she ran for it, rain pelting her face. Her feet splashed in puddles, adding to her sogginess.

Her breath huffed out in clouds and she realized the temperature had suddenly dropped. Not only wet, now she was chilled to the bone. Her teeth chattered and she couldn't stop the uncontrollable shivering. The castle she'd seen was her only salvation out of this dreadful Scottish weather.

Maggie paused, her lungs stinging from her mad dash. Her arms ached from holding her suitcase. Her legs burned from the exertion. Now at the top of the hill, she glanced around, perplexed. No castle. Had she officially stepped into the *Twilight Zone*? Had she merely hallucinated the castle in her desperation to get out of the elements?

She waited for the next flash of light. Perhaps she had misjudged and blindly ran the wrong way. Her heart throbbed painfully as she waited.

Overhead, thunder rumbled. Maggie stared hard into the darkness, holding her breath in anticipation of the lightning that was sure to follow. Seconds later, not one but two flashes came. She was only ten steps from the entrance of the castle.

She ran toward it as the glow faded and smacked into the wooden door. She nearly bounced off but managed to maintain her footing. Even so, her suitcase slipped out of her hand, landing with a muffled thud at her feet. She reached out and ran her hand down the solid wood. It was real. She wasn't hallucinating. Should she knock? Would anyone answer? It seemed deserted. Couldn't hurt if she opened the door and stepped in. Right?

The hinges groaned with displeasure as the door swung open wide. Inside it was dry. Dark, but dry. Maggie picked up her suitcase and stepped across the threshold of the deserted castle. Instantly, warmth surrounded her as she stood in the doorway. Her clothes dripped on the stone floor, the only sound in the deafening silence.

"Hello?"

No answer. But something made her shiver. And it wasn't merely the cold rain running down her back.

She glanced left and right. No furnishings, no nothing. It would also mean no telephone and no hot meal. Or blankets. Or running water.

Still, it was better than nothing. To her left, she saw the flicker of yellow and orange light, which beckoned her. Had it been there before? She didn't remember seeing it when she first stepped inside. She shrugged and headed toward it, looking forward to drying off and warming up. She hoped she wasn't about to get shot for trespassing. But as she ventured farther inside, she saw no signs of life.

"Hello? Is anyone here?" Her voice echoed through the empty depths.

Maggie stepped into a room with a gigantic hearth on one side. She'd had a fascination with castles from the time she could imagine herself as a princess waiting at the top of the highest turret for Prince Charming to come riding to her rescue on his white steed. Seeing pictures and being inside one was very different. This seemed to be the great hall, where those past inhabitants sat at long wooden tables feasting on roast boar, loaves of crusty bread, wheels of cheese and roasted vegetables. At least, that's what her stomach and imagination thought.

The room was empty except for a warm fire blazing in the hearth, crackling with life and lifting her spirits. She dropped her suitcase and wrung out her hair, squeezing the excess wetness out of it.

Thunder rumbled and Maggie was very glad she was inside, creepy castle or no. At least she was out of the cold. But how could there be a fire in a deserted castle? It didn't make sense and she was too tired and too soggy to go searching about. She hoped whoever she shared her warmth with was friendly.

In the morning, she would have to explore the ruins. The historical junkie in her couldn't walk out of here without at least taking a few notes and pictures. Her new digital camera, bought for the trip, was tucked neatly under folds of clothes inside her suitcase.

Remembering technology still existed she fumbled in her

handbag for her cell phone. She scowled at the words NO SERVICE at the top of the screen. It figured.

Finally, she plunked down on the cold stone floor, stretching her hands toward the fire. She'd have to stay here tonight. Despite the warmth, a chill ran through her. Gooseflesh rose on her arms and the hair on the back of her neck stood at attention.

She peered into the shadows and strained her ears to listen for any faint sound. She saw no one. She heard no one. The castle was dead silent save for the crackling fire. Even though it stood to reason whoever built the fire was still nearby.

"Is there anyone here?" she called again.

Was she insane to stay in the middle of a ruined castle all alone? What if there was some vagrant spending the night here? What if they were a serial killer? What if she didn't wake up in the morning?

Get a grip, Mags.

She chastised herself for allowing her thoughts to run away into the dark and dangerous. The place seemed deserted.

When silence was her answer, she shrugged off a shiver and reached for her suitcase. Glancing around the shadows, she flipped it open and rummaged around until she found a cardigan, a long-sleeved shirt, jeans and dry underwear. She peeled out of her wet, muddy clothes, dumping them to the side, and quickly pulled on the dry ones. She double-checked to make sure her camera was indeed safe and dry.

She took another pair of jeans, rolled them up and wrapped another sweater around the pair. It would have to do as a makeshift pillow. She bunched it under her head and lay down on the hard, stone floor. As she gazed at the warm fire, her eyelids became heavy and soon she was fast asleep.

Sir Finian McCullough watched the lovely lass from his prison in the spirit world as she entered the castle. The moment she stepped across the threshold he couldn't stop watching her. He wanted to touch her, to feel that creamy, damp skin on his. *Och*, to *feel* anything. This lass was the one who'd come to be his savior. She was here because she could see the castle, which was invisible to all but the one person who could break the curse.

I curse you to live in solitude until someone with a noble heart comes to right your wrongs.

She was tall and lithe and wet. Dripping from head to toe. Her long dark hair hung limply down her back. Her clothes clung to all her curves.

The castle—his family's castle—was nothing but a ruin on the hilltop. Uncared for, unloved, unneeded. He had felt the same, becoming long forgotten through the pages of history. Or so Elyne said. She had made sure of that. Penance, she'd said, for she constantly reminded him, for killing her lover. As if his curse of being stuck between the Otherworld and the human world wasn't penance enough, he had to be stalked by the Fae princess.

"Hello?"

The girl's voice was soft but with a sexy undertone that made him wish he was human again. Oh, the things he could do if he weren't but a wisp of air.

The lass stared into the darkness, her clothes dripping circles all around her and leaving water spots on the stone flooring. Mayhap she looked for signs of life. He inched closer to get a better look, reaching out a wispy hand to touch—

"Don't even think about it, Finn," Elyne said, making him stop short.

The bloody princess of Faery always showed up at the most inopportune moments. He suppressed a growl of annoyance.

To his surprise, the lass shuddered as if she'd heard the warning.

"Ah, but look at her, Elyne. The poor wee lassie's cold and wet."

Elyne snapped her fingers and the fireplace in the great hall flamed to life. The woman picked up her case and walked towards it.

"Like a moth drawn to a candle flame," Elyne said, shaking her head. "She shouldn't be here, Finn. You know that."

"If you dinna want her here, then why then did you let her see the castle?"

"I didn't *let* her see it," Elyne protested, propping her hands on her hips. "She saw it on the hill of her own accord."

Finn clucked his tongue. "*Och*, lass, dinna lie. 'Tis verra unbecoming."

Elyne furrowed her blonde brow, fire flashing in her cornflower-blue eyes. "All right, so I did. She was stranded. Her car broke down. I couldn't leave her out there in the rain."

As if on cue, thunder rumbled the castle.

"Alas! So ye *do* have a heart," Finn said. "And here I thought ye lacked one."

"If I do, it's because of you." Elyne folded her arms and scowled.

Six hundred and sixty years in ghostland would cause lesser men to go mad. But not Finn. No, he had to be saddled with the Faery crown princess who followed him everywhere in this empty, drafty castle who never let him forget he'd killed her love, a Fae knight.

Hard as he'd tried to convince her otherwise, Elyne couldn't be persuaded the knight's death had been an accident. Finn's lance had been tipped to make it look like murder. He'd been framed by someone he loathed, someone to whom he owed a great deal of money. He'd paid for it with his own life and, in death, Elyne had cursed him. Trapping him for eternity in his invisible castle, which—blessedly—wasn't so invisible to this bonnie lass.

Finn followed the pretty stranger into the great hall, Elyne hot on his trail. Orange and yellow light flickered on the lass's pale features. She had high cheekbones and a straight, narrow nose. Her damp hair hung down to her waist, and when she wrung it out, it made a large puddle on the floor. Then she held some strange silver device, peering at it before tossing it back into her bag. The lassie plunked down, stretching her hands to the fire.

Finn glanced at Elyne, who narrowed her eyes at him. "What?"

"I was thinking…"

"Always dangerous," Elyne interjected.

"You said one with a noble heart would come to break the curse. She's the only one that's stepped foot in the castle in centuries."

"So?" Elyne shrugged one thin shoulder.

"Are ye going to tell me she isna the one?" Finn demanded. "She's here, is she no'?"

Elyne flushed a deep crimson, the color high in her cheeks. "Ah…aye, she's here."

"Or did ye tell me a falsehood? Is the curse real?"

"Oh, no falsehood. The curse is very real. It's that…I…well…" She paused, her finger curling around one long tendril of pale hair.

"Out with it."

"I'm not sure how to break the curse."

"What do ye mean?" Finn thundered. He clenched his fist, his jaw tight. "Ye cursed me and now ye canna uncurse me?"

"I'm rather a novice when it comes to curses, Finn. And I never really thought this scenario would play out." She flashed a sheepish grin.

"*Och*, so ye thought to put me in this purgatory for eternity? For killing yere knight? That wasna even my fault. It was set up." He paced back and forth. "If I wasna nothing more than a wisp o' air, I'd wring yere Faery neck."

"Well, you are and you can't." Elyne folded her arms across her chest and pursed her lips. "I made a mistake, all right?"

"Aye, and how do ye intend to fix it?" he demanded.

"I'm working on it. The girl is here, though. She can clearly see the castle so at least that's a start." She chewed on her lower lip, looking thoughtful. "There is…one thing I could do."

"Aye? What is it?"

Ignoring him, she shook her head, waving away whatever she'd been mulling over. "No, no. I can't do that. 'Tis forbidden. Against every law of magic there is. And aside from that my mother will kill me."

"I'll kill ye if ye dinna stop babbling tell me what it is," Finn demanded.

"It's a crazy idea," Elyne said. "And if I do this then I could get into serious trouble in the Otherworld."

"Do ye mean to use yere Faery hocus-pocus?"

"There is magic involved, aye." Elyne nodded. "But what I'm considering, Finn, has major repercussions."

"Well, out with it then. I'll be the judge of that." He pinned her with a glare.

"The curse states you're doomed to live out eternity alone until someone with a noble heart can right your wrongs. Well, here is your someone." She pointed to the girl in the great hall. "One could only guess she has a noble heart to help right your wrongs."

"And…?"

"And so, I'm thinking she can help you. The past you, I mean. At least that's how I'm interpreting the curse. I could send you back in time. With the girl."

Finn was silent as he considered this. He hovered near her, enjoying the view. A bonnie lass, to be sure. Her face was like porcelain, as if carved by the angels themselves. Her eyes were the color of green jewels winking in the firelight. She shivered then and hugged herself, glancing around. Her gaze met his. But of course, she couldn't see him.

"Is there anyone here?"

When she spoke, her breath came out in white plumes. Her voice shook. He hadn't intended to give her a fright and backed off, moving away so she couldn't feel his presence. She shrugged, then, and opened her strange case, rummaging through it.

He watched her with interest as she pulled out garment after garment. He never really expected her to take off her wet clothes and he chided himself for his surprise. Of course, she would. She thought she was alone.

A warm yellow glow flickered over her glistening skin, the curves of her youthful body. She had a flat stomach and long, muscular legs. He couldn't find one flaw. He longed to feel her warmth, her touch. Finn watched as the woman, now dressed, curled up on the stone floor, pillowing her head on rolled up clothes in front of the fire.

"Well? What do you think?" Elyne asked, snapping him out of his longing.

"What are these...repercussions?" he asked.

"Sifting humans to their past is forbidden, for one thing."

"*Och*, but think of it, Elyne," he said, never taking his eyes off the girl. "With the bonnie lass at my side, things will be different. Going back, I willna kill yere knight with the tipped lance. Ye will get him back and I willna be cursed. 'Tis perfect."

Returning with what he knew already, he could stop things from happening before they happened. He'd know his lance was tipped and could do something about it before going into that round.

"Oh, but there's one teensy little problem. If—and I do mean if—I send you back, you won't remember a thing about the last six hundred years. That's one of the inevitable side effects about, you know, time travel and Fae magic."

So much for going back with his memory intact. He scowled as he looked at Elyne, his mind working. If he wasn't allowed to keep his memories, he'd need another way.

"Then 'tis no' only up to me, lassie. 'Tis up to you, too."

"What do you mean by that?"

"Yere coming with us."

"No, I'm not."

"Oh aye, ye are. And yere gonna to help her see how great I am. The bonnie lass will keep me out of the gambling tents, I've no doubt."

"I am *not* going to play matchmaker." She said this in her best haughty tone.

"It shouldna be too hard for ye. All ye have to do is give her a nudge in my direction. My charms will work after that."

"You are an overconfident jackass. I won't do it." She crossed her arms, looking indignant.

"Ye will if ye want yere knight to live." Finn lowered his eyes, glaring at her but keeping his voice calm.

"Bloody hell," Elyne muttered. She huffed out a long, exasperated sigh. "If she fails—"

"She willna fail," Finn said. He would make sure of it…though he wasn't sure how he would make sure of it.

There was a long pause as Elyne hovered nearby. She propped her hands once again on her rounded hips, watching the woman sleep. "I should never have brought it up. It's against Fae Law."

"Ye wouldna mention it had ye not already made up yere mind. Ye willna give up yere one chance at having yere love back, will ye?" Finn pressed on despite Elyne's huffing.

Elyne scrunched her face in a scowl, knowing Finian had her right where he wanted her. She'd agree to the idea, they'd all go back in time, and he wouldn't kill Derron. Then Elyne could send the lass back once all was done and she would be happy while Finn would live out the rest of his days in his castle.

"You really push me too far, Finn."

He shrugged. "'Tis up to ye. But seems to me worth a try."

"You know I'll do it and you know why I'll do it. But I warn you, Finn, kill him a second time and you will cease to exist. Understood?"

"I canna agree to that when I willna remember it on the morrow." He flashed a wicked grin.

"Oh, fear not, sir knight. You'll remember. Eventually. I'll make sure of it."

Chapter 2

When Maggie woke up, she had a splitting headache. Probably because she'd used a pair of rolled-up jeans and a sweater as a pillow. She strained her ears to listen but all she heard was silence. The rain had finally stopped and she could still feel the warm glow of the fire, which had to be embers by now.

Yet she couldn't quite bring herself to open her eyes. She did a quick mental survey and thought it odd she wasn't freezing to death on the cold stone floor. In fact, she felt positively warm and snuggly.

She rolled over with a groan, the mattress sighing with her weight and the linen covering swishing with her movement. *Wait a second. I didn't fall asleep on a bed.* Her eyes blinked open to the pale morning light and focused directly on the fire blazing in the hearth, sending a warm golden glow across the room.

Maggie sat bolt upright, her head objecting to the sudden movement.

"What the hell?" she blurted.

She hadn't fallen asleep on a bed. Nor had there been fine linen sheets to cover her. Her heart sputtered a fast cadence and her breathing increased to a rapid rasp, loud in her ears. She put a hand to her head, rubbing the taut skin at the hairline. She squeezed her eyes shut, hoping she was in some weird dream. Yet when she opened them again, she was still faced with the blazing fire in the hearth.

She hiccupped, her breath catching in her throat as she realized she was not in the abandoned castle's great hall with the blazing fire. This hearth, it seemed, was nestled into a stone wall surrounded by tapestries. The stone floor was covered in a thick rug.

No, this wasn't where she'd fallen asleep last night at all.

"This is a dream," she said aloud.

It had to be, right? It wasn't real. Because it was the only explanation her tired mind would accept. Maggie slid to the edge of the bed, her bare feet hitting the cold floor and sending a shiver up her spine. Glancing down, she wore the underwear she had changed into last night—her lacy black bra and matching panties. But where were the rest of her clothes? Her suitcase? How in the *hell* did she get in this bed?

Staring into the fire, she mentally retraced her steps. The car breaking down, walking in the rain, getting soaked to the bone. And then the castle on the hilltop that was there and then wasn't there. *Yes, the castle.* She glanced around. Was she still in that castle now? This one was fully furnished, it seemed. Whereas the one she ended up in last night was empty. And cold. And dark.

Maybe someone had found her sleeping on the floor? She'd been so tired she didn't notice when that someone had lifted her and brought her back to a warm bed. And any minute now that someone would bring her a steaming mug of coffee.

A groan behind her made her spin around, grabbing the linen and holding it to her bosom. On the bed, a dark-haired man she had never seen before rolled onto his back. He was shirtless, showing off every ripple of muscle and fantastic pectorals, the likes of which she had never seen in her life. Smooth, hairless skin with tremendous biceps and a narrow waist disappearing into the bedding that made her imagination run away with hot fantasies.

"Oh, dear me," she breathed.

Who was this man? More importantly, where the bloody hell was she?

A soft snore escaped him and Maggie couldn't stop staring at that beautiful chest rising and falling with every breath. His long dark hair spilled around him. And his face…

"Wow."

The word slipped out before she could stop it. His chiseled face hosted a strong square chin with a tiny indention in the center covered with a day's growth of beard, a perfect nose, pronounced cheekbones, dark eyebrows. She propped a knee on the mattress, scooting closer to lean over him for a better look, amazed at how powerful his face appeared. Fierce. A man not to be trifled with. A man who knew what he wanted and wasn't afraid to get it.

Maggie cocked her head to the side, enjoying her view, a smile tugging at the corner of her mouth. For a moment, she had forgotten she was in a strange place. Her long, auburn locks cascaded over her shoulder and brushed against him. The baby-fine strands must have tickled his skin, for his eyes popped open and stared back at her.

Gorgeous silvery eyes met hers and she blinked and pulled back.

But he was faster than she. He grasped her by her upper arms and dragged her to him, placing her on his lap as his large, powerful hands gripped her hips. Maggie was completely aware of all of him now. A hot fantasy splashed through her mind as she shifted on top of him. What was under the linen was apparent between her legs. Every last inch of him. Her hands landed on his chest, her senses delighting in the warm, soft skin beneath her palms.

His gaze lingered on her face a moment before gliding down, pausing on her lace-covered breasts and then continuing his downward jaunt. He fingered the waistband of her panties, running the pad of his forefinger over first one hipbone then her abdomen then back again.

The small movement sent white-hot heat shooting through her, awaking parts of her that weren't used to being on alert so early in the morning. Especially without a cup of coffee.

His hands moved up her sides then, desire evident in those depthless silver eyes…and the appendage on which she happened to be sitting.

"Now, lass, ye best be telling me who ye are and why yere in my bed. No' that I mind, but I canna recall tupping ye last eve and I always remember bonnie lasses I tup."

His deep-timbre brogue purred the words and sent a delicious rumble right through her. She resisted the urge to shudder. She liked this dream-state that put her in a strange place with a very sexy man beneath her hands, straddling his lap with nothing but a breath of linen and cotton between them. It wouldn't take much for her to remove that material and get exactly what she was feeling.

But she wasn't the kind of girl to have sex with a stranger, was she?

I could be.

Besides, this was just a dream. She would wake up any minute in the cold, deserted castle all alone. And then she would be faced with the problem of how to get herself back to civilization. In the meantime, she could do anything she wanted in her dream. Couldn't she?

"I certainly don't mind being in your bed," she told him. He really was quite delicious. She ran her hands along the smooth skin of his chest and leaned toward him.

He grasped her wrists in iron fists and pushed her back. "Ye are the one trespassing."

How in the world could he have the nerve to look angry at her? Maggie wrenched her wrists free and sat up, crossing her arms over her chest. She could play that game, too. She was good at it. Sitting on his lap, she thought, gave her a position of being in control. She glared down at him, though even she had to admit it was hard to glare at a man that looked as good as he did.

"Maybe you should tell me who *you* are, then?" she demanded.

The burly man gripped her hips and flipped her onto her back in one swift movement. Suddenly her position of control and power was removed as he hovered over her, pinning her against the mattress. His brawny weight pressed into her. With one hand on his shoulder, Maggie tried to push him away but he quickly captured her wrist in his big hand and held her arm above her head, thereby removing any chance she could wiggle free.

"Ye best not play games wi' me, lassie."

Ohhh. With his words, his chest rumbled against Maggie's breasts, sending all sense from her mind and threatening to melt her into a pool of jelly. Much to her surprise and delight, his thick waist and hips had managed to nestle between her thighs. Wait— how *did* he manage that? Was she completely pliant in his arms so quickly? She didn't even know him. All she did know was he had the most gorgeous eyes she had ever had the good fortune of staring into and that his hardened body was on top of her.

Maggie couldn't resist, she reached up with her free hand and ran a fingertip over his chiseled jaw, feeling the strong curves and pausing under his lower lip at that sexy cleft. Even his mouth was beautiful with a thin line of lips desperate for her to kiss.

He blinked, complete surprise on his face. A breath shuddered out of Maggie, her chest rising and falling against his naked one. Her lips parted in anticipation and she ran her tongue over them, still mesmerized by his kissable mouth.

A guttural moan rumbled deep in his throat before his head dipped and his mouth met hers. An experienced mouth that knew exactly how to kiss a woman. It was slow and thoughtful at first, as though testing her, and then deepened into something fiercer. The strong hardness of his lips seemed made for hers, as though Maggie had been waiting all her life for a mouth like his to kiss her.

Her thighs tightened around his hips, the bones biting into her flesh. She rocked against him as blissful heat surged through her and made her want more of him. He groaned into her mouth, his hand loosening on her wrist. She slipped her arms around his neck, pulling him closer as his weight pressed into her.

Maggie flattened her foot against his calf, sliding down ever so slowly along the sinew of muscle and brawn. She had officially deemed this *the best dream ever.*

The chamber door banged open and he jerked away from her, leaving her breathless and her lips swollen and damp in his fiery aftermath.

Typical. Dreams always got interrupted when they were getting good.

"Good morrow, Sir Finian. 'Tis time to—oh. A thousand pardons, good sir."

A wiry young man with big blue eyes and fiery red hair stood staring at the two of them tangled up on the bed, leaving Maggie feeling exposed. He cocked a grin as he looked at her.

"I dinna ken ye had company."

"Nor I, Fergus." Finn glanced back down at her, his eyes lingering with hers. "A fine lass she is, too."

Her cheeks flushed hot with humiliation. For a dream, Maggie's embarrassment was certainly real enough. She punched him in the shoulder, her blood pounding as she shuddered with mortification. "Get off me, you brute."

Surprise flickered across his face as he leaned back, lifting his weight off her. She wiggled out from under him and snagged the sheet, bouncing from the curtained bed. Her dream-state allowed her to be the wanton hussy about to get hot and sweaty with a hot stranger. But in real life she was so not that kind of girl. Especially if someone was watching.

"Interrupted. That figures. Go away. I'm not done yet." Maybe if she squeezed her eyes shut, she could will away the young man and get back in bed with the Scottish hottie.

Finn slid to the edge of the bed, giving Maggie a glorious view of thick, muscular thighs. To her relief, the covering on the bed managed to hide his most masculine part. She tried not to think about that, especially when only moments ago she'd had the good fortune to feel it. Still, she couldn't stop staring at the almost-naked man before her. Broad chest, thick thighs, wide shoulders...*oh-so-nice.*

"Mayhap ye should be telling me who ye are, lass, and how ye managed to get into my keep," Finn said, his gaze hardening into something almost fearful.

Maggie stood her ground and glared right back. She wasn't about to let some over-muscled thug intimidate her, even if he was a figment of her delicious imagination. Her head still throbbed from sleeping on a cold stone floor.

Or had she really fallen asleep on the floor? Maybe she'd dreamed the castle ruins, too.

"I don't think I like your tone, buddy."

Somehow during their stare-down, young Fergus had inched toward his master, a tartan in his hand. Finn snatched it from him and stood, wrapping the plaid around his thick waist. In the few seconds the linen covering fell away and he covered his hips, Maggie caught a glimpse of something spectacular.

"Mayhap I'll leave ye to her then." Fergus skittered from the room.

The chamber door banged closed behind him. Maggie and Finn continued their staring contest and she wasn't about to lose this one.

"A silver-tongued she-devil, are ye?" he asked, breaking the silence.

Maggie had been called a lot of things in her lifetime, but a silver-tongued she-devil had never exactly been at the top of the list. She tucked a lock of her wavy auburn hair behind one ear.

"I'm not going to argue with you because this is all a dream and any minute now, I'm going to wake up in a deserted castle," she said.

Finn quirked a black eyebrow. "Ye have a strange accent, lass."

"I do, eh? And I suppose you don't?" To her American ear, he sounded Scottish and sexy.

She stepped closer to him, leaned toward him to get a better look. As if she needed one. His golden skin was taut over thick muscles with a sprinkling of dark hair on his forearms. She reached for him, placing her hand on his hardened biceps. Not that she didn't know what he felt like from before—he was as hard as a rock and more powerful looking than any man she'd ever dated.

This was certainly a departure from her reality. The men she was used to were far from this hunky. In fact, her ex-boyfriend had been a beanpole compared to Finn. Her ex was wiry and tall with round-rimmed glasses and sandy-brown hair drawn back into a ponytail. Scholarly, she thought now. A typical professor-like appearance to go with his expensive doctorate in medieval literature.

Finn was nothing like her ex. Intense, powerful, aggressive. Yes, those were words she'd use to describe him. Straight from the pages of history. If this man was real, she'd want to talk to him for hours, find out what made him tick, learn about his life. And Dad, as a professor of medieval history, would be so jealous.

She glanced up through her thick, dark lashes to see him giving her an inquisitive look. The fire had dwindled in his silver eyes to embers with an underlying belligerence.

With a long, cool smile, Maggie took a piece of his taut skin between her thumb and forefinger and pinched. Would her dream-induced mind let her envision such a flesh-and-blood man? He certainly felt real.

"*Och.*" Finn jerked his arm out of her grasp. "What do ye think yere doing, lassie?"

"Okay, first of all, stop calling me lassie. Second of all, I'm trying to wake up. *This* is a dream. I know it is. And you're not real. Even though I wish you were real because you're really hot." He had all the parts she needed to make all her parts stand up and cheer. She extended her arm to him. "Here. Now pinch me."

"What?"

"Did I stutter? Pinch me," she said.

"Are ye daft? Mayhap ye fell and hit yere head, lass."

"Cute. You're a real funny man, aren't you? Now will you pinch me already?" Maggie shook her arm at him to press her point.

With a huff of annoyance and a shrug of one massive shoulder, Finn reached over, took the skin of her forearm between his meaty fingers and pinched. Hard.

"Ow!" Maggie slapped his hand away, covering her arm where he had left a red mark.

"Ye bid me do it, lass." Now he regarded her with hauteur, crossing those hefty forearms over that magnificent chest.

"It hurt." She pouted.

But then she realized—*it hurt*. Like hell.

And she was still standing before an almost naked Scotsman—almost naked herself—in his keep. With the fire continuing to burn behind her. In a strange place that was not where she had ended up the night before. And her head still pounded.

Crap.

"Okay," she said slowly. "Clearly that didn't wake me up." Still convinced it was a dream, she took a tentative step toward the man. He had pinned her against the bed and she had felt every ounce of him. He had kissed her with a wild passion she had never experienced—and she had felt it. A pinch later and she was sure she felt that, so why was her mind convinced she was dreaming?

Something had to make her believe she was really standing here. She leaned toward him, reaching for him. He stood rock still as her hands slipped over his biceps, caressing his taut skin. She stood on tiptoe, tilting her head back to look up into his heavenly eyes. She guessed he had at least eight inches on her five-foot-six height. Never taking her gaze from him, she ran her hands over his chest, dared to move lower to cup his package…and squeezed.

He jerked back from her staring at her in utter disbelief before his dark brows drew together in a scowl. "*Och*, lass. Ye have lost yere mind."

"That's all I've got," she said at last. "The only other thing I can think of is asking you to hit me." She eyed his broad hands. "And I really don't think I want that."

"Aye?"

She walked around him, eyeing him up and down, dragging the sheet behind her. "Still, I have to wake up. And even though this is a fantastic dream, I really do have to get going. I have to find a phone and call someone about the rental car. And then I have to call my dad before he starts to worry. He's a worrier."

"Phone?" he repeated, the word sounding quite foreign on his tongue.

"Yes, a phone. Don't tell me you don't have one here?"

Finn sighed that heavy sigh again. "Nay, lassie."

"Figures." She huffed out a breath, her hands on her hips. "All right then," she said, pacing back and forth and muttering. "Clearly, I'm not dreaming. You're real. I'm real. This has to be some strange re-enactment. Or maybe some weird cosplay." She paused, turned to Finn. "And you're awesome at it."

"I dinna ken what yere talking about, lass." He looked at her as though she'd grown another head.

"Wow, you *are* good." She smiled from ear to ear. "I get it now, though. The joke's on me. Ha. Ha. Ha."

"Mayhap it'd be best if ye lie down." He waved her toward the bed.

"Are there hidden cameras?" Maggie peered into every corner of the room. But she saw nothing but the bed, a wardrobe, a chamber pot, two chairs, rugs, the grand fireplace, tapestries…her mind halted.

Wait. She walked to one of the chairs, ran her hand over the fine grain wood. It didn't feel as though it was anything that had been manufactured. In fact, it felt hand-carved by the imperfections in the wood. She dropped to her knees to examine the bottom and look for a manufacture date. Nothing.

"Lass, have ye taken leave of yere senses?"

She sat on her heels and dragged her hands down her face. "Oh, God. It's real. It's all real." She looked at Finn, then, who stood over her with a perplexed look on his face. He must think she was mad, crawling around on her hands and knees. "You're real."

"Aye?"

But by the way he lifted the word at the end, it made it sound more like a question. Maggie climbed to her feet and stood a breath away from him. He was massive, exuding power. His muscles weren't from pumping iron in any gym, they were probably from swinging a sword. She was quite certain he could put her over his shoulder as though she weighed no more than a sack of potatoes.

"Are ye all right, lass?"

She *hmmed* her response by placing her hands on his chest, running up the length of his smooth, warm skin to his shoulders where she rested her palms. She stood on tiptoe again to satisfy an urge. Instead, she pressed her face into the crook of his neck, inhaled his woodsy scent…and then flicked her tongue out and licked him. He tasted salty and sweet.

His hands clamped down on her wrists and jerked her away. She saw anger, then surprise, then desire flash over his chiseled features before he gave her a shove and released her. But her legs tangled in the bed sheet and she stumbled to the ground.

"Ye canna be doing that."

Tasting him sent a heat wave shooting right through her. He was definitely real. She was tossed back into the past, though how far she had no idea. She feared if she asked him the date, he'd have her committed.

"Hells bells," she muttered. "I guess this really isn't a dream and I'm not in Kansas anymore."

Chapter 3

There was a gleam of interest in the big Scotsman's sharp, silvery eyes as his gaze fixed on her face, making her want to squirm. She refused to flinch, intent on showing Finn she wasn't mad. Now she had to figure out *when* she was and she frantically searched her memory of All Things History. Her studies were primarily of literature, not history. That was her dad's forte. She would have to fake her way through fitting in.

I should have listened to Dad. She should have heeded the warnings of the universe and stayed put. Dad was right—it *was* all a sign. From her best friend, Beth, falling to the flu and unable to travel with her, to the flight delays due to the volcano, to the car breaking down in the driving rain and then the deserted castle.

Heat prickled Maggie's senses as she thought of that castle. She had curled up on the cold stone floor in front of a fire that had magically appeared. Her heart did a quick *ka-thunk*. Was the castle enchanted? Or haunted? Did some otherworldly spirit conjure the fire for her? She hadn't touched anything, so she couldn't have tripped some magical stone. She certainly didn't step through a stone circle, either. How did she end up here?

She had sensed something in the castle as she sat by the fire. Or thought she did. She'd played it off as her imagination. That her mind was playing tricks on her. What if it wasn't? But that was crazy. No ghost would carry her up to a bedchamber and dump her in a bed with a terribly hot Scotsman.

The kiss they'd shared charged back into her mind. That had certainly felt real, as did being pinned underneath him before they had been rudely interrupted. His body was hard as a rock and, well, awesome.

Mags, you're in over your head.

"Are ye English?" he asked finally. "Ye speak like the English."

What was she supposed to say to that? The Scottish were never fond of the English and, depending on where she was in history, it could be a very bad thing for her to be English.

"Ah…Irish, actually." That was a bit of a stretch. She was presently only one quarter Irish but it would have to do. She knew there was a smattering of English and Scottish in her lineage, too, but that wouldn't matter to Finn.

"Ye don't have the lilt of the Irish."

Maggie felt like a fibbing child, as though he could see right through her. She tried not to squirm. "My, ah, father's side was part English." *Mostly true.*

"Ah, so ye do have English blood."

Could he give her a break already? "Yeah, I do. So…where exactly am I?" A change of subject was needed.

"In my keep," he said. "And I still dinna ken how ye got here. What's yere name, lass?"

"Margaret Anne," she said. "My family calls me Maggie."

"What clan do ye hail from?"

"Clan?" She would have to think fast. What clan could she hail from? Did they *have* clans in Ireland? She thought so. But she wasn't sure so she'd have to switch tactics. Her mother had Scottish roots.

"Aye, clan, lassie. Ye do have a clan?"

"Um…Campbell." Her mother's maiden name would have to do.

"Ewan Campbell's clan?" He towered over her and looking at her with a suspicious gaze. "Did he send ye here to spy on me? First ye tell me yere Irish and now ye tell me ye belong to the Campbell."

"What? No." *Crap. That figures.* Maggie gathered up the bed sheet and tried to stand but her legs were tangled. She ended up falling back on the floor with a muttered *oomph.* "I don't know any Ewan Campbell and I'm certainly not here to spy on you."

"Then what are ye here for?"

She craned her neck to look up at him, unwilling to allow him to bully her. She scrambled back to her feet. "I have no idea how I got here. I'm just *here.*" She charged him, poking him in the chest with her forefinger. "Listen, you. I'm as much at a loss as you are. I have no idea who you are, where I am and telling me it's your 'keep' isn't enough information. *Where* is your keep?"

"Ye would be in Innisborough, lass," he said. "I'm laird of McCullough Castle. 'Tis been a stronghold here for the last century."

The blood whooshed from her head. Innisborough? Scottish Laird? She quickly did a mental calculation of where her car had broken down. If she remembered right, the last sign she saw was for a town called Innisborough, several miles after she'd gotten lost outside of Dumfries. She had no clue which direction Innisborough was from Dumfries, though. That was part of being directionally challenged. She could read a map all day but she couldn't follow it.

Could she have broken down near his castle ruins? And by some miracle ended up in the laird's castle for the night?

And a super-hot laird, too.

She shook her head, forcing her mind away from the fantastic pectorals before her and back to her dilemma at hand. It didn't make any sense because she stood in the middle of a bedchamber with a flesh-and-blood man. It was clear to her this castle was *not* deserted.

"Being of the clan Campbell, ye ken that." He folded meaty arms across his chest.

"Well…I, ah…apologies, sir, for the intrusion." She dipped a quick curtsy then gathered up the sheet and did a scan of the room. Her clothes were nowhere to be found.

She took a step toward the door, but he caught her by the arm. "Ye canna leave."

"Oh, yes, I can." Maggie tried to pull her arm free but he held fast.

"I canna let a spy of the clan Campbell out of my sight."

"I am no spy. I told you that."

"And I dinna ken that until ye prove otherwise."

Exasperated, she said, "And how am I supposed to prove that?"

"I dinna ken yet. I canna let ye out of this room. Ye aren't decent." He wiggled a finger at her sheet-clad body.

"Then bring me some clothes."

"Not until I ken ye are no spy."

That again? She huffed out a breath then released her hold on the linen. It pooled around her feet in a shimmer of cloth and left her standing before him in nothing more than her lacy bra and panties. His face flushed scarlet before he lifted his hand to shield his eyes, as though he were blinded by the sun.

"*Och*, lass, do ye have no decency?"

"After a kiss like that, you'd think we'd be on a first-name basis." She scowled. "At any rate, I have no clothes. And if you won't let me out of your sight, then you give me no choice. I can't wander around in a bed linen, now can I?"

"Ye make a valid point, lassie." He still wouldn't look at her.

"Mayhap, sir, you'd get me something to wear then?"

He stole a glance around his hand-shield and for a moment she thought she saw his pulse flutter in his neck. "Aye, indeed. I best be finding ye some clothes. And then I'll decide if ye will be going wi' me."

"Going where?" Maggie's senses suddenly went on high alert. If she were indeed back in time, she had bigger problems than she first thought. Like how to get back to her *present*.

"I was to be leaving by daybreak, but yere intrusion has slowed me down."

"I'm not going anywhere with you. I have to get back to, ah, my clan."

"'Tis no time for that now, lass. After tournament season is over, then I'll take ye back to the Campbells."

"Tournament? What sort of tournament?" Blood throbbed in Maggie's ears. Could it be? She would actually be able to see a real live jousting tournament?

"By Saint Mary, lassie, ye best be jesting for these senseless questions are trying my patience."

"As in you're going to *joust*?" she asked, her voice hitching at the end. She hadn't been this excited since she'd ridden her first roller coaster at age seven.

"Are ye going to cover up now, lass?" he suddenly thundered.

It was then Maggie realized she hadn't bothered to pick up the sheet and there she stood before him in her unmentionables. Evidently, her breasts were as excited as she was and stood at pert attention. Flushing hot, she pulled up the linen and wrapped it around her, tucking the end between her breasts.

"My apologies."

He lowered his hand, his eyes sharp and assessing. Why the sudden embarrassment at her unclothed state, she couldn't understand. Only moments before he'd had her pinned under him in the massive bed with her lacy cups crushed against his awesomeness. She loudly cleared her throat.

"Sir?"

He blinked, focusing on her face. "After tourney, I will find yere kinsman so I can return ye back to where ye belong. I'll send one of the chambermaids with clothes for ye. I have preparations to make for the journey."

Finn turned on his bare heel and banged out the chamber door, slamming it closed behind him. Maggie drew out a heated breath.

When the door slammed shut, Maggie sat on the edge of the featherbed. Glancing down at her shaking hands, she clasped them together and held them in her lap to keep them still. She sniffed, trying to keep the tears at bay.

How was it she ended up in a Scottish laird's castle? How could she explain to Finn she had no clansmen here? Telling him she belonged to the Campbells seemed appropriate at the time but now she worried what would happen if he decided to deposit her with said Campbells.

If her head throbbed before, it pounded as if it was about to split in two now. The emotional roller coaster she suddenly found herself on had only agitated her headache. She put her head in her hands and rubbed her forehead, squeezing the skin between her fingers.

A quiet knock on the chamber door interrupted her thoughts and before she could grant access inside, it swung open. A young woman entered. She carried an armload of dresses and paused inside the doorway, staring at her with piercing cornflower blue eyes. Her wavy blonde hair was whisked back, tied at the nape of her neck with a satin ribbon.

Maggie wasn't sure what to make of her, so she put on her best fake smile. "Hi."

The girl dumped an armload of gowns on the bed next to her. She turned back to her, folding her arms over her chest and staring at her.

"Thank you," Maggie said. "What's your name?"

"You may call me Elyne," she said, her words hinting at an unmistakable brogue.

"That's a pretty name," Maggie said, still smiling and feeling her cheeks ache.

"Aye, it is." Her tone was haughty.

Maggie's smile faltered, drooping at the corners. "I'm Maggie."

"Oh, aye, I know who you are."

"I guess you would." Maggie blew out a breath and went back

to massaging her forehead. God, she felt like hell. She probably looked it too, judging by the way the girl kept staring at her. Or maybe staring wasn't quite the right word. Maybe regarding was a better word. "I suppose his lairdship told you about me?"

"Aye, he did. But I knew you were here before he did."

"You did?"

"Of course, I did. He asked me to bring you here."

Maggie jumped off the bed and reached for Elyne, wrapping her hand around the girl's arm. Elyne glared down at her hand until Maggie released her.

"What does that mean?" Maggie asked. "How could you have brought me here? I woke up in his bed."

"Aye." Elyne nodded. "I put you there."

"How?"

"You might remember wandering into a deserted castle last night, drenched to the bone and freezing. You also might remember a fire sprang from nowhere."

"Are you saying you did that?"

"Indeed, I did. Then his lairdship asked to have you returned to a time in the past. *His* past. By your calendar, that would be the year 1347."

Maggie's stomach roiled and she pressed a hand against it. She was really in the past, in a laird's castle, soon to leave for tournament.

"Why would he do that?"

"The Finian McCullough of your time was but a ghost, trapped between the human realm and the other side. He saw something in you—what, I have no idea." Elyne had a look of disgust, like she'd swallowed something bad. "He demanded you be sent back in time to keep him from dying at tourney."

Maggie's eyes grew wide. *But I have a thesis to write.* She had to finish researching Sir Derron. She was *this* close to getting her master's degree and now this?

"You send me back right this instant." Maggie tried hard not to shout the words, but they still came out loud and terse.

"I cannot." Elyne shook her head then glanced over her cuticles with disinterest. "You're stuck here until after tournament is over."

"But why?"

"Because that's the way it works, all right?" Fire flashed in the blue eyes as Elyne looked at her then. "Think you can handle it?"

"I don't know. How am I supposed to prevent him from dying? I don't know how it happened. Was it an accident? Or something more sinister?"

Elyne gave her a thin-lipped smile. "I suppose you'll have to figure it out on your own."

"Who are you? How did you send me back in time?"

"*I* am Fae royalty, a princess of the Otherworld—you humans call it Faery—and you're nothing but a gnat on the map of the world."

"Fae?" Dawning began. "You seriously can't mean Faery?" Then Maggie snorted. "You're telling me you're part of the *Tuatha dé Danaan*? Yeah, as if."

"Believe it, human." The Fae princess glared at her, a hint of an Irish lilt coming out in her speech now. "I'm a direct descendant of the Daughters of Danu, the royal bloodline who protects all Fae magic and those within the Otherworld realm."

"If you're Fae, then how old are you?"

"Older than time itself," Elyne said. "Older than *you* can comprehend. I've seen your past, your present, and even your future. A future you could not imagine."

"So, you snapped your fingers and *poof* here I am." Maggie snapped her fingers to enunciate her point.

"No, I did not snap my fingers." Elyne snapped her fingers back. "It took a lot of effort to sift the sand of time and put you here, where you certainly do not belong."

"Did you wave your magic wand? This fairy tale—sorry, no pun—keeps getting better and better."

Maggie giggled and perched on the edge of the bed. She could believe in standing stones that possessed a certain magical ability on certain days of the year such as Beltane and Samhain. In fact, she did believe in them. But magic? Magic wasn't real. It belonged in bedtime stories. The ones Dad used to read her before she'd fall into blissful slumber as she dreamed of fair princesses in towers and sugarplums that danced in her head.

"You would be wise not to mock me, human, or I can make your life a living hell while you're here in what you refer to as the Middle Ages. I am a princess and you will address me as such."

"I know history, *your highness*," Maggie said, thumbing at herself. "I've spent the last six years studying it and I've *never* heard of the Fae meddling in 'human' affairs. It's not history. It's myth and legend."

Elyne took a step toward her, standing toe to toe. "*History*," she hissed. "Not myth. Not legend. History. *My* history and I'll thank you not to mock it or me."

Touchy, wasn't she? Maggie held up her hands in surrender. "Sorry."

Elyne crossed her arms, giving Maggie a superior look. "It happens among you lesser folk. At any rate, your knowledge should come in handy where you're going."

"And where am I going?"

"Like Finn said. To tourney. Middleham, England, if you must know. South of the Scottish border. It's about a week's ride from here."

"You can't make me do anything."

Maggie's eyes narrowed as she looked at the blonde-haloed wispy woman. She didn't look all that tough. In fact, she looked nothing more than a servant girl. Perhaps she was playing an elaborate hoax on her.

Or somewhere in her sleep-deprived mind, her imagination had run amok.

Elyne laughed, a surprising bellow of a chortle from the pit of her lungs. "Silly human. You think you have so much control." She punctuated the sentence with a lift of her head, looking down her straight, pointy nose at Maggie as though she were nothing more than pond scum. She leaned forward, her voice dropping to a dangerous level. "You have no control of your own destinies. You are nothing but simple fools."

A pounding on the door made them both jump. "Lassie?" It was Finn, his voice muffled through the thick chamber door.

Maggie huffed out a breath. "Not ready yet," she called, hoping to stall.

"Ye best be in the next few minutes or I'll be dressing ye meself."

Maggie tried not to think of his hands on her trying to dress her. It sent too many erotic images through her fertile imagination. She held her breath, waiting for him to boom through the door again but he must have left since all fell silent. She turned back to Elyne.

"Send me back."

"As I said, I cannot. Not until tournament is over."

"And what if I can't keep Finn alive? Then what?"

"Then…well… Then that's on *your* pretty head, isn't it?" Elyne reached for a plain white dress that looked at least ankle-length with long sleeves and a tie at the neck. A potato sack would have been more exciting. "Here. Put this on."

Maggie snarled.

"It's a shift, you dolt."

"I know what it is," she snapped, taking the shift. "I've never seen one in real life. I'm holding, in my hands, history."

"How nice. Get dressed, will you?"

An unwelcome blush crept into her cheeks. "Yeah, uh, I don't know how to put this stuff on."

Elyne huffed out a breath. After several embarrassing and harrowing minutes of her assisting, Maggie left the chamber. She stepped into the drafty hallway, wearing the shift underneath the soft brown gown—Maggie refused to give up her bra and panties, though. She needed at least some comfort from home. Elyne had even taken the time to coil her hair around her ears and head in the fashion of the time. Despite her predicament, Maggie couldn't help but feel like a princess.

Now Elyne led her down the stone steps outside the castle. The courtyard was a bustle of morning activity with servants running about to do their lord's bidding. Several groomsmen busied themselves with brushing horses but still giving her a cursory glance as she and Elyne walked by. A couple of young men packed a cart with supplies of armor and lances, swords and archery.

"What happens now?" Maggie panted, trying to keep up with Elyne.

"Now you go to tournament."

"You're not coming?" Maggie demanded. "You brought me here yet you're not even coming to Middleham?"

"Nay. I have other matters to attend in the Otherworld."

"You can't leave me with these men. It wouldn't be proper."

"I can. And I am. You, human, are on your own."

Maggie clamped a hand on her arm, her fingers digging into her smooth flesh. The princess raised a brow at her, her eyes hardening, as if to say *you dare touch me?* Maggie glared right back as if to reply, *yeah, I dare. Get over it.*

"You're not getting off so easy, princess. You *are* coming with me as my maidservant. And when this is all over, you *will* send me back."

Before Elyne could retort, she heard the men's voices in a low murmur and one of them she immediately recognized as Finn. He had donned a shirt along with his plaid and looked incredibly attractive with his wild long hair and two plaits on either side of his face. She nearly swooned.

"Ah, there ye are, lass. And fully dressed I see," he said when spotting her.

Maggie recognized the boy next to him as Fergus, the young lad from the chamber earlier that morning. Fergus hadn't stopped staring at her since her arrival. Feeling self-conscious, she smoothed her hand over her skirt and then clasped them in front of her to keep from fidgeting.

"Fergus, saddle the horse for the lass and her companion," Finn commanded. "'Tis time to be leaving for Middleham."

At that, Maggie's stomach rumbled loudly and she pressed her hand against it. "What about something to eat?"

Finn gave her a cursory glance. "Ye dinna break yere fast yet?" He glared at Elyne and fired another question at her. "Ye dinna take her to the great hall for food?"

"Your pardon, sir—" Elyne began.

"Take her back inside," he roared. "Get her some provisions and then bring her back here at once. I've wasted enough time with both of ye. We must be on the road to Middleham."

"Sir Finian, I cannot—" Elyne started, her tone full of snootiness.

But Finn cut her off again. "Ye will do as I request, lass, or face a thrashing. Now go. The both of you." All the cords stood out on his thick neck and Maggie held her breath.

"You can't talk to me that way." Elyne projected an aura of arrogance. Tension crackled the air between them. Maggie waited for the sparks to fly.

Finn clenched his jaw, a muscle ticking along the edge. "Dinna give me trouble. I canna waste any more time. 'Tis time to make haste for Middleham." He had lowered his voice, though Maggie could tell it took some effort for him not to yell. "Fergus," he said slowly, "see to it the horses are ready when they return. And as for ye—" He turned toward Elyne, pointing at her. "Ye'll be taking her and bringing her back to me when she's done."

Finn spun away from her and stomped out of the stable. Only

when he had disappeared completely from sight did Maggie blow out the breath she was holding. She glanced over at Fergus whose face was stark white. Elyne scowled, her pretty features scrunched into a frown.

"Dear princess, I think you made him mad." Maggie suppressed a snicker as the princess flashed a look of death.

Elyne sat Maggie at the long table in the great hall, the very room she had fallen asleep in the night before. Or rather, six hundred plus years in her future. There were the two giant fireplaces on either side of the room, both featuring a cheerful fire. The wood table Maggie feasted upon was scarred from longtime use. Faded tapestries hung along the stone walls. Maggie smiled. Here she was in a working medieval castle and she longed for a pen and paper to write down everything she saw, heard, and smelled.

Her breakfast was a thick porridge in a bread bowl and various dried fruits. The servants who placed the meal in front of her stared at her with big round eyes and gave her a look that said she had no business there. Maggie wondered if Finn was notorious for having strange ladies in his keep and she was another one in a long line of bonnie lasses.

Elyne poured her a tankard of a pale liquid and slid it her direction. Sniffing the honey sweetness sent her stomach plummeting. She wasn't fond of sweet drinks, especially early in the morning, and she wrinkled her nose.

"It's mead." Elyne rolled her eyes.

"I'd rather have a cup of coffee with cream."

"I'm not a short-order cook. You better get used to it if you plan to survive here. I thought you knew about history?"

"I *do*. But I studied medieval literature. Not food and drink." Maggie waved toward the feast in front of her.

Elyne snorted in response.

"I don't understand why you can't just snap your fingers and send me back," Maggie said, taking a bit of the steamy porridge.

"It doesn't work like that," Elyne said, an edge of impatience creeping into her voice.

"How does it work then?" Maggie was truly interested. She'd never laid eyes on a Fae, much less a royal one, and she wanted to know more about her.

"That's none of your concern."

"It is my concern. You brought me here. Besides, I'm not all too sure you're really Fae. Prove it to me."

Elyne's mouth pulled into a sour grin. "I don't have to prove anything to you."

Maggie shrugged. "Have it your way."

The princess puffed out a short breath. "Fine, then. I'll prove it to you."

Elyne clenched her fists at her sides and her body shimmered in gold and silver hues while Maggie watched. Her blonde hair sparkled with an otherworldly light, making Maggie shriek and drop her food, shielding her eyes from the blinding brightness. But not before she spotted the distinct pointed tips of Elyne's ears.

"This is my true form," Elyne informed her. "But you humans cannot look upon us for very long."

"Why not?"

"Because it's like looking directly at the sun."

Meaning it would burn her eyeballs right out of their sockets. She got it. "Turn it off."

"Are you sure? Have I proven myself, then?"

"Yes, yes. Turn it off."

Elyne's image muted, the tips of her ears and the rest of her returning to normal, and a smirk appeared upon her face.

"All Fae wear glamour to protect us from those who would harm us. Satisfied?"

Maggie nodded, clamping her open jaw shut. "I am, your highness. But you're still coming with me."

"Am I?" she asked, cocking her head in a sort of mocking way to one side.

"You are," Maggie confirmed as though it was fact. "And you'll *like* it."

"I agree it would not be proper for a lady to go without an escort, but——"

"Good, then it's settled. I've never had a maidservant before. This should be fun."

At Elyne's grimace, Maggie flashed the brightest smile she could muster.

Maggie and Elyne arrived back at the stable where Finn and Fergus loaded more equipment onto a large cart. Lances, swords, armor, tents, furs, linens, food rations. Maggie wished she had a notebook so she could take notes. Or even her camera so she could take pictures.

She leaned against the barn door and watched Finn's solid biceps, admiring the muscles there, the thick vein popping out under the bronzed skin. She noticed he had a silvery scar along his right forearm. She'd read a lot about jousting in the Middle Ages, knew it was a wildly popular form of entertainment and knew some knights grew very rich from it.

It had occurred to her as she ate breakfast there was a chance she'd meet the subject of her thesis in the flesh, Sir Derron. From the old texts she'd found, she'd followed his jousting career, how he rose from a virtual unknown to one of the most famous. He was undefeatable, it seemed. No one could touch him.

Sir Derron was the jousting champion across England, Scotland, and France, and yet not a lot was known about him other than he was a real ladies' man. Until there was an unfortunate accident in the lists one day and he died. Fans were devastated by his untimely demise. Women flung themselves off towers in despair. It was all so strange, Maggie thought. And yet romantic. Would she fling herself off the highest turret for a man? Not likely. She liked living too much.

Elyne cleared her throat loudly, snapping Maggie out of her deep thoughts. "Sir Finian, her ladyship. Per your request."

"Ye best get into the saddle, lassie," Finn said. "The day is waning."

Maggie flashed him a sour look before glancing at Elyne, who tried desperately to slip out of the barn unnoticed. Maggie clamped her hand on the princess's wrist and gave her a gentle tug.

"Come along, Elyne." Then she whispered, "Not so fast, princess."

"Wait." His gruff voice made her stop. "Ye canna bring *that* girl. Any other maid would be fine but no' this one."

"And why not?" Maggie demanded. She glanced at Elyne whose brows arched in surprise.

His jaw tightened and his mouth thinned with displeasure as he looked over the princess, mistrust in his eyes. Maggie could read his expression like an open book and understood.

"Elyne is the only maid I can depend upon to have with me. We've already formed a rather unbreakable bond." She gave him a winsome smile in hopes he would believe her, even though her words were a lie and she knew it. She wasn't all too sure she trusted the Fae either, but she didn't exactly have a choice. And Elyne was coming whether she liked it or not.

Maggie knew Elyne was the only one who could get her out of this world and back to hers and she wasn't about to let her slip away. She would keep the princess close. Plus, it would give her a great opportunity to find out more about the Fae. Perhaps she could work that into her thesis somewhere.

Despite the fact he towered over her, she didn't back down. Really all she wanted to do was take all that pent-up anger and put it to good use by tossing him to the ground. Naked.

And she had been so close to his nakedness in the bed earlier that morning. Finn pursed his lips, apparently trying hard not to lose his cool and then blew out a heated breath, exasperated.

"I simply can't leave Elyne behind," she continued.

He growled then. It was a low, guttural sound deep in his chest that sent a tingling sensation right through her. He started to reply, but before he could get the words out, Elyne interjected.

"Your pardon, sir, but I've already packed for the both of us," Elyne said and flashed a superior grin.

Maggie looked at her, surprised Elyne had managed to pack their things in such a short amount of time. But then, she *was* a Fae. Finn, however, gave them both a look of disgust and defeat.

"Fine then. Bring the girl," he said through thin lips. Without another word, he turned back to loading the equipment.

Maggie knew she had agitated him once again. She squelched her guilt for making him angry and tried to concentrate on the thought of heading to her first real live jousting tournament.

It was early afternoon before they headed away from the castle walls and onto the road toward Middleham, England. Maggie tried to quash the apprehension crawling through her as they left the safety of Finn's castle behind. It was her last link to her world and she couldn't help but steal a glance over her shoulder as it disappeared into the distance.

Turning forward again, she took a deep breath and faced her new future.

Chapter 4

The group arrived in Middleham after a week of hard riding. Maggie did her best not to complain, but riding a horse left her saddle sore, tired and cranky. The only good part about riding nearly nonstop was the beautiful English and Scottish countryside and stopping every night at small country inns and taverns for food and sleep. She began to look forward to a hot meal and a good night's sleep.

Even so, it was still roughing it for Maggie. No hot and cold running water, no toilets, uncomfortable straw beds. Not to mention the numerous flea bites she had along her arms and legs. It made her long for her twenty-first century comforts like Egyptian cotton sheets and, most of all, a bathroom. Oh, how she longed for toilet paper. How did these people manage to get out of the Middle Ages?

Finn didn't want to waste any more time so he insisted on pressing through, stopping late and starting again at the first light of day. Tournament was to last over a week, with masques and banquets following each day's events, celebrating the safe return of King Edward from France. All worthy and notable knights were invited to attend and participate.

As they headed past the practice field, Maggie could see Middleham Castle sitting atop a ridge in the distance. She so loved seeing a working castle in real life, with turrets and heraldry boasting the owner's colors and symbol of lineage.

They entered the encampment surrounding the tournament field to a bustle of colorful activity. Red, green and yellow tents dotted the grounds, with knights ordering squires about and squires dashing to do their lord's bidding. Boisterous men's laughter could be heard, followed by the titter of a woman's giggle. Maidens huddled together, talking with one dashing knight who seemed to be signing autographs on parchment with a quill pen while his squire dutifully held an ink well.

Seeing it all made Maggie forget her severely saddle-sore butt. Excitement burned inside her, tingling up and down her spine. Passing through, she noted each tent's occupant was signified by the large banner flying outside, boasting the knight's heraldry. There were shields with crosses, shields with lions, shields with dragons.

Across the field, a knight rode astride a large white destrier, his horse draped in scarlet and emerald and ladies on his heels clamoring for his attention. The ladies fair, it seemed, came from near and afar to join the festivities and most of them trailed behind this knight with black hair and a broad smile in a perfect chiseled face.

Finn claimed two tents, one large one for him, his squires, and all their equipment and a smaller one for her and Elyne.

"Geoffrey, help me unload the armor and equipment," Finn ordered. "Fergus, take the horses to the stable. Get them fed, watered and brushed. I want them well rested before tourney begins on the morrow."

Fergus nodded and bustled about to do his lord's bidding. Geoffrey, a young boy of barely fourteen with flaxen hair, removed several lances from the cart and placed them inside the larger tent.

"So, this is home for the next week." Maggie watched Finn at work, her hands on her hips. She couldn't stop staring at the muscles in his arms and back as he lifted equipment and handed it to Geoffrey.

"Aye, it is." He never made eye contact with her, which had been the norm for the last few days. It irked her. He paused then, and turned to her. "Ye should get some rest. 'Twas a long journey."

"Aye, it was," Elyne agreed, carrying an armload of fur. She ducked inside their tent, disappearing from view.

"We have banquet tonight," Finn said. "I expect ye to wear something befitting a lady. Elyne can help ye."

"I can?" Elyne popped out of the tent. "I'm supposed to dress her now?"

"Ye packed for ye both, did ye no'?"

"I did, but I'm not your handmaiden," Elyne snapped.

"Do ye forget yere place?"

"We're going to a banquet tonight?" Maggie interjected, trying to diffuse the situation. A real medieval banquet. "You and me?"

Finn threw his hands up in the air. "Aye, we're going to the banquet. Just dress her." His gaze fixed on Elyne as he pointed to Maggie. Then he stalked off and ducked into his tent.

"Sheesh," Maggie said. "He's so temperamental."

"You have *no* idea."

Elyne stomped into their tent, leaving Maggie alone with Geoffrey the Squire. She searched her mind for something useful to say to the kid but she couldn't come up with anything that didn't sound dorky. She was about to ask him why he'd decided to become a squire when there was a burst of noise from the practice field. Lots of loud male voices and women laughing. Giving in to her historian's curiosity, Maggie picked up her skirts and headed away from camp to the practice field to see what the commotion was all about.

Once he'd calmed down, Finn emerged from the tent to help Geoffrey continue unload and reached for his jousting armor. The lassie was infuriating beyond words, yet there was something completely disarming about her. He hadn't intended to turn on her angrily and he had to tell himself to calm down. Having her with him was actually a blessing in disguise. He hoped having Maggie appearing in public with him would do his reputation good.

He heard a shouted greeting and glanced up. He handed off the breastplate to Geoffrey as Sir Drake Attenborough approached. A tall, broad man with black hair and piercing blue eyes, he extended his hand to Finn.

"Finn, it's good to see you're still among the living, my friend."

"Aye, and you as well, old friend." Finn grasped his hand, wincing at the knight's iron grip. He knew his friend alluded to the previous tourney that had turned into a disaster for him. Sir Drake had been his friend for more years than Finn could count.

"I had no idea you would be in Middleham." A broad smile played on Drake's face.

"Nor I until a servant of the king's arrived with my invitation."

Drake released a low whistle. "With what happened last time, I was sure I'd never see you again in the lists. Indeed, I thought you'd be stretched on the rack. Was it wise to accept, man?"

"Aye, and I intend to win."

"Well, then, I'm afraid we may face each other in the lists.

Something I daresay I'm not fond of."

"A guest of the Litonshire's, are you, then?" Finn's eyebrows rose, impressed his friend had been invited by the wretched earl.

"It was either come to Middleham or go to war in France, and I had no such desire to go to France. Should we meet in the lists, I'll try to go easy on you." He laughed and clapped his friend on the shoulder.

"Are you sure it isn't *I* who should go easy on *ye*?" Finn grinned, matching his friend's confidence. Drake laughed heartily again.

"Will you be at the banquet this evening?" Drake asked.

"Aye, I'll be there."

And escorting the lovely lass who had ignited a fire within him. The week-long ride had been near tortuous for him as he tried to ignore his attraction for Maggie. He couldn't deny it was instant and powerful, so he kept her at arm's length as much as possible. Now they were in such close quarters and he wasn't sure he could do that much longer.

"There will be a fair amount of lovely young maids there, I'm sure." He winked.

"Still chasing everything in a kirtle, I see." Finn grinned broadly. "I'll see ye there then."

"Excellent. Now I best tend to my squires, make sure they're shining the armor and brushing the horses. At times, they need too much supervision." He scowled at the thought and gave a jaunty wave as he walked away. "See you at banquet."

As Finn watched the man saunter away, he caught a glimpse of someone else headed in his direction and grimaced. Earl Byron de Fortier of Litonshire approached. A rail of a man with thinning brown hair cropped short above his collar, he wore the finest clothes in England. He had an unusually skinny nose, which Finn supposed made his voice sound the way it did, and his thin lips stretched into a sneer.

Finn suppressed an inward groan. He had become the earl's sworn enemy at the last tournament—when he'd made the grave error of playing a few rounds of dice with him and lost. It wouldn't have been so bad—only he'd bet the family estate in Innisborough in a desperate, drunken stupor. If he won the tourney in Middleham, it would earn him almost enough to pay Litonshire and get him off his back for good. The rest, Finn had already decided, he'd have to earn in the gambling tents.

"Ah, 'tis the illustrious Sir Finian McCullough," Lord Litonshire said in his nasally voice.

"Lord Litonshire," Finn greeted with a nod of his head.

"Come to soil another lady's good name?" The earl looked him over, one eyebrow raised in contempt. The contempt then turned to a surly smile. "Or perhaps you've come to try another round of Hazard with me. Have you forgotten the tidy sum of money you owe me? Not to mention your lovely estates."

Finn clenched his fists at his sides and reined in his temper. It wouldn't do for him to be hitting Lord Litonshire. At least not until he had won the tournament. How he would prove he hadn't laid a hand on his sister he wasn't sure yet. Paying him what he owed him was another problem.

"I haven't forgotten. Or was I not invited here?"

"Aye, you were invited. I couldn't allow the tournament to pass without having you here." Litonshire's smile reminded Finn of a wolf. "Hence the reason I made arrangements to request your presence."

"I've come to win, my lord."

"Win what?" the earl asked, giving him a smug look. "Ladies' favors so you can steal their innocence?"

"I never laid a hand on Lady Juliet," Finn said and pursed his lips.

Anger flushed through him. Litonshire's insinuation he'd forced himself upon Lady Juliet was unfounded. He never even bedded the lass, nor had he ever bedded any lassie who didn't want him. He'd discovered Lady Juliet in the stable only after the deed had been done and tried to help her.

"That's not what the bishop told me when she was examined." Litonshire inspected his nails, perfectly trimmed, as if bored with the entire conversation.

How could Finn explain to the man he'd been set up? He would never under any circumstances steal the innocence of a lady of noble birth, nor would he hit a woman. Seeing Lady Juliet with a black eye, a bloody lip and her gown torn had pushed him into action. He had wrapped her in his tartan, intending to carry her off to the healer when the earl found them.

"I haven't forgotten about our duel, either," Litonshire continued. "Fortunate for you, immediately after the last tournament, I was called away for business in France at the king's behest. But rest assured we *will* duel once tournament is over and I not only win your lands but win your life."

"We'll see, won't we?"

"And what of the money you owe?"

"I intend to pay ye back once tourney is over."

"Ah, I see. You hope to win back the money, do you?" Litonshire nodded in understanding. "I wish you the best of luck, Sir Finian, in your endeavor to win. By the end of the tournament, I expect to be paid or I expect to ride home to Innisborough. Following our duel, naturally."

"Ye'll never see the inside of that castle."

"You best be careful, Sir Finian. T'would be a shame should anything happen and you were unable to compete during tourney," he continued.

"Is that a threat, my lord?" Finn clenched his jaw so tight his muscles ached.

"If you perceive it to be one, then aye." The man leaned toward him. "And a word of warning, sir knight. If you so much as breathe close to the Lady Juliet, you will have to contend with me."

Before Finn could give Lord Litonshire an appropriate response, he turned on his heel and walked away with elaborate nonchalance. Finn pinned his back with a scorching look, hands fisted at his side before unclenching them. He wasn't a fool. He knew a threat when he heard one.

He swiveled from the disappearing earl and turned back towards his work, suddenly agitated. Mayhap what he needed was to release his pent-up anxiety before the opening ceremonies. Making the snap decision, he snatched his sword still on the cart and headed for the practice field in search of someone with whom to spar.

Maggie made her way through the maze of tents to an open field where, in the distance, she could see a crowd of onlookers hanging on the wooden fence around the practice field. When she reached them, she saw a knight sitting atop his black-and-white destrier, holding a lance. At the other end was a real quintain, a post with a revolving crosspiece with a target on one side and a sandbag on the other.

Excitement skittered through her, her heart doing a happy dance in her chest. She couldn't believe she was actually *here*.

Holding a lance under his arm, the knight charged toward the quintain, lowered the lance at the right moment and smashed it against the shield. The lance splintered into a thousand wooden toothpicks to the cheers of the small crowd gathered around the fence to watch. Even a few maidens swooned, sighing heavily, their bosoms popping out of their gowns as they batted their eyelashes.

Maggie looked and gasped, understanding why. The knight on horseback was *gorgeous*—with a sort of ethereal beauty not normal for a man. What man could be called beautiful? Serene? Intoxicating? Those were all the words jumping to mind when she looked at him. For whoever the mysterious man was, looking at him made Maggie's pulse pound like the Energizer bunny banging his drum.

The handsome knight handed the broken lance off to his squire, flashing a bright smile with deep-set dimples on either side of his oh-so-kissable mouth. He had shining blond hair like a halo, and his eyes were the brightest blue she'd ever seen. He wore no armor, instead a padded tunic and padded breeches. Maggie could see his muscles straining against the material. Hard muscles she wanted to run her hands, legs and tongue over. She quickly shoved those thoughts out of her head. *No, Mags. You have a hot Scottish knight, remember?*

"Sir Derron! Sir Derron!" One fair maiden standing next to her waved her favor at him.

Maggie blinked, surprise snapping through her. It was *Sir Derron*. In the flesh. The man with no surname she'd been studying for years. The subject of her thesis. No textbook had mentioned how good-looking he was or waxed poetic about his deep-set dimples. Maggie wished she had a pen and paper so she could start composing an ode to his thighs. And arms. And that smile!

Her heart thudded hard, sending chills shooting through her. Every inch of her skin prickled with anticipation and excitement as she soaked him in, memorizing every plane of his face, every line, every strand of hair as it fell over his forehead. He trotted over on his war horse, looking calm and cool. Maggie was fairly certain he hadn't even broken a sweat in his practice run. And why would he? He was perfect. Enchanting. Fascinating.

"Take my favor, Sir Derron," a girl said, lifting a champagne-colored piece of opaque cloth toward him.

He leaned toward her from his mount, taking her cloth and hand in his, kissed her delicate knuckles and slipped the material from her all in one smooth motion. The girl sighed.

Elyne harrumphed next to her, making Maggie jump. She hadn't realized the Fae princess had followed her.

"Show off," Elyne muttered.

"You know him?" Maggie nodded in Sir Derron's direction.

"Oh, aye. I know him all right."

Glancing at her, Maggie could see the angry lines creasing her forehead. Angry lines? Or concerned lines? Maggie couldn't decide which. Sir Derron caught her gaze then, flashed a bright smile and dismounted the horse, surrendering it to his young squire.

"I see you decided to make an appearance," he greeted, bowing with a flourish to Elyne. "I'm truly honored by your presence." Dimples framed his mouth as he gave her a crooked smile.

"You endanger yourself here and you know it."

"Ah, but what other time can I practice my skills than at tourney?"

"You don't need to practice any skills. You should be—" She paused, giving Maggie a sidelong glance. "You know where you should be."

"Court is so boring." Derron yawned to prove his point. "Why should I waste my time lounging around there with those hangers-on who want nothing but to serve, serve, serve. It makes me weary. And don't get me started on all the bores in the rest of the Otherworld."

"It's your *duty*." Fire flashed in Elyne's eyes as she bit out her curt words.

Maggie watched the verbal volley between the two, trying to deduce exactly *who* Derron was to Elyne. Clearly, he was a Fae of some importance. And Maggie knew Elyne was a princess. Was he related to her somehow? They argued as if they'd been together a long while.

"Humans are much more interesting."

Was Sir Derron a Fae royal? Could it be possible? Maggie had lived nearly twenty-six years not believing in faeries and yet in a fortnight she'd met two.

Derron turned to Maggie then, upping the charm. "Mine eyes

hath seen nothing as bonny as you, fair maiden, so pray forgive my rudeness." He bowed low. "May I ask your name?"

"Lady Margaret." Elyne answered before Maggie could. Her gaze clawed him like talons. "And she's none of your concern."

Clearly unflustered by the irate princess, Derron took Maggie's hand, kissed it with warm lips soft as velvet. His touch sent a wave of desire right through her, shaking her to her soul. "The pleasure is mine, Lady Margaret."

Oh, she had a thousand and one questions to ask the man. She had to know everything about him. She wanted to know how he managed to win so many tournaments without so much as an injury. Was it because he was a Fae he cheated death? How many hours did he practice? What made him so good? If he was a Fae, did he have magic like Elyne? Did he use it to make him a god in the lists?

"I'm delighted to make your acquaintance, Sir Derron."

Still holding her hand in his, he chuckled. It was a deep sound, rumbling around in a broad chest.

"Shouldn't you be getting ready for the banquet?" Elyne ripped out her words impatiently.

"All in good time, dear Elyne. First, I intend to get to know Lady Margaret." He tucked her hand in his elbow.

Standing so close to him, Maggie sensed something very ancient and otherworldly about him. It had to be the Fae in him. Even so, her knees nearly buckled at the thought of spending time alone with her idol. What could she learn? How she wished she had a mini recorder.

Still ignoring Elyne, he said, "Will you be attending banquet tonight, Lady Margaret?"

She blushed, lowering her gaze to the ground as a delicious shudder tingled her spine. "I will, sir knight."

"Then, aye, I should make my way posthaste to my tent and begin preparing to meet you again."

"Stop using your Fae charms on her," Elyne demanded.

He blinked, feigning innocence, and Maggie suddenly realized that's why she felt so weak and lightheaded. He was doing something to her on purpose.

"Unhand her."

The big booming voice sounded through the practice field, turning heads. Derron kept his grasp firm on Maggie's arm, meeting Finn's feral gaze as he charged across the field, sword in his hand gleaming in the afternoon light.

"Uh oh," Maggie whispered.

"You're not kidding," Elyne agreed.

Finn stopped, pointed the sword a mere inch from Derron's face. "Release her."

"I don't think she really wants to be released." Derron offered Maggie an arresting smile, pulling her closer. His ancient, spicy scent pressed into her, making her head spin.

"I said, let the lass go."

"And then what? You'll take her under your protective wing?" Derron laughed. "Much like you did Lady Juliet?"

"Oh, here we go." Elyne rolled her eyes.

Maggie gasped. The last person she'd want to make angry was Finn. He was the only one who could keep her safe in this wretched place after all. She tried to pull free. "Really, I should probably go—"

"Now, why would you do that, Lady Margaret, when we're just getting to know each other so well? You don't want to go with this brute of a man, do you?" Derron wasn't even bothered by the sword pointed in his face.

"*Release her.*" Finn snarled through clenched teeth, his face turning an odd shade of red.

Maggie wished a large black chasm would open in the ground and swallow her whole. All she could do was stand there and watch the sultry Fae insult her Scotsman.

"I think I should see what Fergus and Geoffrey are up to," Maggie said, trying again to pull her arm free.

But still Derron held fast. "Lady Margaret tells me she'll be attending the banquet tonight, Sir Finian. Did you know this? Oh, of course you did. Mayhap you'd hoped to escort her yourself to ease your tarnished reputation."

"My reputation 'tis none of your concern. I'm asking ye to release the lass. She's with my camp."

"Indeed?" Derron clucked his tongue and released her. Finn lowered his sword, relaxing. But Derron wasn't finished yet. "'Tis a shame, really. Perhaps she will come to her senses, though. Lady Margaret…" As he addressed her, he bowed. "Allow me to be your escort tonight."

"Oh, I, um…" Maggie glanced toward Finn, who had a look of

the devil on his face. She knew she should say no but part of her wanted to say yes. It would give her ample time to talk to Derron, learn about him, and help write her thesis. How could she refuse that? It was too good to be true.

"I dinna think that's wise."

"Nor I," Elyne interjected. "It's not for you to be meddling in, Derron." She wagged a warning finger at the knight.

"Aye," Finn agreed. "She goes with me."

"Mayhap an old-fashioned duel should decide with whom she goes. Squire, my sword." As he called for his sword, he released Maggie.

"Finn, don't." She crossed to him in one step, gripping his arm. "Don't fight him over me."

"Aye," Elyne agreed, nodding. "She's not worth it."

"You stay out of this," Maggie snapped, giving Elyne a hostile glare.

The two exchanged silent, angry glares. Maggie glowered at Elyne. Elyne gave her a sardonic grin that did nothing but inflame her temper even more. She wanted to tell the Fae princess to shove off except she knew she couldn't since Elyne was the only person who could get her back to her world. But then she remembered she had to keep Finn alive, to save his life, to get back there.

"If it's a fight he wants, 'tis a fight he'll get. Step aside, lassie." With that, Finn nudged Maggie out of the way.

It occurred to Maggie this could be how Finn dies and the twenty-first century would be lost to her forever. She had to stop their duel. And if she did, then he wouldn't die and she'd be able to go home. She did the only thing she could think to do. She flung herself in front of him, pressing her body against his, her hands on his shoulders.

"No, Finn. Don't do this."

He gave her a look of warning that translated to *don't get in my way* when he calmly removed one hand from his shoulder.

"Ye will stand aside, lass, or I'll have ye restrained."

Fear knotted inside her, she had no choice but to do as he asked and watch with numbed horror as Derron took his sword from his squire. The two men stepped into the practice arena. Those who had hung around gathered at the fence line once again to watch them square off. Fair maidens and dirty-faced commoners alike all gaped with eager looks on their faces. Maggie even saw money change hands and guessed they were betting on who would be the winner.

She prayed it would be Finn.

"I hope you're happy," Elyne spat. "This is your fault."

"*My* fault? How is this my fault?" Maggie wanted to know.

"You incited them to fight."

"Can't you wave your fairy magic wand and do something?"

"It doesn't work like that."

"Isn't that how you got me here?" Maggie fired back.

But the first clang of swords crossing made them both stop bickering and look up. Maggie surged towards the wood fence, standing on the bottom rung to get a better look. She shielded her eyes against the afternoon glare, watching with her heart in her throat as the two men started to spar. Elyne stepped up next to her, gripping the fence so hard, her nail beds turned pale pink.

"He better live," she said.

"Yes, he better," Maggie agreed, taking her to mean Finn.

If he died here and now, what would happen to her? Would she be stuck here? Or would Elyne still be able to send her back to her own time? Maggie felt completely responsible for keeping Finn alive, so she'd have to find a way to jump between them and stop the fighting. She already tried once to no avail, so she wasn't sure how she would get between the two men with swords.

Especially two angry men. She bit her thumbnail.

Finn pushed Derron backward, their swords clanging against each other over the din of the crowd cheering them. The crowd that suddenly doubled in size at the sight of the two men battling it out. Maggie and Elyne both held their breath when Finn took a swing and missed Derron's head—he ducked, missing the blade by a narrow margin.

Derron fought back, the cords in his neck straining against his skin. But the Scotsman was bigger and more muscular and Maggie could see nothing good coming of this entire so-called practice. She would have to find a way inside that ring and quickly before one of them got seriously injured. She discovered she could squeeze between the two rungs of the fence. Bending, she stepped over the bottom rung, intending to go through when Elyne grabbed her by her sleeve.

"Where are you going?"

"To stop this madness," Maggie retorted. "Since it was my fault and all, then I best make them stop."

Maggie needn't have worried since the match didn't last long. A shout from Derron and the two ladies looked up to see him flat on his back, disarmed, staring up at Finn and Finn pointing the tip of the sword in his face.

"Do ye yield?" Finn asked.

"You give me no other choice, do you?" Derron gave Finn a sour look of defeat. "You win, this time."

Finian lowered his sword, exuding a smugness Maggie hadn't thought possible for any man. "Aye, then. The lass goes with me. Dinna think to be stealing her away from me again."

"The week is long, Sir Finian," Derron replied, his words acid. "We'll see about that."

Finn grunted and held out a hand to Derron. By now the crowd had dispersed, some counting their winnings since they'd picked the burly Scot against the Fae knight. Derron took his hand and Finn helped him to his feet.

"I'll see you in the lists." Derron brushed his dusty hands off.

"Aye, ye will."

Finn turned his back, grinning broadly with his win, and headed over to Maggie who had resumed her position on the outside of the arena fence. She caught the evil glint in Derron's eyes as he charged Finn. She barely got a shout out when the Fae jumped on Finn's back, knocking him forward and punching him in the side of the head.

"What are you *doing*?" Elyne shrieked and scrambled through the fence. "You bloody fool."

"Men are so stupid," Maggie muttered and huffed out a sigh. Despite her nonchalance, it was impossible to steady her erratic pulse.

Finn plucked him off his back and tossed him to the ground with a loud *ka-thud*, knocking the wind out of Sir Derron. He propped his foot on his chest, leaned on his knee.

"Not one of yere best ideas, eh, Derron?" Finn's grin broadened in approval, completely pleased with his reaction.

"Let him go, Finian." Maggie had followed Elyne and now stood next to him, hands fisted on her hips, peering at him with her best withering stare. "You two have fought enough for one day."

"Aye," Elyne said. "Save it for tourney."

"I thought…you didn't approve of tourney." Derron huffed out the words as he spoke to Elyne, never taking his eyes off Finn.

"I don't, but if you're going to act like bampots, then at least save it for when it counts."

"Finn," Maggie said. "Remove your foot."

"Ye fancy the pretty lad here?" Finn pointed to Derron sounding like a jealous man. Any other circumstances would make Maggie giggle with glee.

"Just let him go."

Finn snarled, curling his top lip upward, and removed his foot, though Maggie could tell it was with reluctance. He fixed her with a level stare. "I'll see ye at banquet."

"As will I," Derron said as Elyne helped him to his feet.

"Oh, be gone with you." Elyne shoved Derron away, then took Maggie by the arm and led her out of the practice arena.

"I don't know how I'm going to keep Finn alive, Elyne."

"Why not?"

"Because I may have to kill him myself."

"I can't say I blame you."

Chapter 5

Once they left the practice area, Elyne took Maggie to the grandstand where they sat side by side with the other spectators to watch the opening ceremony, which Maggie came to learn was called the Invocation. The parade of contestants and judges sat upon their horses filing into the lists. One by one they entered, each knight wearing his finery and the squires carrying the heraldry of his lord. Some knights wore bright plumes upon their helms, their new armor polished to a high shine, the late afternoon sun winking off the silver.

Maggie spotted Sir Derron first, riding his destrier and waving to the crowd with a broad smile on his handsome face. He looked as though the altercation in the practice arena hadn't even happened. One glance by him through the crowd and the ladies cheered louder, fanning their silks toward him, shouting his name and hoping for more.

"All the ladies fair all want a knight to take their favors," Elyne grumbled, watching Derron ride through.

"And I suppose most of them want Sir Derron to take their favors."

"Oh, aye. Look how they fling themselves at him. Those fecking wenches." Elyne grimaced.

"Do I hear a note of jealousy in your voice, Ellie? Or is that contempt?" Maggie nudged her with her elbow, grinning.

Elyne bristled at the nickname and gave Maggie a sour look. "Ellie? You dare call me this?"

"You don't like it?" Maggie asked. "I thought it fit you."

"You may call me princess, your highness or Elyne, and nothing more." A shadow of annoyance flickered across her face.

Maggie only shrugged, unruffled by Elyne's irritation. "If you insist. Tell me all about Sir Derron. How do you know him?"

"'Tis nay your concern," Elyne bit off, her lilt coming through loud and clear.

"He's a Fae, isn't he?"

Elyne paused, the silence stretching before she finally replied. "How did you know?"

"It was rather obvious when he said humans were much more interesting."

"He needs to keep his fecking mouth shut." Elyne glowered.

"Ah ha. So, he is then. And he's a royal?" When Elyne gave her another sour look, Maggie shrugged. "He said court was boring."

"I see nothing gets by you."

"I'm observant. I have to be." Her future thesis depended upon it.

There was a pause before Elyne answered looking down her nose at Maggie as if she were a cockroach doing a rumba on her clean kitchen counter. "Aye, he's a Fae. But a royal he is not. He is a knight, a sworn protector of the Otherworld, and son of one of the Guardians of the Four Treasures."

Maggie looked at Derron again, wondering what a sworn protector of the Otherworld did exactly. She had no idea what a Guardian of the Four Treasures was either but both sounded important. More important than jousting for fun. She made a mental note to ask Elyne about that later. "Why does he joust?"

"He likes to play with humans."

"And that's something you're not happy about, I take it."

"Humans are lower than the Fae." Elyne presented her haughty look again.

"Hey, I resemble that remark."

The princess flicked a disgusted look over Maggie, leaving her feeling as though she should apologize for her race. "You do nothing but destroy your world, fighting each other for tiny parcels of land and power. Killing each other in the worst possible ways. Vying for more subjects, more gold, more everything. I've seen more death and destruction, more famine and greed than I thought possible. Don't give me that look. Your future is no different."

She had a point. Maggie had seen the horrors of war and terrorism via CNN. Watched with horror as the twin towers fell in New York. War and death and destruction were very real in her future. That was why she'd escaped to her history books.

"And I suppose your people, the Fae, are not like that?" Maggie asked. If only she had a voice recorder. She could be getting this all down. She concentrated hard to keep it all filed away in her mind.

"The Otherworld has its own problems," Elyne retorted.

When she didn't elaborate, Maggie prompted, "Like what?"

"Nothing *you* could understand." Elyne gave her a sidelong glance, closing the subject.

"Because I'm human?"

"Aye, indeed. Because you are human."

Maggie kept her gaze on the parade of knights and chewed on her lower lip. Elyne thought humans were nothing more than killing machines. And thinking back on her history, she had a point. War after war hadn't solved anything. All it left behind was a lot of widows and fatherless children.

Finn rode through, still wearing the altercation of the arena on his face. Even so, Maggie could see through it to the handsome Scot beneath. She knew underneath that growly brusque exterior, there was a gentle man waiting to get out. She saw it the morning she landed in his bed and the way he looked at her with reverence.

"We're not all like that, you know," Maggie said. "Not all of us are greedy or violent. Some of us just want to be loved."

"I've not seen a human yet worth anything," Elyne said.

And that, Maggie thought, was all the reason she needed to prove her wrong.

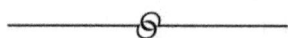

After the Invocation, the two ladies returned to their tent in the pavilion. Elyne had dressed Maggie in a deep-purple sideless surcote cut low in the hips over a jade-green kirtle and had wrapped her long hair around her head, leaving tiny tendrils to curl about her face. Elyne finished the look with a crispinette. Maggie had protested loudly at the time, but once her hair was up, she was amazed at how she looked. She stared at her reflection in the polished mirror inside their shared tent, turning to and fro to inspect the outcome.

"You'll pass."

"Gee, thanks." She peered at her reflection once more. "I feel like a princess."

"Don't be getting the big head," Elyne warned.

"Oh, don't worry, fairy princess, I shan't. I'm well aware who is princess here." She bowed to Elyne, who merely scowled in response. "My first real banquet. This is so exciting. I only wish I had something to take notes on. I would love to be able to write everything down for my thesis. Why aren't you dressed?"

"I'm not going," Elyne said. "I'm seen as your servant. That wouldn't be proper."

"Proper, schmoper. Get dressed, Ellie. You're going, too."

"I told you not to call me that, did I not?" Her blonde brows lifted toward her hairline, creasing her smooth forehead. "Yet you persist in using this...name." The way she said the word *name* made it seem as though it were something vile.

"You don't like that nickname?" Maggie let her irritation roll off her.

"I've never been addressed as anything but 'your highness' or 'princess' and certainly not Ellie." She lifted her head and looked down her nose giving Maggie that haughty look she was all too familiar with.

"Pardon me, then. I'll not use it again." She said the last in her best singsong voice, trying to sound like someone from this century. Though she didn't think she succeeded very well.

Elyne's expression softened as she relaxed. "Actually...maybe you could be the only one to call me that."

Maggie held back the smug smile she wanted to give her. Instead, she nodded. "It's a deal. Now get yourself dressed. I'm not leaving without you."

She grasped the Fae princess by the shoulders and spun her toward the sleeping quarters of their tent. She pointed, giving her a stern look and nudged her forward. With a sheepish grin, Elyne disappeared inside as Maggie blew out a breath. She couldn't help but feel as though they'd finally had a breakthrough.

Elyne was her ticket out of the Middle Ages. If she could make friends with her, then perhaps she could find out how she was supposed to keep Finn alive. Though she was still unsure how that was supposed to work. Elyne didn't exactly offer up any help in that department. She wondered if it had anything to do with Sir Derron. The two were clearly rivals in the lists.

Which made her wonder about other things. Derron mentioned something about a Lady Juliet and Finn's tarnished reputation. Who was this Lady Juliet? What had happened between her and Finn that tarnished his reputation? She made a mental note to get to the bottom of that before all of this was over. There was more to Sir Finian than he let on and she was determined to get the scoop.

Plus, it made excellent drama for her thesis. Thinking of the paper she'd soon write about her medieval men made her giddy with glee.

Elyne stepped out looking radiant in a gown of dark blue. It set off her lovely blue eyes and highlighted her beautiful creamy skin.

"Wow, Ellie," Maggie breathed. "You look lovely."

"Aye, I know." She dismissed her compliment with a wave of her hand.

"Good to know you're not conceited. Let's get to banquet before the man comes bursting in here wondering what we're about."

Outside, Finn waited, dressed in a fine tunic of pale green, which made his silvery eyes stand out all the more. He'd changed from the padded breeches to taupe ones that draped his muscular legs and ended in a pair of soft shoes. He was deep in conversation with a dark-haired man who stood as tall as Finn. As she and Elyne emerged from the tent, he gave her his attention.

"And who have we here?" He stepped toward Maggie, reaching for her hand. "Finn, I believe you're holding out on me keeping this beauty hidden. What's your name, my lovely?" He planted a soft kiss on her knuckles.

"Lady Margaret," she said, an amused smile on her lips. "And you are?"

"Sir Drake Attenborough, my lady. It's a pleasure to make your acquaintance." And he kissed her knuckles yet again.

Flattered, Maggie gave her best disarming smile. Finn immediately reached for her hand still in Sir Drake's grasp and tucked it into his elbow. He gave the man a sour look. She stifled a giggle.

"I must admit, I'm terribly surprised you've picked an Englishwoman, Finian. 'Tis not like you. Tell me, my lady, what part of England do you hail from?"

"She's no' English. She's part of Campbell's clan," Finn corrected. "And 'tis where she'll go once tourney is over."

"I didn't realize Campbell had such a bonnie lass amongst his kinfolk." An appreciative smile ruffled Sir Drake's mouth.

"I'm a, ah, distant cousin." Improv was not one of her strong skills. She would have to get better at it, though, the longer she walked through this world.

"A cousin, you say? All this time and he's never mentioned it to me. I daresay I'll have to inquire about that next time I see him."

Crap. Figures Sir Drake would know the man. Thinking fast, she said, "Oh, I'm afraid we're a part of the family branch that no one speaks of. Due to the illness, you know."

"Illness?" Drake looked rather taken aback.

"Oh, yes. Madness, it seems. Strikes every other generation. 'Tis why Campbell stays in Scotland." It *sounded* plausible to Maggie but when she glanced at Elyne, she rolled her eyes. Some help she was.

Finn cleared his throat. "We best be going to the castle." He eyed his friend, impatience flaring.

"Indeed," Sir Drake agreed. "Off we go then."

"Elyne will be joining us," Maggie said.

"*Och*, but she's a servant."

Maggie could see Elyne ready with a biting retort, but she cut her off, lest she get herself in more trouble with the laird. "She's *going*," she insisted and glanced at Sir Drake. "Mayhap you'd do the honor of escorting her? I simply shan't go anywhere without her."

"'Twould be my pleasure, my lady." He held out his arm for Elyne.

Elyne flashed Maggie the dirtiest look she could muster before taking Drake's arm. The two of them headed through the pavilion, past all the colorful tents to Castle Middleham. Maggie and Finn fell in step behind them.

"Yere Lady Margaret now are ye?" Finn asked, his voice low so only Maggie could hear.

"Thanks to Elyne."

"'Twould be a shame if yere lying to me," he warned.

"You still think I'm some sort of spy?" Looking up at him, the waning light of the afternoon shadowed his face, making him more handsome than she thought possible. "I don't believe you think that, Finn, for if you did, you wouldn't have fought Derron over me this afternoon."

His jaw tightened, a muscle ticking along the edge.

"Ah. So. You *are* jealous of him." Elyne's self-satisfaction must have oozed onto her. She couldn't help but feel a little smug. "Why do you dislike him so much?"

"Why do ye fancy him so much?" Finn retorted.

"He's a legend," Maggie said without thinking. Of course, in her time, he was a legend who died when he was in his prime.

Finn snorted. "Aye, so he kens. Ye'd be wise to avoid him, lass. Take my word for it, eh?"

"Is he trouble, then?"

"More trouble than he's worth."

Maggie pondered this as they approached the castle. The foursome paused at the entrance to wash their hands in a giant stone bowl. Servants waited with linen towels for them. Squires stood about after they entered, ready to show them to their table. Two young men bowed and then led Elyne and Drake followed by Maggie and Finn through the crowd to the great hall.

Many of the lords and ladies turned out for the festivities after the opening ceremony earlier that afternoon. They mingled throughout the room, talking in soft voices, holding tankards of ale, and goblets of wine. They wore the finest linens, velvets, and silks in the brightest colors Maggie had ever seen. Musicians played joyful tunes on stringed instruments—a lute and a mandolin—and a recorder.

This beat any re-enactment she'd ever seen. Better than any renaissance faire she'd ever been to. This was the real deal and she was really standing here, next to the biggest, brawniest Scotsman she'd ever laid eyes on. She was one lucky girl. And terrified beyond words. Her feet froze, refusing to move, and her stomach knotted in a nauseated lump.

Could she really trust a Faery princess to send her back to her time? Everything Elyne had told her thus far had seemed to be true, yet Maggie wasn't so certain saving Finn would send her back home. And, for that matter, she wasn't certain she *could* save Finn. How could she when she hadn't a clue as to how he died in the first place? If Finn lived, then what would happen to history? Would it alter it? Would his castle no longer be ruins? Would she end up lost in Dumfries? Or would she even take the trip in the first place?

So many questions boggled her mind.

"What fashes ye?" Finn's voice cut through her thoughts.

She couldn't tell him all her fears because he would never understand she was from the future. Or that she was sent to keep him alive. Instead, she said, "I've never seen anything like it." Nor would she ever again. She wanted to pinch herself to make sure she wasn't still dreaming.

"Dinna be nervous, lass. 'Tis a fine time, banquet."

He patted her hand in the most reassuring way and gave her a knee-melting smile. She nearly dissolved into a puddle at his feet. Another indication Finn was a man who had a big heart and she wanted to break down all the walls around it and get to him. He had huge potential. And she knew something else huge to match.

The banquet hall tables were set up in a giant U-shape with the honored guests at the high table in the middle. Finn was on Maggie's left while Elyne sat next to her with Drake on the other side. They were seated at a table to the left side of the high table, toward the middle. Which meant they weren't as important as Sir Derron, who was across from them near the high table. Maggie stole a glance at Finn, who glared across the banquet hall at him and Derron beamed right back, looking arrogant as usual.

Loaves of bread were stationed up and down the table. In front of each of them, they had a knife, a spoon and a trencher of bread instead of a plate. But Maggie had been prepared for that from her earlier meal at Finn's castle when she ate porridge out of a bread trencher. Servants poured wine and ale for those already seated and those who had been mingling made their way to their seats.

At the high table, a tall, thin man rose and the hall quieted.

"Welcome, honored knights and ladies fair," he greeted in a nasal tone. "Let us say grace."

Heads bowed but Maggie couldn't help herself. She tipped her head up enough to peer around the room and see a priest stand up from the high table, intoning his benediction.

"Amen."

The spread of food lined the high table in a stepped buffet covered in richly colored drapes—scarlet, violet, emerald. It had to be the biggest buffet Maggie had ever seen and was still surrounded by a bustle of activity as cooks and servants came and went, serving a soup in the trenchers before them.

"Soup? That's all we get?"

"'Tis merely the first course, lass." Finn leaned down to speak in her ear, his warm breath tickling her tender skin. Gooseflesh erupted over every inch of her.

"The first course?" She turned her head to look at him, their faces mere inches apart. His eyes were like liquid silver, inviting her to dive in, stay awhile.

"Aye. Barley pottage." He gave her a wicked smile, one that said he remembered what she looked like in her delicates, and reached for his spoon, the spell broken.

Her stomach rumbled in response and she realized she hadn't eaten anything all day. She took up her spoon.

The man who greeted them at the high table, Maggie noticed, stared first at Finn then at her and back again. It made her uneasy.

"Who is that man?"

"The Earl of Litonshire." Finn's voice was deep and dusty, tinged with anger. "Lord Byron de Fortier."

"I take it you're not on good terms with him." Maggie sipped her pottage, pleased with the rich flavor. "He stares at you as though he holds a grudge."

"Lord Litonshire holds a grudge against any man he can't marry off to his sister," Sir Drake said, leaning forward to join the conversation.

"What's wrong with her?" Maggie asked.

"Nothing," Drake replied. "But no one wants him for a brother-in-law." He laughed then, as though it were a hearty joke. "Despite how fetching his sister is."

"Aye, 'tis true. The man is a beast to contend with," Finn agreed.

Maggie looked around the banquet hall. "Is she here? His sister?"

"I haven't seen her," Drake said before Finn could reply. "Rumor is one of the knights at last tourney stole her innocence."

Maggie might have missed the quick exchange of glances between the two men if she hadn't been looking. She saw the look of guilt and shame pass over Drake's face as he finished saying the words, as though he hadn't meant to say it. She also saw the look of death Finn gave Drake. Pieces fell into place, then, and Maggie realized the horrendous truth. Finn had been accused of stealing Lady Juliet's innocence. So why, then, would Finn come to tournament with that dark secret hanging over his head? There had to be a good reason for it.

"'Tis best not to spread falsehoods," Finn snapped.

Lord Litonshire continued to give them a dark stare. Maggie smiled sweetly at him and slipped her hand around Finn's biceps, splaying her fingers so the earl could clearly see she had her hand on his arm. Finn opened his mouth to protest but she nodded her head in his direction and he saw Lord Litonshire refusing to look, his face a deep shade of red.

"Ah, lass. 'Tis kind of ye but—"

"Hush now," she said.

The bustle of activity resumed as servants brought trays of covered meats from the kitchens and served it. This course was a lovely roasted boar and some sort of boiled fowl. Other meats followed and, according to Finn, they were more delicate in flavor, consisting of wild stuffed bird, a sturgeon cooked in parsley and vinegar, and fresh fish.

All of this was promptly followed by tarts and pies and fritters. By the time the food had been cleared out from in front of her, Maggie was pleasantly stuffed. As the music got louder, the knights and ladies began to dance.

Maggie drifted through her food and wine stupor while Drake and Elyne made pleasant conversation next to her when she noticed Sir Derron weaving his way through the crowd toward them, his gaze fixed on her. She sat up a little straighter, pleased to see her idol heading right for her.

"Lady Margaret," he greeted and bowed. "Will you allow me the pleasure of a dance?"

"She will not," Finn answered before Maggie could even open her mouth to respond.

"I wasn't asking you." Derron's eyes flashed hot.

"She willna dance with ye."

"Oh, yes, I will." Maggie stood quickly, her chair scraping over the floor.

Derron smiled, pleased as she hurried around the table and took his outstretched hand. This was her big chance to get a moment alone with him and she wasn't going to let anyone—not even Finn—stand in her way.

They took the dance floor, Maggie trying hard to follow his lead. She was unfamiliar with this dance, though, so it was difficult not to step on his toes or bump into other dancers. As they went by, she'd catch Finn's irritated glare. Quickly looking away, she pasted on a bright smile and focused on Derron.

"I suppose he'll not be very happy with your decision to dance with me," Derron said.

"He won't be but I'm sure he'll get over it." Eventually. Hopefully he wouldn't trot her out to Campbell's clan and dump her off anytime soon. She did have that to worry about.

Derron chuckled. "Tell me, my lady, why I find you so

fascinating."

"Mayhap for the same reason I find you fascinating." He whirled her away from another dancer who tried to intervene. "I know who you are."

His blue eyes glittered with a mischievous glint. "Ah, so Princess Elyne has revealed my true identity, I see."

"She mentioned you were protector of the Otherworld and Guardian of one of the Four Treasures," Maggie said.

"She makes it sound more important than it really is," Derron said, though he made no effort to elaborate.

Maggie couldn't resist asking. "What exactly does a guardian do?"

Derron's smile showed off his deep dimples. "Nothing you need to worry your pretty head about."

His vague answers frustrated her. "Evasive, aren't you? Then tell me this. Why does a Fae knight want to put his life in danger by jousting?"

"And swordplay. Lest ye forget."

"Indeed," Maggie agreed, feeling a little out of breath. Either from the exhilaration of dancing or from being next to the man she'd been researching for the last year, in the flesh, she didn't know. Nor did she care.

"I prefer to live rather than waste away in some dull court, waiting to become Guardian of one of the Four Treasures."

"Ah, a real answer at last. I thought you already were guardian?"

"My father is guardian until his death." His smile faded. "And since the *Tuatha dé Danaan* are immortal..."

"You'll be waiting a really long time," she finished.

Derron nodded. "I have no interest in guarding a dusty old relic for the rest of my days. Tell me, my dear. What else do you know about our race?" He spun her away from him then brought her back and held her close. So close the heat of him pressed into her, sending spine-tingling excitement trickling through her. He was breathtaking.

"I know you don't like humans very much," she said.

"Elyne doesn't like humans very much," he corrected. "I, however, am quite fond of them. As I am of you." She blushed as he pressed on. "Coming to the human realm is strictly forbidden. You wouldn't know that, would you?"

"And yet here you are."

"Aye, here I am. I do as I please and ignore those stuffy old rules."

"By shirking your duties in the Otherworld?" Maggie asked.

"My duties consist of nothing but waiting. A boring existence, to be sure. I come here to fill my days with banquets and jousting and beautiful women."

"And Princess Elyne?"

He snickered. "Turning green with envy at the moment."

As he turned her, Maggie could see the Fae princess fuming with indignation. Even when Sir Drake tried to coax her onto the dance floor, she shook her head, preferring instead to stare them down, which didn't make sense to Maggie. She acted as though she hated the man yet at the same time, she seemed insanely jealous.

"Are you two related?" she asked.

"Gods, no." He laughed out loud then, a melodious laugh that vibrated through her. "She is my betrothed."

"She's your *what?*" Maggie stopped dancing so abruptly he stumbled over her.

"I see I've caused you quite a shock. Come, let's go where we can talk and not cause any more disorder here."

He took her by the hand and led her from the great hall into the bailey. She followed as he led her outside into the evening air where the crickets chirped. Moonlight spilled over the manicured grass, lush and green. They sat on a stone bench and he took her hand in his, holding it quite pleasantly.

"She didn't tell you, did she?" he asked.

"No. I had no idea."

No wonder Elyne was all bent out of shape over the fecking wenches, as she called them. No wonder she glowered at Derron at the practice arena. No wonder, indeed. It all made sense now.

"'Tis a betrothal in name only."

"You don't love her?"

His eyes were black orbs in the shadowy darkness. Even so, she could see the faraway look in his gaze.

"We have been affianced for the last half century. It's a match her mother and my father arranged since Elyne is crown princess and I am Knight of the Realm."

Maggie noticed he eluded answering that question as well. Did Derron love Elyne? She sensed there were some feelings there, but she couldn't decide if he was masking his love for her or if there was something else. "Why haven't you married then?"

"She's rather...difficult at times. An arranged marriage is not for me. I prefer to marry someone of my own choosing." Holding her hand, he put it to his lips, kissing her. "Let us not talk of such things anymore, for it does not matter."

Oh, but it did matter. Maggie wanted to shout it, to rip her hand away but instead she sat there, letting him hold her fingers in his. Elyne didn't want her to know Derron was her betrothed for some reason. It was also clear he and Finian were enemies when it came to the lists. She would have to get Elyne and Derron together somehow, to figure out why there was a rift between them and mend it. And in the meantime, keep Finn from dying.

She clearly had her work cut out for her.

"Tell me, Lady Margaret, what do you see in that big oaf of a Scotsman."

"He's not an oaf." Maggie tugged her hand free of his grasp.

"Surely you don't intend to continue to stay with a man of his ilk," Derron said. "He's nothing but a ruffian."

"He's no ruffian, Sir Derron." Maggie stood now, the fire flaming inside her.

"Ah, I've insulted you." He clucked his tongue and reached for her, trying to get her to sit down again. "A thousand apologies, my lady. I don't want to see you get hurt."

"Hurt how?"

"Surely you've heard the whispers through the pavilion. Sir Finian is a bit of a cad when it comes to the ladies."

"And you're not?" she fired back.

He chuckled. "Indeed, no. I would never steal a lady's maidenhead."

"What are you saying?" Maggie couldn't believe it. Not Finian. No way. He wouldn't treat a woman like that. At least, she didn't *think* he would.

"Seems Sir Finian was found with the Lady Juliet in the stables, her lip swollen and bleeding and the blood of her maidenhead on her thighs. She was wrapped in his tartan," Derron said. "It's been quite the scandal."

"Are you telling me he *hit* her?" She couldn't bring herself to voice the other horror. That didn't add up. Even when Maggie had tested Finn, he'd never exhibited violent tendencies. He would never hit a lady, she was sure of it. She was also sure he'd never force himself on a lady if she didn't want it. The morning in his bedchamber was a big clue to that. "I don't believe you."

"You can ask Lord Litonshire, if you must."

"What does *he* have to do with it?"

"Why, my lady, Lord Litonshire is Lady Juliet's brother, of course. He had the bishop examine her and prove she was indeed violated. And since Sir Finian was the knight found with her, it was clear he was the one, despite vehement denial on both their accounts."

"He didn't do it." This smelled of a set-up. Somehow Finn had been blackmailed by Litonshire.

Derron laughed, a hearty bellow that came from his depths. "How could you know that?"

"He just wouldn't. And I mean to prove it."

"How might you do that?"

Maggie paced, her hands balled into fists. "I don't know yet but I'm going to figure something out." She was a twenty-first century woman, after all. She was smart and savvy. She could come up with something. And she decided she'd start with Lord Litonshire, as smarmy as the man might seem. He was the key to Finn's tarnished reputation, but why she didn't know.

"Come sit down, my lady. Let us not talk of such unsavory subjects." He reached a hand to her, coaxing her next to him.

She stopped pacing and intended to sit when she saw Finn charging toward them. Her heart nearly stopped when she saw the fierce look on his face. After her moment of terror passed, she nearly swooned, feeling rather lightheaded over the fact he'd come for her.

"Sir Finian—" she began.

But he ignored her and went for Derron. He punched the Fae in the face. He went flying backward, off the bench and into a bush. Maggie squealed as she saw his feet in the air. He hadn't moved a muscle.

"Sir Derron." She started to dive in after him but Finn caught her by the arm and held her in place.

"Dinna even think to go after him, lass." His voice was dark, angry, with a powerful edge that sent gooseflesh rising across her arms and a smug thought crossed her mind. He certainly was possessive for a man who wanted to rid himself of her.

"But…he could be hurt."

She glanced up into Finn's eyes, those silvery molten eyes, and she was immediately silenced. Okay, so she wouldn't be going after Derron after all. Derron, meanwhile, had managed to extricate himself from the offending bush. His nose dripped dots of blood on his tunic and he wiped it away with the back of his hand.

"You'll pay for that," Derron said. Even his lips were bloody.

Maggie couldn't help but feel sorry for him. She wanted to help him but Finn kept her rooted in place with his viselike grip on her arm.

"Take it out on me in the lists."

"Oh, I do intend to do that." His gaze landed on Maggie then. "He's a barbarian."

"You leave her out of this," Finn shot back before Maggie could defend his honor. "And I'll be thanking ye to stay away from the lass."

"She can decide that for herself."

"Yeah, I can. I'm a grown woman, Sir Finian."

"Aye," he agreed. "And ye'll be doing what I tell ye."

"I will not." Maggie crossed her arms, defiant. "And I'm not finished talking with Sir Derron."

"Oh, aye, ye are and yere coming with me."

"No." She sounded like a petulant child and stopped short of stomping her foot and sticking out her bottom lip.

Finn's gaze narrowed and she felt immediately she'd made a grave error in judgment. She also noted his burr became more pronounced the angrier he got. Fiery pangs of desire shot though her and for a moment she was completely distracted by his hot accent.

"*Och*, aye. Ye are."

Before she could protest further, he whisked her up and threw her over his shoulder as though she weighed nothing. He darted off, back toward the pavilion and their tents.

"HEY!"

But he ignored her shout. As he hurried away, she could hear Sir Derron's bellowing laugh following them.

"Put me down."

"Nay, lassie."

He said it so calmly, as though he often carried women around on his shoulders. They garnered a few glances here and there as he stalked through the pavilion, but he seemed unaffected. Finally, he put her back on her feet when they arrived at their tents. They stared each other down. Maggie with her hands on her hips. Finn with his powerful arms crossed over his chest.

What could she say to him? That she was embarrassed for being treated like that? That she wasn't his personal property? That he shouldn't have punched Derron?

To which he would reply he didn't care she was embarrassed. Maggie *was* his personal property until he returned her to Campbell, a clan to which she had no intention of going. And Derron deserved to be punched in the face and his nose bloodied. He was an insolent Faery and even she knew that.

"God's teeth, woman." His voice was low with an edge as sharp as a sword. "Have I no' told ye to stay away from him?"

"You have," Maggie said matter-of-factly. But she couldn't explain to Finn she had to interview the man before her time here was over.

"And ye disobey me anyway?" Again, the burr left her feeling warm and tingly all over. "Are ye daft?"

Oh, if she wasn't so ticked at the man, she'd jump into his arms and kiss him senseless. Maybe that was what he needed.

"It's your fault if I am." She gave him an angry shove, which was like shoving a brick wall, and spun on her heel, about to duck into her tent.

He snatched her by the arms, pulling her to him. She crashed against his rock-hard chest so hard it vibrated through her entire body. She nearly swooned.

"Ye best do as I say from here on, lass. Or I'll take ye across my knee."

Maggie wrenched free and turned to peer up at him. "You. Wouldn't. Dare."

"Oh, wouldn't I?" There was a mischievous glint in his eye, one eyebrow slightly cocked, and she knew he wasn't kidding.

The mere thought of lying across his lap while he spanked her sent her mind reeling. How could he even *think* to do such a thing? How could she even *think* it sounded appealing? No, no, she would never permit something like that to happen. She'd rather dance naked under the full moon.

With him.

Followed by a raucous round of lovemaking under the stars.

She quirked a half-grin, enjoying the visual despite the fact she was still annoyed with him. Perhaps that's what made him soften. Finn's gaze turned to mercury, liquid silver slipping over her, lingering on her breasts as she tried to calm her enraged breathing. Perhaps he remembered what she looked like in her lacy bra for his eyes lowered and sparked. Maggie's breathing turned from enraged to excited and she totally got the heaving bosom thing. She never thought she'd do that.

He brushed the back of his large hand across her cheek, his touch sending her pulse into high gear. She felt short of breath when he rested his palm on her neck, the warmth of his fingers spreading through her. He slid his other hand against her waist around to the small of her back, pulling her towards him ever so slightly, and she realized—OH—he was going to kiss her. She ran her tongue over her dry lips in preparation.

His mouth was a breath away from hers. Maggie focused on the straight line of his lips, the way they parted—

"What is going on here? And why does Sir Derron have a bloody lip?"

It was Elyne who suddenly burst onto the scene, interrupting them. They jumped apart as though they were caught doing hanky-panky by a parent.

Maybe it was for the best they'd been interrupted because Maggie wasn't sure how much longer she would wait for him to plant that kiss. She was about to fling herself at him and get after it, which is what he needed to make him to be nice to her. He had practically purred at her when they'd been in his bed and they'd shared the only kiss they'd had.

Finn stepped away, back toward his tent. It was then Maggie noticed his two squires had stepped out of Finn's tent, wide-eyed watching the two of them. Had they seen everything? She blushed.

"Well?" Elyne asked when neither of them offered a response.

"I have a match in the morning." Finn flung aside the flap to his tent, disappearing within. Maggie fought the urge to follow him.

"Nice timing," Maggie grumbled. "I'm going to bed."

Unable to sleep, Finn left the pavilion to head toward sin. There was something about the gambling tents that pulled him, almost as though an invisible hand beckoned him. He knew he shouldn't go.

He should ignore their existence but the debt lingering over him outweighed his common sense.

If he could win back even a little of the money owed, if he could pay off some of that debt...then mayhap he could get Litonshire off his back and out of his life forever.

He paused to watch a game of Hazard already in progress. While he enjoyed cards, dice was his weakness. With his small purse of coins in one hand, he entered the tent as a gamer won his round. He knew most of the men here. They were the usual crowd that haunted the gambling tents. He also recognized a few of the men from the clans Montgomery and Stewart.

"Good eve, Sir Finian." He recognized his old friend and fellow Scot, Angus Duncan. "Come for punishment at a game of Hazard?"

Laughter filled the tent and Finn held his temper in check. He and Angus got along fine when it came to jousting and riding, but in the gambling tents, they were mortal enemies.

"Aye, I have." Finn threw his two gold pieces into the game, feeling good about this round of play.

"I thought ye'd have had enough of the game after last tourney," Angus said, continuing to dig into the old wound. "Seems ye canna get enough."

The others chuckled at Angus. Finn's jaw clenched.

"Are ye going to be the caster or not?" he boomed in his baritone voice.

"Aye, all right. I'll go, then." Angus couldn't hide the wide grin behind his red beard.

He started the round by throwing out the die until he managed to get the main number, which was a five. He continued to cast the dice, rolling a five several times and getting a nick. But Angus' luck ran out quickly, as he couldn't hit the five again. He threw out once when the dice rolled into a double one, then again when he landed on one and two. He managed to lose three times in a row and, with a frown, passed the dice to Finn.

"Ye dinna seem to be so fortunate that round." Finn didn't bother to hide his grin.

"'Tis merely a setback for now," Angus said. "We'll see how well ye can do, aye?"

Finn shook the two dice in his hand, blew on them for luck, and tossed them out. He landed on eight, which became his number he had to hit to win. He threw again, landing a nick with twelve and another by hitting the main number, eight. He continued to win round after round, racking in the coins much to the dismay of his fellow players and Angus.

"Huzzah!" the dice players cheered when Finn scraped up the last of the coins.

"Ye fare well, McCullough," Angus said. "Though I admit I dinna expect to see ye here."

"Indeed?" Finn closed the purse with the drawstring. "'Tis enough playing for one night, I should think."

"Ye misunderstand," Angus said. "I dinna expect to see ye at tourney at all. Not with that Litonshire in charge."

It appeared no one had any love for the earl, especially Finn. He pursed his lips. He hadn't realized the earl had taken charge of the tournament. Mayhap it was a mistake to come after all, though he knew if he didn't, he'd surely lose his lands.

"Litonshire is nothing but a swine-breathed knave," Finn said.

"Aye, he is," Angus agreed. "But a powerful swine-breathed knave."

"Mayhap," Finn agreed. "But 'tis no' enough to keep me from trying to win, aye?"

Angus laughed. "Well, then. Another round of Hazard, my friend?"

Finn couldn't resist. "Aye, then. Let's see who's better at this game, me or you."

"A challenge," Angus said and laughed heartily. "And should ye win, I'll be the gracious loser and allow ye to buy me a tankard of ale."

With a grin, Finn tossed two more coins into the pot.

Chapter 6

Maggie had a restless night, unable to fall into a deep sleep. She blamed that on Finn and the kiss of which Elyne robbed her. She hadn't heard Elyne come into the tent that night and she half wondered where the Fae princess had wandered off to. Perhaps she'd flitted off to Faery. If she didn't need the wench, it'd be good riddance. As it was, she did need her.

As Maggie rolled over on her side on the pitiful excuse for a mattress, she thought of Derron and Elyne and their betrothal. If Elyne had no feelings for the Fae knight, then she wouldn't have been jealous while they danced.

Maggie couldn't help but feel sad for Elyne, but she kept that closely guarded. She would never want Elyne to think she pitied her. Still, it must be difficult for her to be in love with a man she was betrothed to who not only didn't want to marry her, but didn't love her back. Maggie was convinced Derron had long-buried feelings for the princess and he hid them well by flirting with the other ladies. She intended to pull them out of him one way or another. He *had* to love Elyne.

When she heard the first twitter of morning birds, she flung off the coverlet and got up, combing her fingers through her hair. She dressed as quickly as she could. She still wasn't used to the shift, the hose gartered at the knee—which were actually more uncomfortable than nylon knee-hi's. That day, she chose a linen kirtle in a reddish brown, finishing it off with a pale-brown sideless surcote. Finally, she stepped out into the early morning, the air fresh and cool. She couldn't face fussing with her hair and left it hanging down her back. The pavilion was already alive with activity. Squires bustling about and knights getting ready for the first day of tournament.

Maggie paused outside Finn's tent, leaning toward the flap and straining her ear to listen for any sort of noise—a rustle of fabric, the clink of armor, heavy breathing. She heard nothing. When she

MICHELLE MILES

got up the nerve, she took a step inside and peered around. His tent was empty and tidy with lances and swords and armor stacked neatly to one side.

Fascination overtook her good sense and she knelt beside the armor. The breastplate had dents in various places, looking well-worn. One place looked as though it'd been cracked and repaired by a blacksmith. She tried to imagine all the lances and swords it must have resisted. She ran her hand over the cool surface, feeling every nick and bump, and yet the armor had been polished to a high shine. Finn's squires no doubt taking extra care of it for him.

Finn had two sets of spurs for his plate boots, which had riveted plates along the top. There were things she recognized, such as the greaves for his calves and ankles and the gauntlets for his hands. The gauntlets sported spikes along the knuckles and she shuddered. Those would leave quite a mess if he happened to punch someone. She thought of poor Derron.

Then there were other things she couldn't identify. One piece looked as if it would fit over his massive thigh and a small part that looked as if it belonged on his kneecap. Another large piece could only be the back plate and it, too, was polished and perfect. His helm had a skirt of mail and a visor with a long slit in it, giving him minimal visibility, but in a joust it would do well to protect his eyes.

He had chainmail neatly piled next to his armor. A small, round shield next to that. A dirk, a dagger, a short sword, a broadsword, a claymore, numerous lances with blunted tips. Of course, she'd seen pictures in some textbooks, but to be sitting here touching it, feeling it, seeing it, sent chills dancing up and down her spine.

All of this must weigh a ton. How heavy would that make him when he was in full dress? She considered this for a moment, staggered by the thought of him wearing nearly two hundred pounds of garb to sit on a horse and carry a big stick. It must have been worth it or the knights wouldn't do it. And in the heat? What a man.

He made all the men she'd known back in her time look like pansies.

A trunk on the other side held all his clothes. Again, neatly folded and stacked. She rose and backed out of the tent, but she couldn't stop gawking at it all. She paused, half-in and half-out. There was another flap inside the tent and through it she could see the sleeping compartment. There was a low bed like hers and the

70

pillow and coverlet were neatly folded. Finn was a neat freak.

A giggle bubbled up her throat. She'd never known any man to be neat and orderly. Oh, how she loved that about him.

"What do ye mean to be doing, lass?"

At the boom of his voice, she nearly jumped out of her skin. He was at the entrance of the tent, one flap held aside as he peered in. His handsome faced was etched with lines of a what-do-you-think-you're-doing gaze. She stepped backward, but somehow got tangled up in the fabric of the second flap—the one he wasn't holding—and tried to wave it away. When she finally got loose, she spun to face Finn. He had moved back, outside the tent, and stood no more than an inch away from her.

"I was looking for you," she managed.

"Aye?"

They stared at each other in a long, awkward silence. Finn wore a tunic and soft breeches. His dark hair hung around his face, the two plaits on either side looked as though they'd been freshly braided. She wanted to ask for that kiss she nearly got last night but thought better of it.

"What are we doing today?"

"We?" One brow quirked, the only expression in his chiseled features. He neither smiled nor grimaced which was more unnerving than anything. "I'm off to the Tree of Shields. Ye stay here." He pointed at the ground, as though she weren't to move from that very spot.

"I will not. I want to come with you." She flashed a smile but stopped short of batting her eyelashes. She knew what the Tree of Shields was and she *had* to see it. "Where's the Tree of Shields?"

He glowered at her before stepping into his tent. She could hear him rustling around, muttering to himself. He emerged a few minutes later wearing a quilted coat and carrying a roll of parchment. He gave her a halfhearted wave to join him.

Maggie picked up her skirts and hurried after him. She had a hard time keeping up with his long strides, but his height kept him visible in the crowd. She could spot that handsome head anywhere. They made their way through the colorful pavilion, Finn nodding to the greetings of knights and ladies as they passed by. She had to admit she was puzzled. For someone with a tarnished reputation, Finn seemed to weather it well. Those in the pavilion smiled and greeted him as though he were any other knight at tourney.

Interesting.

She was sure more than ever Lord Litonshire had something to do with these rumors. She decided she would need to find out the truth. She knew it was unconventional to be roaming around tournament without her maidservant and could quite likely cause a stir, but she was never one to follow the rules anyway. She wanted to talk to the people here to get to the bottom of it all.

Just outside the pavilion was the Tree of Shields. And what a tree indeed. It was a massive oak with sprawling branches that looked like it'd been there at least a hundred years. Under the tree in the shade, were two stiff-looking men, one with a thin, perfectly trimmed goatee while the other was clean-shaven. They were dressed well, like nobles. Above them, hanging from the tree, were two long rows of shields, each one with a different combat symbol.

She should have known that's what it was as soon as she saw it. Her fingers itched to write down all the details of the Tree of Shields, how it looked. If she had any artistic ability, she'd draw it since she had no camera to snap a picture.

Maggie watched, entranced, as each knight stepped up to the heavy wood table, handing over a roll of parchment. The clean-shaven man unrolled the parchment, speaking in low tones with the other as they looked over whatever was on it and then rolled it back up. At the goateed man's nod, the knight would then take a mallet and hit several of the shields above their heads.

"Next."

Finn stepped up to the table, Maggie hovering around behind him.

"Papers, please."

She peered over his shoulder, watching with keen fascination as he handed over the rolled parchment. Clean Shaven unrolled it, held it open while Goatee checked it over, tracing his hands over the carefully written words and the perfectly drawn lines. It was Finn's family lineage, showing the roots of his nobility. It showed his parents, grandparents, great-grandparents and even further back than that. She was supremely impressed with the detail and the artwork.

"Choose your combats, sir knight," Goatee said as Clean Shaven rolled up the parchment.

Finn picked up the mallet and hit the shield with two swords crossed and the shield with the lances.

"Sir Finian McCullough has chosen the sword and the lance," Goatee said and Clean Shaven scrawled something with a quill into a large book that looked like a ledger. "Your first match is the sword. Next."

Dropping the mallet, Finn turned and sauntered away from the Tree of Shields. She had to find parchment soon so she could start writing this all down. This was awesome research material.

"So, you're signed up?" she panted, trotting to keep up with him.

"Aye," he said curtly. His long strides seemed to get longer as he walked back into the pavilion, heading for their tents.

"What now?" Maggie finally caught up to him. "Could you slow down?"

"I havna time to slow down, lass. I'm headed to the practice arena."

"Can I come?" She felt like a child, asking her parent's permission.

"I'd rather ye not."

"Why not?"

"'Twould be a distraction."

"I'm a distraction?" Smug satisfaction crept through her. Perhaps she was finally breaking through that tough exterior.

"Ye ken what I mean."

"No, I don't. What do you mean?" If he'd been looking at her, she would have fluttered her lashes and grinned.

"*Och*, lass." He stopped so fast, she had to skitter to a halt. "Do ye wish me to get injured?"

"No, of course not."

"Then ye must stay away."

Maggie loved that his burr became more pronounced with every word. Good. He was clearly flustered. He needed to be flustered. Still, if she wasn't tagging along with Finn, then what?

"But...what am I supposed to do instead?" She sounded more pitiful than she had intended.

Finn softened and his bunched shoulders relaxed, drooping a bit. A small smile quirked the corner of his mouth, something she'd not seen him do. Not yet. She liked it. He needed to smile more. It crinkled the corners of his eyes in a sexy way she found highly appealing.

"Mayhap ye and Elyne can visit the market."

"There's a market here?" She perked up at that. "Where is it?"

"Elyne can take ye. Come. I'll give ye a few coins to spend."

He started to walk again this time slow enough for her to keep up. By the time they reached his tent, Maggie was smiling and her gait had a happy cheerfulness. Happy to have something to fill her time until Finn's first event. Even happier thinking of all the trinkets she might buy. Or parchment. She could actually some scribe words on medieval parchment with a quill pen and an inkwell. Excitement bubbled up through her. He ducked into her tent and came out a moment later with a small bag with a drawstring top. He handed it to her.

"Here now. Dinna spend it all at once, aye?"

"Thank you, sir." She dipped a quick curtsy and pocketed the coins. "I promise I won't."

Maggie had wasted nearly an hour searching for Elyne. The Fae Princess was nowhere in sight and not in the pavilion either. She wandered from tent to tent looking for her, garnering wary glances from others. The only good thing about that was she managed to chat with some of the others. Specifically, the other ladies.

"By your leave, you're with Sir Finian, are you not?" one pretty young thing twittered. She was blonde and green-eyed and looked barely old enough to drive had they'd been in Maggie's time. She wore a pale-pink gown with gold trim and had her long hair flowing in soft waves over one shoulder.

"Yes, I am. Do you know him?"

"I wish. He's so handsome." The girl giggled, fluttering her lashes and looking every bit a teenager with a giant crush. Maggie imagined if she could, the girl would have posters of the dashing knight plastered all over her bedroom wall.

"Oh, indeed." Maggie decided to use this opportunity for a bit of recon. "Tell me. What do you know of Sir Finian and Lady Juliet?"

The girl scrunched up her face. "Oh, merely the rumors I've heard."

"'Tis only a rumor then?"

"No one knows for sure." She shrugged. "No one's seen Lady Juliet since last tourney when it happened. I heard she took to her bed beset with a deep sorrow."

"What happened to her?"

"Some say she was attacked. Others think she's a bit of a vixen."

"And therefore, brought it upon herself?" Maggie asked.

"Aye, so I've heard."

Maggie couldn't pass judgment on the woman until she met her, though. Vixen or no, if she was attacked, Maggie had to get to the bottom of it. "I see then. She was badly injured, I understand."

The girl glanced around and stepped closer, lowering her voice. "My da would have my head if he heard me gossiping, but I heard whoever he was, he beat her up right good."

"And you don't believe it was Sir Finian." It was more a statement of fact and not a question.

"Oh, not at all." The girl shook her head. "Sir Finian isn't like that and we all know it. 'Tis a shame he was in the wrong place caught with her. No one seems to know who the boor was, though."

"You think he was there to help her?"

"He follows the Code, my lady," the girl said. "He'd never disrespect a lady."

Maggie asked if she'd seen her maid but she hadn't seen Elyne either. They lapsed into a bit of small talk. Maggie learned her name was Lady Grace de Mauly, the youngest daughter of an English noble whose brother was participating in the tourney. Thanking her, Maggie went on her way. The more people she talked to, the better understanding of Finn she got. He was a big, brute of a man, but he always followed the Code of Chivalry. Another tick mark in the pro column for the Scotsman.

The only place she hadn't looked for Elyne was the practice arena and it was the last place she went. She headed there next but was intercepted by Sir Drake, her anticipated excitement of getting to the market waning.

"Good morrow, Lady Margaret. What brings you out so early this fine morning?" He bowed low to her and she curtsied.

"Good morrow, Sir Drake. I'm looking for my maid, Elyne. Have you seen her?"

"I daresay I have. Over at the practice arena. Shall we go there straightaway and fetch her?"

"Yes, but in a moment, if you will. I should like to ask you a question or two," Maggie said. "About Sir Finian."

"Ah, yes, I thought you might. I shouldn't have said that about the rumors last night. Sir Finian was quite unhappy with me."

"Are the rumors true?"

"I would never believe Sir Finian would do such a thing," Sir Drake replied. "'Tis no proof but the evidence is rather damaging, wouldn't you say? Lady Juliet had his tartan wrapped tightly around her."

"I'm assuming she was…without attire?" It was the most delicate way Maggie could put that question.

"'Twas very damning," he said, nodding.

"Should I fear for my own reputation, then?" Maggie hoped not. If anyone was going to take advantage of her, she hoped it would be Finn. She was certain he could make her purr like a kitten.

Sir Drake chuckled. "Do you fear for your reputation?"

"Honestly, no' one wee bit." She smiled, showing all her teeth and he laughed.

"Come, then, and let me escort you to the practice arena."

He held out his arm and she took it, and together they walked in amicable silence to the practice field.

Maggie found the Fae princess standing with her arms crossed, glaring at Derron while he flirted shamelessly with the ladies. He had just finished a practice round, Maggie surmised, judging by the way the sweat beaded on his forehead and his upper lip and yet he managed to look as though he hadn't really exerted himself at all. Maggie wondered why Elyne stood there and watched it all happen without intervening.

It was time to put a stop to Derron's flirting and get those two together.

"Ellie, there you are."

"Ah, finally awake I see," Elyne said when she saw Maggie.

"Good morrow to you, too," Maggie said, dropping a quick curtsey and flushing with embarrassment. "Sir Drake was kind enough to escort me here."

She gave him a cursory glance before retuning her glare to Derron. It was clear the woman needed an intervention before she blew a gasket. Maggie pressed on.

"I understand there's a market nearby and Sir Finian gave me a few coins to spend if you want to go with me."

"You want to go *now*?"

Sir Drake cleared his throat. "I would be more than happy to escort the two of you."

Elyne glanced between Maggie and Sir Drake. "You do realize Sir Finian's first match starts in a few minutes, right?"

"Oh, I didn't realize. He never mentioned it when I saw him this morning. Well, other than saying I'd be a distraction."

By the look on Elyne's face, it told her she should probably get thee to the match—wherever that was—to make sure Finn didn't die in this particular event.

"Some other time, then," Sir Drake said. He gave a quick bow before leaving the two of them.

Elyne flashed one more look full of daggers at Derron—who was blissfully unaware—before she grabbed Maggie by the sleeve and led her from the practice arena.

"You haven't forgotten our bargain, have you?"

"I keep Finn alive and you send me home. How could I forget?"

Elyne flashed a flat look that said she wasn't amused. "Why are you wandering around the grounds alone? Don't you know how dangerous that is?"

"I don't have time to sit around and wait for you to show up, princess." Maggie's tone dripped with sarcasm. "Besides, it's not like *you're* following the rules, either."

"What is that supposed to mean?"

"I mean by talking to me like that in front of Sir Drake. He thinks you're a servant, after all, and not my equal."

"Sir Drake is the least of your worries, you know," she chastised. "You should stop worrying about everyone else and worry about Finn. And, furthermore, I'm not your equal. I'm Fae royalty."

"What's going on with you and Derron?" Maggie asked, steering the subject away from her and Finn. She was aware of her responsibilities and she didn't take them lightly.

"Nothing. That's what."

"Even though you two are betrothed?"

"We are, but that doesn't mean he wants to marry me."

"But you *want* to marry him, don't you? You're clearly jealous when he flirts with the other girls."

"I am not." Elyne huffed out the words.

"Uh huh." Maggie hid her knowing smile.

"You don't believe me?" Elyne stopped, put her hands on her hips. "I don't care what he does with those fecking harlots and I never have."

Maggie lifted one eyebrow. "They're fecking harlots now?"

Elyne rolled her eyes and started walking again. Maggie had to hurry to catch up with her. "If you two are betrothed, why haven't you married?"

"You think it's that simple?" Elyne spun on Maggie, her hands flying wildly. She paced back and forth then. "He doesn't want to marry me."

"Why not?"

Elyne huffed out a breath. "A long story you won't be interested in."

"Try me. I'm a good listener." And she was sure she could fix the problem if she knew what it was.

Sighing, Elyne resigned to tell the story. "Our betrothal was arranged long ago by my mother and his father. We were children at the time. We spent so much time together, it seemed natural we'd marry when were grown. But I wanted nothing to do with an arranged marriage, even though Derron courted me. He pursued me relentlessly until one day he finally professed his feelings. He told me he loved me and that he intended to petition my mother, the queen, for my hand in marriage. That's when I rejected him. I thought I didn't want him. That he was nothing more than a nuisance."

Maggie remembered what Derron had told her previously—that an arranged marriage was not for him. After so many years of wanting Elyne, he must have used that lie to convince himself it was the truth. Elyne came to halt and lapsed into silence. Color stained her cheekbones as she remembered.

"It crushed him. He wouldn't speak to me for years. That would be centuries in your human world. I spent so much time wanting him to leave me alone and then when he did, I felt empty. Like something was missing. I realized what I was missing was him. The way he teased me, followed me around, seemed to know what I wanted before I wanted it. I tried to apologize, to make amends, but he wouldn't even speak to me."

She paused and clasped her hands, lacing her fingers in front of her. Her cheeks still flushed red.

"You love him, don't you?"

Elyne bit her bottom lip and marched away from Maggie. At last, Elyne was giving her something to work with. Broken hearts she could help mend. Maggie could tell her feelings for Derron were strong and he didn't give her a passing glance and now she knew why. She was also surprised at the very human emotions the Fae princess exhibited now.

"You do, don't you?" Maggie asked, panting to keep up with her.

"'Tis none of your concern," Elyne snapped, her lilt pronounced and her composure regained.

"Well what happened next? You can't leave me hanging like that."

"My mother decided it was time I marry. Because she's the Queen of the Otherworld, she gets to choose who that is. Imagine my surprise when she picked Derron. He was outraged. I thought in time he would forgive me and that he might still feel something for me again. But the damage was done and it didn't seem as though there was any way to mend it. As the time of the wedding neared, he became more distant. Then I noticed he started disappearing for long stretches of time. He comes to the human realm," she continued, "to get away from his duties at court and that includes me."

Maggie understood now, her matchmaking ideas completely destroyed, though she contemplated this new turn of events. She glanced toward the practice arena, watching Derron leave with a trail of women after him and one on each arm. What a cad. How could he be interested in them when he had such a beautiful princess to marry?

"What happened with the wedding?"

"Postponed indefinitely at Derron's urging," Elyne said tersely.

Elyne was in love with the stuck-up knight-errant of the Otherworld and too proud to admit it. But then maybe he wasn't as stuck up as he presented himself to be. Maybe Maggie could figure out a way to get these two love birds together. Unless, of course, he truly felt nothing for Elyne. That would be a problem.

"I'm sure there's a way we can get Derron to forgive you,"

Maggie said.

"There is no *we*, Maggie. It's a lost cause and one that I will have to live with. Even if we do marry, he will never feel the same for me."

"Maybe I could try."

She snorted. "All you need to worry about is Finn and nothing more," Elyne said in her scolding tone.

The subject was now closed according to Elyne. But Maggie couldn't let it go. There had to be something she could do to help. She would have to probe Derron and see if there were any feelings there. Perhaps he was a master at hiding them. It would also give her an excuse to spend more time with him for her thesis.

Finn was all suited up in his armor, ready for his first sword match. The swordplay was in a small box of an arena near the lists. His first opponent was short and squatty next to the massive Scotsman. Elyne and Maggie arrived in time to see Finn swing first. His sword clanged against the other man's. Despite the other man's size, he managed to hold off Finn in the initial attack.

"You must be Lady Margaret."

The nasal voice pierced her ear. She turned and came face to face with Lord Litonshire.

His skinny hawk nose perched over even skinnier lips as they stretched into what could only be called a smirk. His thinning brown hair was cropped short above his collar. He wore the finest velvet clothes in a deep blue, but even that didn't make him appealing. When she turned to him, he took her hand and planted a cold, lifeless kiss on her knuckles. His lips felt like a dead fish and she tried hard to keep the bile from rising to her throat. His beady, blue gaze landed on her bosom before finally meeting her steely glare.

Maggie slipped her hand away as casually as possible, not wanting him to see her recoil. She resisted the urge to wipe the back of her hand on her gown.

"It is an honor to meet you at last, my lady."

"And you are?" As if she didn't know. She lifted her chin an inch higher to look down her nose, practicing the look Elyne had so often given her.

"Earl Byron de Fortier of Litonshire, champion of the Tournament at Windsor. Mayhap you've heard of me?" He gave her an oily smile.

"No, actually, I can't say that I have." She turned back to the sword match, watching as the short opponent ducked one of Finn's lethal swings. Next to her, Elyne snickered under her breath.

"I've made a point to find out who you are, my lady," he said, sidling closer.

"Is that so? And to what do I owe the pleasure of your attention?"

"Sir Finian and I have a bit of a..." he paused, looking at Finn, "history."

"Truly?" Maggie asked, looking as innocent as she could. She wasn't all that impressed by this Lord Litonshire, though he seemed clearly quite impressed with himself.

"I'd like to know exactly how you've come to find yourself in Sir Finian's presence."

"I find myself quite happy in his presence, thank you." She beamed.

"You know of his...reputation, I gather."

"His reputation?" Maggie gasped, pressing a hand against her chest as she feigned surprise and gave him her best innocent look. "Why, I'm sure I don't know what you mean, my lord."

"I would advise you to be careful of him."

He leered at her, leaning as close as possible. She could smell his rancid breath and turned her head. Why wouldn't this vile creature go away?

"Would you be referring to the rumors about your sister, Lady Juliet, then?" she asked pointedly.

"Rumors?" His eyes narrowed so slightly she would have missed it had she not been looking. "They are but fact."

"Oh, I don't know about that," Maggie said airily. "Sir Finian has been nothing but gracious and kind to me. I can't imagine him being anything but the chivalrous gentleman he is." She kept her gaze focused on Finn. He'd managed to corner the other knight.

"Quite noble of you, my lady," he said, his voice greasy. Next to her, he observed Finn's match. "However, my sister hasn't quite recovered as yet."

"It does trouble me to hear it." Maggie put on her best heartbreaking look. "Are there any repercussions to the errant knight?"

"The errant knight, my lady, I'm convinced is Sir Finian."

"And yet he and your sister deny it." Maggie had never been so glad she'd stopped to talk to people today. She actually had ammunition for this guy. "Surely there was other proof?"

"His tartan was wrapped around her. That's all the proof I need." The words slithered out of his mouth and over her, like something slippery and vile. Lord Vile, she decided would be his name henceforth. He quickly changed the subject then. "He's quite good with a sword, I daresay."

"Indeed," she agreed. "Mayhap he should show the one who started the nasty rumors a thing or two."

"Are you suggesting a duel, my lady?"

"Oh, I don't know about a duel. A lesson instead?"

She gave him a winsome grin as Finn pinned his opponent to the ground with this sword. There was no chance of the man getting to his feet. The arena master declared Finn the victor and everyone cheered. Maggie clapped wildly. Lord Litonshire's thin-lipped mouth drew down in disapproval and he gave a half-hearted applause.

"I do thank you, my lord, for your concern," Maggie said, once the cheering died down. Finn had removed his helm, his hair damp against his head. She, however, tried to focus on Lord Litonshire. "But I can assure you, Sir Finian has taken no liberties with me."

"I would tread cautiously, my lady, though it appears my warning falls on deaf ears. My apologies for disturbing you."

He stalked off, his tall, lean form walking upright like a stick. Elyne blew out a breath.

"You shouldn't pick a fight with that one," Elyne said. "He's bad news."

"I'm sure he is," Maggie agreed. "I recognize a veiled threat when I hear one."

"And a threat it was," Elyne agreed.

"I have a feeling he has something to do with all these rumors flying about, though," Maggie said. "I intend to get to the bottom of it."

"And get yourself into trouble? You think that's wise?"

"Do you think it's wise that I'm here trying to keep a man alive I barely know?"

"Point taken," Elyne said.

"Here comes Finn. I don't want him to know about the encounter with Lord Litonshire."

"Oh, he'd have your head if he knew," Elyne said.

As the other knight struggled to get to his feet with the help of his two squires, Finn exited the sword arena. He handed his helm off to Geoffrey as he walked toward the pavilion, his armor clearly impeding his gait. It clinked with every labored step. Maggie picked up her skirts and followed, having to take two strides for his long ones.

"Sir Finian," she called.

"Awful match," he muttered. "'Twas not verra challenging."

"I thought it was marvelous."

He spun on her, making her stop short and nearly bouncing off his brick wall form. "And what would ye know, lassie, since ye spent most of it talking to Lord Litonshire."

He *saw* that? She gulped. "He approached *me*."

"And ye dinna think no' to speak to him."

"Hey, I defended you." She poked him hard in the chest to press her point for all the good it would do. He probably didn't feel a thing through the steel. "When he started saying things about how dangerous you were, I told him to bugger off." Well, not in so many words but that was the gist of it.

"Did ye now?" he asked.

"Aye, she did," Elyne said and Maggie hadn't even realized she'd been following them. "And a fine job of it she did, too."

Finn glanced from Elyne to Maggie, his gaze settling on her full of appreciation. He smiled, the corners of his mouth upturning barely visible. "'Tis true, lass?"

"It is. He's a vile man, to be sure. So much so I think from now on I shall call him Lord Vile."

Finn threw his head back and laughed loud and hard. It was so infectious she couldn't help but giggle. She heard even Elyne snicker. When he finally regained his composure, he held his arm out to her.

Maggie was momentarily stymied by the gesture. He was actually *giving* her his arm? Willingly? Her heart pounded a hard cadence in her chest as she slipped her hand over the cool metal of his armored forearm. They resumed walking together toward the pavilion. A quick glance behind her revealed Elyne following, her hands clasped in front of her.

"Have ye had a chance to get to market yet?" he asked as they neared their tents.

"No, I haven't."

"Aye, then. I'll put on some breeks and escort ye."

"Really?" She felt the flush of pleasure on her face. "I'd love that."

He leaned down and lowered his voice. "Mayhap then ye can tell me who you *really* are."

Her wall of defense flew up and pinpricks of heat stabbed her skin. "I'm sure I don't know what you mean."

"*Och*, lass. 'Tis clear you dinna belong to Campbell or his clan."

"How do you know that?"

Maggie licked her lips that had suddenly become dry. A wave of acid welled up from her belly, burning the back of her throat. If he knew she didn't belong to Campbell, what would happen to her? What would he do to her? If he knew she lied about that, then what else would he think she lied about?

"Because he'd have come searching for ye by now."

"Oh. Well, I, um…" She paused, unable to figure out how to answer. She couldn't very well tell him she was from the future. He'd never believe that. She glanced behind her now, looking for help from Elyne, but the Fae princess was nowhere in sight. Of course. She was never around when Maggie really needed her.

"I ken ye have the tongue of the English. Nothing like Campbell and his clan."

"I do?"

"Aye, and ye were speaking with Litonshire now. Are ye working with him to destroy me? Did ye bring along that maidservant because ye knew she'd keep yere falsehoods for ye?" As they walked, he moved closer to her, his large form looming over her. He was formidable in his full armor, making her wish to shrink back. "Who are ye really?"

"I'm not working with Litonshire," she blurted. "I swear to you, Finn, on my mother's grave I'm not. I'm here to help you. I don't like Litonshire any more than you do."

He searched her gaze as he visibly relaxed. Or at least as much as he could in a full suit of armor. "I still canna understand how ye came to be in my bed that morn, though I canna say 'twas all too unpleasant."

"I don't understand it either," she lied, even though she knew

Elyne was the one who had put her there at ghost Finn's request. He'd surely never believe that one either. If she told him he was dead and told a Fae princess to do it, he'd think she'd gone mad.

Finn cupped her chin, tipping her head as he moved to stand closer to her. "Such a bonnie lass ye are. I canna remember tupping ye that eve, though I wish I could."

Heated pleasure warmed her from her toes upward thinking about what could have been had they not been interrupted by Fergus.

"Mayhap because we didn't...tup." Have sex? She hoped that's what he meant but she'd never heard the word before. Although they hadn't been together, it didn't mean they never would be. She had plans for him and she intended to see them through.

Finn raised one thick eyebrow at her, those silvery eyes still peering into her soul. As though he could see right through her and into her heart. "'Twould be a shame should we never remedy that, aye?"

Her heart did this funny thing in her chest where it suddenly felt as if it wasn't there anymore when she realized Finn intended to kiss her and for real this time. He bent to capture her lips as her eyes fluttered closed and she prayed Elyne wouldn't interrupt them. At first, she didn't feel much of anything and then his mouth touched hers and she thought she might melt into a puddle.

Her knees threatened to buckle, but he'd wrapped an arm around her, pulled her close. She pressed against his armor, unable to feel the warmth of his body, save for the kiss. His gauntlet pressed into her back while the cold steel of his breastplate sent chills through her. His tongue slid deftly into her mouth, touching, teasing, tasting. They did a bit of an oral tango, each one fighting for control of the other. Maggie was only vaguely aware of his other hand, not yet wearing the gauntlet, brushing through her hair, resting on her neck. Something he'd done before when he tried to kiss her. And now she relished in the touch of his hand, so warm on her skin.

Maggie lost her senses, as though everything around them fell away and they were the only two in the world. As though no laughter surrounded them or cheers from the lists or people bustling through the pavilion. She completely forgot about Lord Litonshire, Elyne and the snooty Sir Derron, the thesis she had to write. The only thing that mattered was kissing Finn as though there was no tomorrow.

Finn drew back at last but Maggie couldn't open her eyes yet. She let her head fall back, memorizing the way his mouth felt on hers. How he held her so close and rested his hand on her neck. She would never forget that moment.

"Ah, there, lass. 'Tis a mite better now, aye?"

She blinked her eyes open then and found him smiling at her. Nodding, she said, "Oh, aye."

"Now then. What say ye, lass? Care to tell me who ye really are?"

Perspiration sprang up on her palms and she ran her hands down her skirt in an effort to remove the dampness, but making it seem as though she smoothed the material. Searching her mind, she tried to come up with a good enough response.

"I can't explain it myself, sir." That was as close to the truth as he was going to get.

"In time, lass, ye'll tell me."

He sounded certain of that as he dropped his hand and went into his tent, leaving her standing there alone. If he didn't think she belonged with Campbell, then what could she tell him? She needed to talk to Elyne and find out exactly why she was here. She was certain there was another reason besides keeping Finn alive, which she still had no clue how to do. She didn't even know how he died.

It seemed forever before Finn emerged from the tent no longer in his full jousting armor. Instead he wore long breeches, soft shoes and a tunic in a pale shade of green. They shared an awkward silence as the soft breeze tousled her hair. He reached up and tucked a wayward lock behind her ear.

"Let's be getting on to market so we dinna miss banquet tonight."

Maggie wasn't sure which excited her more—going to the market or banquet with Finn. She decided, as she took his arm for the second time, that both were pretty spectacular.

Chapter 7

The market sprawled over two acres of land near Middleham Castle with buildings butted against each other. People crowded the dirt streets, shoving their way through as hawkers shouted descriptions to entice buyers to purchase their wares. Maggie could smell freshly baked bread mingling with the scent of unwashed bodies surrounding her, heard the squawk of chickens and the honking of geese, and spied a cart draped in colorful scarves.

There were filthy beggars on the streets, asking for handouts from anyone who walked by. There were fair ladies escorted by nobles who bought them anything they asked for. There was a man pushing an overloaded cart of freshly grown vegetables down the street, trying to dodge people and calling out curses when they got in his way. It was dusty and dirty and terribly delightful.

Maggie paused at the display of silken scarves, running her hand down the length of a pale-blue one. The material was soft and better than any silk she had in her time. She'd never seen anything so lovely.

"Do ye fancy that one?" Finn asked.

"It's very fine," Maggie replied.

"How much?" he asked the seller who hovered impatiently, hoping for a sale.

"Oh, Finn, that's not necessary," she protested.

"I think it is."

"Two gold pieces," the seller replied.

Finn handed him the coins, then reached for the delicate material. He held it out to Maggie, who stared at it a long moment, awestruck. He'd bought her a scarf? Could it be he'd finally warmed up to her? As she took it, their hands brushed and she flushed.

"Thank you." She held it a moment and then an idea struck her. "Will you wear it in tourney?"

She lifted her gaze, meeting his. For a moment she felt as though she floated, as though her heart had stopped beating in her chest and moved to her throat. He looked at her with such heartrending tenderness, it made her lightheaded. His hands closed over hers, though he resisted taking the scarf.

"Aye, lass, I will."

"Well, well. How romantic, indeed."

This from Lord Litonshire, who had managed to push his way through the crowd and pause next to Finn. Next to him stood a frail-looking girl with pale-brown hair and big doe eyes. She was so thin she looked nearly anorexic, the pink velvet grown practically hanging off her bones.

Finn dropped his hands, leaving Maggie's feeling cold. She still held the scarf, though, and slowly wound it around her hand out of nerves.

"I'm sure you remember my sister, Lady Juliet," Litonshire said, nodding towards the girl.

So, *this* was the infamous Lady Juliet. Maggie examined her carefully, trying to decide if she and Finn really did have a thing for each other. Litonshire's sister looked mostly like a lost little child and had a deer-in-headlights look. This was certainly no vixen. Next to Finn, who was massive in every way, she had the appearance of a stick figure, like she'd break in half at any moment. Maggie wondered if she hadn't eaten in a week or so, because it certainly seemed that way to her. She had dark circles under her eyes and her cheeks looked hollow. She might have been beautiful if she hadn't looked so emaciated. Maggie felt sorry for her.

Lady Grace had been right—beset by a deep sorrow didn't quite cover it. More like a deep depression.

Seeing Lady Juliet now sealed it for Maggie. There was no way Finn would take advantage of a girl like that. He wouldn't even take advantage of *her* when he'd seen her in her underwear.

Finn bowed low to Lady Juliet out of respect. "My lady."

Maggie remembered Lady Grace saying Lady Juliet hadn't been seen since last tourney and who could blame her? She looked awful, the poor girl. She did a quick mental calculation of how she could help Juliet in her already busy schedule. She had Finn to protect, Elyne and Derron to get together and now she had to find a way to help this frail creature.

"'Tis a pleasure to see you again, Sir Finian." When Lady Juliet spoke, her words were so soft Maggie could barely hear her over the din of the market.

"Did you hear that? She said it was a pleasure to see you again. And what a pleasure indeed." Litonshire laughed, his tinny voice carrying and calling attention to them. When he said it, he leered at Maggie and she could smell the alcohol on his breath.

Maggie wanted to belt him. She made a note to do that before this was all over.

"I see ye've been into the bottom of a whiskey barrel," Finn said. "And we'll be taking our leave of ye." He grasped Maggie's hand, ready to lead her away.

"Not so fast."

Litonshire had the nerve to grab Finn by the arm. Finn's gaze turned to molten silver.

"Ye best let go."

"You best do right by my sister," Litonshire snarled. "You stole her innocence. I still insist upon that duel."

Shock rolled through Maggie as she glanced from Litionshire to Finn. Her shock turned to fear when she saw the dark look on Finn's face, the way his jaw clamped close so tight she could see the muscles working there. The cords on his neck stood out and she could tell it took everything he had to maintain his composure. When the slime ball refused to remove his hand, Finn took his fingers in his and pushed him away.

"I'll not be dueling ye or wedding yere sister." Then to Juliet, "Apologies, my lady. I mean no disrespect."

"Your refusal dishonors yourself, Sir Finian," Litonshire shouted.

"Lity, please stop—" Juliet began, reaching for her brother.

But he slapped her hand away. "Nay, Juliet. He disgraces our family and you by not wedding you right away. I'll not stand by and allow him to continue disrespecting our family name."

"I don't want to marry him against my will," she said in her very soft way.

Litonshire backhanded her then, so hard he left a red handprint on her cheek and her hand flew up to cover the spot. She took a step back, tears welling in her eyes. She looked ready to bolt any minute.

"Do not speak to me in that insolent tone, you ungrateful wench."

"Hey," Maggie said, unable to stand by and let Juliet take the abuse. "You leave her alone, you bully."

Finn's hand landed on her shoulder and pulled her back and it was only then she realized she'd charged forward, her hands in fists. Lady Juliet blinked wildly, trying to hold her emotions in check.

"I canna have ye attacking the lady," Finn said calmly. But Maggie knew, by the heat radiating from his palm, he held his temper in check.

"Tell me true, then," Litonshire taunted. "What do you intend to do about it?"

"This."

Before anyone could move, Finn punched the man square in the nose. Maggie never saw that coming. Litonshire dropped like a bag of bricks to the ground, wailing and holding his nose as blood spurted from it, seeping through is fingers. He'd broken the man's nose.

Not that he hadn't deserved it.

Lady Juliet made no move to help her brother and everyone else around who'd stopped to watch the altercation quickly resumed minding their own business. Maggie stepped around Lord Vile and put her arm around Lady Juliet's shoulders.

"Lady Juliet, you're coming with us," Maggie said.

"You unhand my sister." Litonshire's nasal voice was even more nasal now that he had a busted schnoz.

"Mind yerself," Finn warned. "Or ye'll get another visit from my fist."

"I'm not scared of you," the earl whined.

When Finn took a step toward him, though, he scuttled back in the dirt. It took all of Maggie's willpower not to laugh at the man.

"We should be getting back to the pavilion," Finn said.

Maggie couldn't agree more. She nodded and, hugging Juliet close to her, they left Lord Vile as he managed to get to his feet. His squires had found him then and fussed over him to make him feel better. But Maggie thought he got exactly what he deserved.

"Are you all right?" Maggie noticed Juliet had a spot of blood in the corner of her mouth.

"I am. I do appreciate the help, but 'tis not necessary." Juliet focused on Finn's back as he sauntered through the market and those in the square parted like the Red Sea to let him and the two ladies through. "Sir Finian has already come to my rescue once. I shan't wish to take advantage of that again."

"I don't think it's an imposition," Maggie said. "You can come with us, stay in my tent with me." Of course, she had an ulterior motive. It would give her a chance to quiz the earl's sister and find out what had happened that day in the stable with Finn.

"Oh, I couldn't. Please don't misunderstand my reluctance as being ungrateful. I do appreciate your help. It's just that my brother can be rather…overbearing and he prefers to keep me close to him."

Maggie couldn't believe what she was hearing. Lady Juliet was afraid of her brother and yet she defended him. The fact that Finn had come to her rescue made Maggie believe he wasn't the one that did that dastardly deed of which Litonshire accused him. She was sure of that more than ever and the only person who would know the real truth was Lady Juliet. And she wasn't talking for fear of her brother. It sent burning anger right through Maggie.

"He shouldn't be hitting you." It may have been a common practice in this time period, but Maggie detested men who hit women.

"He forgets himself sometimes."

How she could be making excuses for the vile man, Maggie couldn't fathom. Finn walked ahead of them, leading the way, but a man about Maggie's height hurried through the crowd toward them. He was young and handsome, with a weathered face and thick, wavy brown hair. His face was smooth, devoid of even a five o'clock shadow. Like he'd never had to shave, yet he clearly showed experience in the lines of his eyes. His gaze was focused on Lady Juliet, never wavering from her face.

Maggie glanced at her, saw the blush creep up the girl's neck to stain her cheeks. A smile threatened to erupt on her face. She even went so far as to flutter her eyelashes at him. It was a definite *aha* moment for Maggie. This man meant something to Lady Juliet.

"I just heard," the man said as he stopped them in the square. "Are you all right, my lady?"

"I'm quite all right, Lord Brian."

"News travels fast, I see," Maggie said.

Finn hadn't realized they had stopped and continued on through the market, heading back to the pavilion. She thought she should call out to him, but they'd already caused enough ruckus in the market for one day. She let him go, thinking she'd catch up to him later. This seemed much more important at the moment anyway. She might actually find out what was going on with Lady Juliet.

Brian took both her hands in his, kissing her fingers. "I thought you wouldn't come to this tourney, my lady, but I'm certainly glad you did. Are you sure you're quite all right, dearest?"

"Yes, of course." She pulled her hands away, placed one on his cheek. "You shouldn't be here, Brian. And I should return to the castle."

"Will you be at banquet tonight, my lady?" Lord Brian asked.

"I don't think so. Fare thee well."

Lady Juliet pushed her way into the crowd and left them behind.

"Wait." Maggie started after her. "Don't leave, Lady Juliet. Let me help you."

She paused to turn back to her, her eyes damp with tears. "You cannot."

Lady Juliet disappeared into the throng of people, blending in with them and leaving Lord Brian and Maggie to watch her go. Maggie wished there was something more she could do for her.

"Apologies, my lady, for not introducing myself," he said then, breaking the awkward silence. "Lord Brian de Mauly."

"Lady Margaret," she said as he took her hand and kissed it.

Something clicked. The young girl she'd talked to earlier that morning was Grace de Mauly, who mentioned her brother participated in the tourney. Maggie wondered if Lady Juliet had willingly given herself to someone—Lord Brian?—or if she had truly been attacked.

"A pleasure to meet you," he said.

"You know Lady Juliet?" She blurted the question out before she could stop herself.

"Aye, I do." His gaze flickered out to where she'd disappeared into the crowd. Perhaps hoping to see her head bobbing through it. "I confess I already knew she was at tourney. I've been keeping a watchful eye on her."

"And you know her brother, then, I take it."

"The man is vile beyond all words." He spat. "He's the one that spread those rumors about his own sister. He continues to defame her by bringing her here and displaying her for all to see."

Maggie knew history was unkind to women who had been destroyed like Lady Juliet had. It stood to reason she would have been confined to a nunnery, but instead here she was. Victim to another one of Litonshire's vile actions.

"Are they true? Was she attacked in the stable that night?" Maggie asked.

"She was attacked, yes," Lord Brian said. "By whom I cannot say, though if I ever find out I will kill him myself. Lady Juliet is a frail creature and he treats her abhorrently."

"So why does she stay?" Maggie was glad to see she wasn't the only one who thought Lord Litonshire was vile.

"He doesn't want to pay out her dowry," Brian said. "He keeps her there because he refuses to marry her off."

"But...he's an earl," Maggie said. "He should have money, shouldn't he?"

"Aye, he has it," Brian agreed. "He's spends it all on ale, gambling and wenches, leaving nothing for Lady Juliet. She's practically a slave in her own house."

"That's terrible." How could she get Lady Juliet away from her brother?

"Indeed. 'Tis up to the king to make a match for the lady, though Litonshire seems to have some sort of hold over him, too. He's yet to arrange her marriage."

This just got better and better. And definitely beyond Maggie's reach. She wasn't sure she could help Lady Juliet. Unless she could find a way to expose Lord Litonshire. But then there was the matter of the king making a match.

"Litonshire is that powerful?"

"Unfortunately, yes. However, I understand the king will be here for the end of the tourney," Brian said. "I should like to speak to him on her behalf should I get the chance."

And that solved that problem. Once the king arrived, Maggie would have to use her wits to figure out a way to get to the king and talk him into making a match for Lady Juliet—hopefully with Lord Brian—not to mention the task of exposing Litonshire for the vile being he was, all the while playing matchmaker to Derron and Elyne and keeping Finn from dying.

She took a deep breath.

If you want something done right, Mags, you do it yourself.

And that's just what Maggie was going to do.

Once Maggie was able to excuse herself from Lord Brian, she headed through the market toward the pavilion. Having lost sight of Finn's head in the crowd, she discovered rather quickly the place wasn't all that easy to navigate. When she thought she was going toward the pavilion, she realized she was going in the opposite direction. Nothing looked familiar and instead she ended up deeper and deeper into the market.

Stopping on the street, she looked up to see a sign swaying gently in the breeze, the ancient hinges squealing disapproval. The sign boasted it was home to the finest apothecary in Middleham. Perhaps the proprietor could give her directions back to the pavilion. Ducking inside, she saw none other than Lord Litonshire at the counter. Maggie paused inside the door and watched as the rotund shopkeeper closed her hand around several gold coins and the earl stuffed a small pouch of something into a pocket. Her heart stuttered to a halt upon seeing him there. She wished she hadn't defied convention and had Elyne with her.

Litonshire turned, his glare falling on her, making her want to squirm. Already his eyes had started to bruise. His nose was bright red, his tunic splotched with drops of blood. His gaze narrowed and he walked toward her, but Maggie was frozen in place.

"Tell your master to be very careful." His rancid breath wafted over her, making her gag.

Maggie kept her composure. "Is that a threat?"

He shoved her out of the way with one thin, clammy hand and it was only then she realized she stood in front of the door. Litonshire yanked it open and disappeared into the road, the door slamming behind him.

"Good day, mistress. Can I help ye?" the woman behind the counter asked.

Maggie's hands shook as she clasped them together and peered out the grimy window.

"Are ye all right? Don't let that tosspot bother ye. 'Tis no' worth the trouble, he is."

Tosspot was a new word to her, but she gathered its meaning and smiled warmly at the clerk. She was older, with salt-and-pepper hair pulled back into a bun at the nape of her neck. Sprigs sprang from around her head, giving her a messy yet charming appearance. She wore a nondescript gray gown and her eyes were bright blue, lighting up when she smiled.

"Now, what can I help ye find?"

"Could I ask what the tosspot purchased?"

"He bought some of me husband's best mandrake, he did. Says he has a spot of an aching head and I can't says as I blame 'im, what with the bloody nose and all."

"Will mandrake help?" Maggie asked. She knew it was a member of the nightshade family only because she'd briefly studied herb lore in one of her classes freshman year.

"Oh, wondrous well, mistress, indeed. 'Tis the best thing for a bit of the aching head. Will fix 'im right up, I should think. Though it'd be best for 'im to stay out o' the drink an' I told 'im so, I did. Oh, listen to me prating on when there's business to be about. Pray pardon me, but would ye be needing mandrake, too?"

"No mandrake for me, thanks. Could you point me in the direction of the pavilion?"

"Ah, here for tourney."

The woman launched into another discussion about tourney and who was about. Maggie tried to concentrate on her words, but her thick accent made her difficult to understand.

"In truth, I think he should no' be jousting 'imself."

"What? What was that?"

"Lord Litonshire. Yon tosspot." She motioned toward the door where Litonshire left only moments before. "He plans to joust. Why, I just saw 'im yesterday in the weaponry, purchasing lances."

Cold fear swept over Maggie. Litonshire had a great hate for Finn and it was clear *he* wasn't so fond of the earl either. She wasn't sure how each knight was eliminated with each match, but she was certain if Litonshire intended to joust—against Finn?—then he would certainly try to harm him. Could it be Maggie had been sent to protect him from the earl? She had to get back to camp and find Finn.

"I do thank you for all the news. Could you please point me in the direction of the pavilion?"

"Zounds. I didn't mean to keep ye, mistress."

Finally, Maggie got the directions she needed and left the apothecary's wife behind. Joining the throng of people in the road, she quickly headed back to the pavilion, weaving in and out of the meandering shoppers. By the time she made it back to the tent, her dress was dusty and dirty, her feet and legs ached and she was out of breath from hurrying. Elyne intercepted her before she made it to their tents.

"Where have you been? Finn's in an uproar." She fell in step beside Maggie, hurrying to keep up.

"I was detained," Maggie said, puffing to catch her breath. "I need to talk to you about something, Ellie. It's about Lord Litonshire—"

"By Saint Mary, woman. Where have ye been dallying?"

Maggie jumped at Finn's outburst, her heart stuttering in her chest. She disliked when he talked to her as though she were an errant child.

"We got separated in the market. I got lost. And don't blame me. You never even looked back for me." Maggie held her temper in check but she couldn't resist the jab.

"Ye could have been hurt. Or worse, accosted." His tone scalded her, disapproving. "Do ye have any notion of what vermin crawl the roads of the market?"

"Why, yes, I have a vague idea. Especially since we ran into Lord Vile." She decided it best not to mention she saw him in the apothecary shop or that he quietly threatened her. It'd only rile him further.

He sighed with exasperation. "Change yere dress. 'Tis time for banquet and we must make haste."

As he marched away from her, flinging the flap of his tent open so he could enter, Maggie decided he was getting less and less growly since they first met. Still, though, he sounded like a grizzly bear.

"You'll never learn, will you?" Elyne's tone was coolly disapproving.

"Don't patronize me." Maggie grabbed the Fae princess by the arm and turned her toward the tent, giving her a shove inside. "We need to talk."

"Don't be so pushy." Elyne's warning was velvet yet edged with steel. "And you better make it fast. He won't wait for you much longer. He's in a foul mood, thanks to your disappearing act."

Maggie knelt at the trunk, tossing out gown after gown, looking for something to wear. She refused to let Elyne trap her with her jab. "Litonshire was in the apothecary shop."

"*That's* what you had to talk to me about so urgently?" She snorted. "So what? That's nothing to be worried about."

"He bought mandrake." She paused to look up at Elyne. "And when he left, he told me that my master should watch his back."

"Empty threats." Elyne waved her hand as though it didn't matter.

"I don't think so. The lady in the shop told me Litonshire plans to joust. Is that how Finn died? Is that who I'm supposed to protect him from?"

Elyne didn't respond right away and Maggie feared the worst with her answer. If Lord Litonshire was the one she had to protect Finn from, she wasn't so sure she was up for the job. The man was a sleazy little worm who drank too much and beat his sister. She feared what would happen to her if she got more involved with Lady Juliet. Still, though, she couldn't leave Juliet to the hands of that brutal man. She'd risk it.

"No," Elyne said at last, drawing out the one-syllable word slowly. "Litonshire is a smarmy bastard, but he wouldn't actually hurt anyone."

"Are you sure? He confronted Finn in the market, demanding he duel for his sister's honor."

"An important nugget of information you left out." Elyne gave her a sour look. "What happened?"

"Finn refused, of course, and when Lady Juliet—"

"Lady Juliet was there, too?" Her brows flew toward her hairline, her eyes wide with shock. "How did she look?"

"Awful, really. Very thin."

"I'm not surprised, after what happened last tourney. I can hardly believe she showed up here after the scandal that went down," Elyne said.

"Litonshire hit her." Maggie wrinkled the fabric of the gown she held in her fist. "And it wasn't the first time, I'm sure."

"Rotten bastard," Elyne muttered. She scraped a hand through her long hair and paced the length of the tent, which only consisted of two or three steps. "This isn't how things happened the first time around."

"What do you mean by that?"

"I mean, the first time around, there was no *you*. But you being here has thrown things off, changed things. I knew this would happen and I tried to tell Finn that."

"So how does Finn die, then?"

"I can't tell you."

"Why not?" She huffed out an exasperated breath and rose, turning to Elyne. "You have to give me something. I'm completely in the dark. I don't know what or who I'm supposed to keep from him or even *how* I'm supposed to keep him alive."

"All right, all right. I'll tell you. Finn dies in the lists."

"During a joust? How am I supposed to stop that? Jump into the lists and distract his opponent?" This made her pause as she thought of the events to come. Finn had already conquered one sword match but tomorrow he had another, plus two rounds of jousting. "And I suppose you won't tell me who his opponent is."

"You suppose correctly."

Defeated, Maggie turned back to the trunk. "Fine. Help me pick out a dress."

Maggie wasn't interested in all the gaiety that night at banquet. Her stomach was tied in knots, leaving her feeling somewhat out of sorts and Finn had barely grunted one word to her since they arrived. At the high table sat Lord Litonshire with bruises on his face and next to him the emaciated Lady Juliet. Maggie watched her all evening, hardly touching her food. Instead she pushed it around on her plate while shrinking away from her brother. Every time Maggie glanced their way, Litonshire would catch her gaze. A cold sliver of fear trickled down her spine and she would quickly look away.

Lord Vile was the best title for the man.

Sir Drake Attenborough sat next to Finn, as he had the night before. Elyne had refused to come to banquet. She begged off, saying she had things to do, though what those could be Maggie had no idea. Could it be the princess had to flit off to Faery for some Fae duty or other? Maggie didn't know, nor did she really care. The only thing she wanted from Elyne was the truth, and she wasn't getting that any time soon.

The other distraction at banquet was Sir Derron. Perhaps that's why Elyne refused to join them. She couldn't stand to see the women—or fecking wenches, as Elyne said—fawning all over him. And could Maggie blame her? Hardly. If Derron were betrothed to her, she'd be rather ticked off to see him flaunting himself.

"Would you care to dance, Lady Margaret?" Sir Drake asked, breaking into her thoughts.

She was about to answer when Finn butted in. "The lass willna be dancing."

Taken aback, Maggie looked up at him. Those silvery eyes became flat and unreadable as stone, though she could see a hint of the fire that smoldered there. "I won't?"

"Just one dance, Finn," Drake said, rising. "The poor girl looks bored stiff."

She couldn't agree more. Maggie opened her mouth to respond but again, Finn spoke for her. "The lass willna be dancing…with *you*." And he looked pointedly at Drake who sank back into his chair, his vexation evident.

Maggie's heart thudded and she suppressed the smile that wanted to erupt. Finn was being protective of her and she *loved* it. She loved it even more when he reached for her hand and closed his fingers around hers, the heat of his skin surging through her.

She rose with him while Sir Drake looked on with a that-was-my-idea expression on his handsome face. Finn tucked her small hand—small compared to his—into the crook of his elbow and led her onto the dance floor as a new song began to play. Standing close to him made her realize how big the Scotsman was and how much she wanted to be crushed under his weight. He seemed to tower over her, though if she were back in her time, she'd gain at least another four inches in heels.

Instead, he had six inches on her and looked down at her with eyes that peered into her soul. A delicious warmth cascaded through her as she gazed right back up at him.

"It's all right with me if you're jealous," she said, and smiled. "I like it."

His face darkened with the scowl. "I'm no' jealous."

Why did everything he said to her sound like a growl? Like he was snarling at her. Maybe he was and she was too blind to see it. Maybe he really didn't like her.

But then again, why would he fight Derron over her at the practice arena?

She could chalk it all up to him sticking to the Code of Chivalry or she could let her fantasies run away with her and pretend he really *did* want to keep her for himself. She much preferred the latter.

"You can't hide it from me," she needled. "And anyway, what's so wrong with being a little jealous. Am I not worthy of it?"

He softened. "Oh aye, lass. Ye are more than worthy."

"But you don't trust me." She filled in the blank for him. She had suspected when she first crashed onto the scene it would take a while to get him to trust her.

"Should I?" he asked as one dark brow rose.

"I'm not here to do you harm," she said. Harm was far from what she wanted to do to the rock-hard, six-foot body of his. In fact, she wanted to crawl over his nakedness and do all sorts of naughty things.

Just thinking about it made heat flush her cheeks.

"Aye?" He sounded inquisitive and curious. Something she'd not heard from him yet. "Then what are ye here to do, lass?"

"To save your life," she said matter-of-factly.

Finn chuckled, a deep rumble in his magnificent chest. The chest she wanted to run her fingers over and feel the curve of the pectorals, the lines of the washboard abs. Mostly because she'd never seen something so splendid before.

"Aye, then? And how do ye plan to do that?"

"I don't know yet." She glanced toward Lord Litonshire, who kept them pinned with his beady stare. Next to him, Lady Juliet looked forlorn as she watched Finn spin Maggie around the dance floor. "But if Lord Vile has his way, he'll see you dead."

"'Tis no reason to fash yerself over him, lass," Finn said. "I dinna believe he would hurt me."

"You may think that, Finn, but I'm not so sure."

She wanted to tell him about the apothecary, the threat Lord Litonshire made as he left the shop, but was afraid Finn would be unhappy with her again. He finally seemed over her getting lost in the market, so she didn't want to remind him. Finn cupped her chin in his hand, turning her face up to his.

"'Tis naught to worry about," he said again.

"If you insist."

"Aye, I do."

He dropped his hand, leaving an indelible mark on her skin. She could feel the warmth of him there still. His eyes continued to pierce her, as though he remembered her near-naked state days ago. A small smile quirked his lips as Finn pulled her closer to him, the lines of their bodies meshing together. His thick, powerful thighs brushed against hers. His thigh wasn't the only rock-hard presence. The glimpse she got of him that day in his chamber reminded her he had a big package up front. She stifled a giggle.

"Yere smiling, lass."

"Aye, I am." She tried to force the damn smile away but she couldn't. Her lips insisted on curving upward…and then doing other positively scandalous things.

"Pray tell, my lady, what amuses ye so."

It was the first time he'd ever called her anything other than lass. Her pulse jumped into overdrive. In only a few moments, it seemed, he changed from surly and angry to sultry and sexy. Not that he hadn't been sexy before, but his constant growling hadn't really done anything for her.

Was she a twenty-first century woman, or wasn't she? Even though he kept his emotions in check, she could read him well enough to know he wanted her as she wanted him. Why did she continue to pretend she had no feelings for him? It was silly. All she had to do was tell him the truth, drag him back to his tent and let him have his way with her. That's what she wanted. That's what she planned to get.

"Finn, I—"

"Pardon me, good sir knight, but might I cut in here?"

It was Sir Derron who managed to shove aside Finn and step in front of Maggie as she was about to confess her desires for the man. Did Fae have an incredible sense of timing hardwired into their DNA? She sighed, deflated.

Keeping her away from Sir Drake had been on Finn's agenda so she looked at him, bracing for an explosion. It never came. She waited instead for him to claim her as his property. He never did. Instead, Finn bowed gracefully and left her alone with the Fae knight.

Finn walked back to the table with irritation crawling through his veins that he'd let Sir Derron take Maggie away from him. His first instinct was to punch the rat in the face, but he didn't want to cause any trouble at banquet. There'd been enough of that with him at the last tourney. This time he needed to stay calm. He didn't want any more rumors going about.

He really needed to win this tourney to pay back the money he owed. He couldn't lose the McCullough estate, the very land his family had been born and raised on for the last few generations. It would be the humiliation of a lifetime. He would never be able to show his face in Innisborough again.

As he took his seat, he kept a watchful eye on the pair. Derron stood a little too close to her for his liking but he couldn't do anything about it except clench his fist and swear under his breath.

"You let that little weasel dance with her instead of me?" Drake asked, sounding put-out.

"He's harmless," Finn said, taking up his tankard and downing the ale.

He wanted to believe Derron was truly harmless and not interested in Maggie, but deep down, Finn feared she preferred the younger knight. He didn't fail to notice the swooning looks of longing she gave the man and it annoyed him to no end. Not only did Derron have youth on his side, but he had looks, too. Finn was never one to admit a man was beautiful, but by all accounts, Derron was. He didn't carry the scars Finn did, emotional or otherwise.

It was enough to make Finn despise the man. That and the fact Derron had bested him in nearly every match he'd had with him.

"And I'm not harmless?" Drake asked, breaking into his thoughts.

"Not in the least."

"I'm deeply hurt, Finn." Drake feigned his best wounded look.

"Oh, I dinna think ye are." Finn flashed his friend a broad smile as a servant girl refilled his tankard. "Ye ken what sort of man ye are."

Drake looked thoughtful, watching Maggie and Derron dance. "Aye, I suppose you're right." He took a sip of ale. "Say, where do you suppose he's taking her?"

Finn looked up in time to see Derron twirling Maggie right out of the great hall. He banged his tankard on the table, sloshing liquid over the rim. "Bloody hell."

Before he could go after her, Lord Litonshire stepped up to his table. "Ah, Sir Finian, have you managed to let another cad steal your lady?" He nodded toward Derron and Maggie as they disappeared.

"If ye'll pardon me…" Finn began but Litonshire interrupted.

"Oh, I don't think so. We have some unfinished business."

"If this is about Lady Juliet—"

"Not at all. It's about another pressing matter."

Finn clamped his hand around the earl's arm and led him away from the table so Drake wouldn't overhear their conversation. "You'll be getting paid once tourney is over. That was the bargain."

"And I've decided I don't like that bargain, after all. Patience isn't one of my strong suits. I'm ready for my money now. Or my lovely country estate in the lowlands of Scotland. I would much prefer the castle on a hill surrounded by a moat."

"Ye'll get nothing but a fist up yere nose again."

"I could take what I want from you by force. You realize that, don't you?"

Finn knew the man was more powerful than he. Plus, he had the king as an ally. But he didn't much care about that. All he cared about was getting Litonshire off his back for good. "If ye do, I will declare war on ye and take back what is rightfully mine."

"Oh, but you lost it to me in a fair game of Hazard. Unless you wish to have a rematch?"

Finn was running out of patience with the man. "Ye give me until the end of tourney, as we agreed."

"And if you lose?"

"Then the lands in Innisborough are yeres. But ye are forgetting I may not lose, in which case, my debt is paid and my lands remain mine."

Litonshire clenched his jaw in aggravation, a muscle ticking. "We'll see, won't we?"

Chapter 8

Shock rolled through Maggie as Finn left her in Derron's care. How could he? Perhaps then she'd really misread his thoughts and he cared nothing for her at all.

But then she was certain he must have felt *something*. The evidence was in his breeches after all. He was a man and wasn't she a decent-looking woman? She was no Angelina Jolie, but she did have her strong points.

"I thought he'd never leave," Derron whispered loudly, though it wasn't meant for her ears only. She knew Finn would have heard him yet he continued walking toward the table.

"Sir Derron, this is quite a surprise," Maggie managed.

He twirled her away from him and brought her back, clutching her close. Derron was more her height and she fit snugly against his frame. Unlike Finn, who seemed more of a beast next to her. Still, she preferred the beast instead of the beanpole.

"Whatever do you see in that ogre, dearest?" He shook his head, as though it were tragic. Then clucked his tongue in disgust. "I'll never understand it."

"You don't have to," Maggie said, trying her best not to be offended and slap him. "Finn is more man than you'll ever be." More man by height and breadth.

"That was low," Derron said, though he didn't sound as though it cut him as she hoped it would. He didn't bother to disagree. Instead, he said, "Tell me, where is Princess Elyne this evening?"

"I wouldn't know. She didn't want to come."

"Oh?" His voice lifted, as though he could finally get away with something. Like a child ready to make mischief now that the parent was out of town.

"Don't get excited," Maggie said. "She'll be back."

"Oh." Deflated, his shoulders slumped a bit.

"Just what is it with you two anyway?" Maggie figured now would be as good a time as any to try to get them together.

"Nothing, that's what." Derron sounded miffed, which was further confirmed by the sour look on his face.

Though why he was miffed Maggie couldn't figure out. "What are you so upset about? You have women falling all over themselves to get to you."

"Aye, I do. And I quite enjoy that."

"Do you?" Maggie asked as he twirled her again.

When she came back to him, he clutched her close. "Sometimes." He gave her a conspiratorial grin.

"Aha."

"No *aha*," Derron corrected.

"Oh, yes, aha. That was an 'aha' moment and you know it." Maggie had no idea he had been dancing her right out of the great hall. "Hey, wait a second."

"Let's not talk about Elyne, though."

Derron clutched her hands in his, holding them close to his chest. He kissed her fingertips so softly she thought she might melt. *Uh oh.* This wasn't going exactly as planned. This was supposed to be about Elyne, for crying out loud.

"All right, if you won't talk about Elyne, then let me ask you questions."

"Like?"

"Like how it is you've managed to stay alive during all these tournaments? Is it because you're Fae? Do you use your Fae magic to win? Or do you play fair?" she asked.

He laughed, a melodious sound that made her smile. "So many questions, indeed. I compete as a human would so, no, I don't use Fae magic."

"So, you win all of them fairly?"

"Ah, Lady Margaret, let's not talk about me either. What I wish to tell you is I'm mad about you."

"You're what?" Oh, this couldn't be happening. He was supposed to marry Elyne. And she was supposed to fall into bed with her hot Scotsman.

"I know it's wrong." He kissed the inside of her wrist, sending hot shivers through her. "But I find I can't stop thinking about you."

"But *why*? I don't understand how you could feel that way about me when we've only known each other a short period of time. Why would you want me? You could have any lady here. You could even have Elyne."

"You're beautiful, smart and everything I want in a woman for myself."

"Elyne is far more beautiful than I am," Maggie said. "And she's a princess...your princess..." Her voice trailed away when he kissed the warm pulse of her elbow. She was strangely flattered by his interest in spite of the fact that she'd rather be hearing those words from Finn. "You and Elyne—"

"I've petitioned the Court to have our betrothal annulled."

"You *what?*" That snapped her out of her headiness and she jerked her hands away. "You can't do that."

"But, my love, it's the only way we can be together. And I have done it."

She took a step backward. He took a step forward, a seductive gleam in his crystalline-blue eyes. No, no, no. This was not going as planned at all. Maggie put her hand on his chest and gave him a shove.

"We can't be together. I'm *human*. And you're only saying this because you know I belong to Finn. You're trying to get under his skin."

"Not at all, dearest. I realize you are who I'm meant to be with. You and no other. Leave that overgrown lout and come back with me to Faery and live as my one true consort." He slid his hand up her arm, pausing at her shoulder. The other hand snaked around her waist, pulling her to him. His lips were on her face, brushing over her cheek, her hair, her earlobe. "You will be pampered to your heart's desire. Given anything you wish."

When he spoke, giddiness gathered under her skin, threatening to boil over. As though she'd imbibed too much wine, which she knew she hadn't. Drunk, that's what she felt. Her skin prickled with passion. She was completely entranced by Derron. No, make that ensnared by him.

There was something enchanting about him that drew her in, as though he could speak to her soul. As though he knew her innermost desires. How did he know she wanted nothing more than to be the star princess in her very own fairy tale?

"All that and more, dearest," he said, kissing her fingers as though he'd heard her thoughts.

She blinked slowly, languidly. As though she floated on air, light as a feather, on the pillow of a fluffy cloud. In her haze, she could see them together, she and Derron. Happy. In a place so beautiful, it defied all sense of imagination.

"It's what you wish, isn't it?"

Focus, Mags. Focus. Maggie shook herself awake. She remembered the distraught look on Elyne's face when she told her he would never marry her. How she tried to hide the anguish and grief on her face.

"Oh, I don't think so." She shoved him away again, breaking the connection. And just like that the spell was broken. "I'm not going anywhere with you and I certainly don't want to be your *consort.*"

The smile in Derron's eyes contained a sensuous flame. "You say that now, but in time, you'll change your mind. Would it be so terrible?"

When he stepped toward her again, she backed up. "Don't come any closer."

"Do not deny me, dearest. Do you not want those things? To be treated as you deserve?"

"And what is that?"

"Like a princess."

Well, sure. Who didn't want to be treated like a princess? But she had Elyne to think of. And Finn. And Lady Juliet. She certainly didn't have time for a dalliance with Sir Derron, even if he was her idol. Though he was beginning to fall from that pedestal she'd put him on.

"Elyne loves you." She hadn't intended to blurt it out and in fact when the words were out of her mouth her hands flew to cover her lips. "I shouldn't have said that."

"Elyne loves the idea of marriage and of becoming queen. It has nothing to do with me." He waved away the notion as though he waved away a common house fly.

"You're wrong." It enraged Maggie. Was he so blind he couldn't see the woman for what she was? For who she was? "She really loves you. She wants to marry you. And if you had half a brain in that Faery head of yours, you'd see that."

A moment of surprise skittered across his face before it turned to amused wonder. "You are charming, dearest. Exactly why we're meant to be together."

He reached for her again but she backed up, unwilling to let him touch her again. When he did, things happened to her she couldn't control and she really needed to be in control right now. She needed to have all her senses. He had the nerve to look hurt.

"No, we are not. *You* and Elyne are." Aggravation crawled under her skin and she huffed out an annoyed breath. "Oh, why am I even bothering? If you can't see it for yourself, then I'll have to *make* you see it."

"See what?"

"Exactly."

Derron would never understand Elyne really did love him. It was then and there Maggie decided she would have to give Elyne a push in Derron's direction and vice versa. He looked as though he were about say something else, when he spied someone coming behind Maggie. He clamped his mouth shut, spun on his shiny boot and darted away.

"'Tis for the best, aye," Finn said from behind her. "His face would have seen my other fist that time."

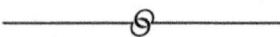

Silence stretched between Maggie and Finn as they walked back to the pavilion from the castle. Their elongated shadows preceded them in the moonlight and somewhere in the distance Maggie could hear music playing, singing, and laughter. She could make out a lute, some sort of flute or recorder, and another stringed instrument of the time.

There was no such laughter between her and Finn. In fact, he seemed to brood as they made their way through the tents. Whatever he moped about—Maggie suspected it was the fact he'd found her with Sir Derron in a precarious situation—made her own mood sour. Where did he get off getting mad at her when he was the one who let her go?

"Why did you let him cut in?" she blurted, unable to maintain her silence any longer.

"Why did ye go?" he countered.

"Oh no, you don't. Don't put it back on me. You're supposed to be the chivalrous one here."

"And ye are supposed to be the lady."

"I *am* a lady. I couldn't refuse Derron publicly, after all. That would be *rude*."

Finn stopped midstride and rounded on her, his shadowed face a menacing mask in the half-light. She took a step back.

"'Tis clear ye wish to be with the man, so I let ye go."

"I don't want him." Maggie propped her hands on her hips. "He was the one who…who…" What did they call it in this time? Making a pass?

"What?"

"He made an advance on me." There. That was it.

Even in the darkness, she could see Finn's eyes narrow. "Unwanted?"

If she said yes, would he pummel Sir Derron? If she said no, would he pummel her? "It's nothing to get your breeches in a wad over. I told him no."

"What do my breeches have to do with this?"

"Nothing. The point is I don't want Sir Derron."

"Aye?" He sounded intrigued now and leaned toward her. "What do ye want, lass?"

Maggie swallowed hard, her throat suddenly dry. This was it. This was her moment to tell him. He stepped closer.

"Or mayhap ye can tell me *who* you want?"

Oh, this was a trick question. He was baiting her. He *wanted* her to admit her feelings for him because apparently, she wore them on her sleeve. And yes, she could admit she wanted him, too. Wanted him to take her back to his tent and ravish her. But she didn't appreciate him trying to *make* her tell him. She pressed her lips together and looked away, staring into the shadows of the pavilion.

"'Tisn't wise to fall in with that of Sir Derron," he warned. "He's no' but the lyingest knave in Christendom."

"Is that so?" Maggie folded her arms now, giving him her best go-to-hell look. She doubted it did much good for he couldn't see it.

"Aye, 'tis so."

He inched toward her, like a wall of brawn. Maggie didn't shrink back into the shadows, though. Instead she tipped her head up and jutted her chin out much like she'd seen Elyne do. Finn's hands slipped up her arms, holding her there as if she were to run away. But in truth Maggie couldn't run anywhere even if she wanted to. She stood rooted in place, looking up into those silvery eyes that reflected the moonlight.

"I canna say it enough that Sir Derron is a dangerous man to be dealing with."

"Why is that, Finn?" she asked. "He doesn't seem dangerous to me."

His hands tensed on her arms, his face creasing with worry. "The man has a reputation. One of ill repute." Leaning closer, he lowered his voice so only she could hear and when he spoke, his warm breath brushed her cheek. "He has a different lady in his bed each night."

A hand closed around her heart and squeezed for Elyne. Sir Derron certainly was fond of women—human women. It didn't seem unreasonable, what with the way he flung himself at her and the way women flirted shamelessly with him.

"I can believe that," she said. "Perhaps you're right about him."

"Aye, I am."

Finn's lips brushed her temple, shoving out any other thoughts of Lady Juliet, Sir Derron or Lord Brian. She swayed but he held her steady, pulled her closer and folded her into his arms.

"Now, lass, answer my question."

"What question?" she asked innocently. She knew very well what he meant, but hoped he'd forgotten the whole thing while discussing Derron.

"If ye dinna want Sir Derron, then who do ye wish to win affection from?"

As if he didn't know. She suppressed a snort. Instead, Maggie tilted her head back, letting him trace her face with a light flutter of kisses. Her eyes closed as she drank in the moment, memorizing every shudder of her heart, every brush of his lips on her face. She didn't want to forget a single thing. She wanted this to last forever.

"I think you know the answer to that. He's standing right in front of me after all."

Finn chuckled, a deep rumble in his chest. "'Tis a fine answer, lass."

His mouth found hers, tentative at first. Soft. Controlled. Then he took the kiss deeper. When their mouths fused with the heat of the kiss, he went from slow and easy to passionate and frenzied. His calm was shattered with the ravishment of his mouth. Maggie leaned into him, letting him take her over like that first kiss they shared in his bed. Though this one, it seemed, was more intense. It sent spirals of ecstasy through her, twisting with the knot of hunger and desire in her lower belly.

She slid her hands up his chest, gliding over the pectorals she'd so longed to touch to his thick shoulders. She stood on tiptoe to slip her arms around his neck. He slowed his exploration of the recesses of her mouth, his touch velvety and warm, and trailed his kisses down her throat. Maggie tipped her head back to allow him more access as his lips whispered over her dewy skin. The feather-touch of his caress turned her knees to jelly, making her feel boneless in his strong arms. Finn planted kisses on her shoulders, neck and face before coming back to her mouth and demanding more, and all the while she enjoyed the luscious ride.

He ripped away from her so violently she stumbled, shattering the moment they'd spun together. He bent over, one arm across his stomach.

"Finn? What is it?"

His response was nothing more than a grunt.

"Are you all right?"

"Aye...I'm fine." But he sounded out of breath and, more importantly, out of sorts. Sweat had popped up on his brow. His cheeks were flushed and red. "I have a match on the morrow so I'll bid ye good night."

He stumbled backward toward his tent.

"Finn? Are you sure—"

"Good night."

And that was the last she saw of him as he ducked into his tent. Perplexed, she stepped into hers, though she was too wired to sleep. Something wasn't right with Finn. As she kicked off her shoes and perched on the edge of her bed, she made a note to check on him in the morning. Whether he wanted her to or not.

"Maggie, wake up." Elyne shook her with such force, her teeth rattled.

"I'm up," Maggie grumbled as she shoved to a sitting position. The tent was still dim, like just before dawn. "What is it?"

"It's Finn," she said. "He's sick."

"Sick?"

Maggie shoved aside the bed clothes and stood up so fast her head spun. She dragged her fingers through her tangled hair. Finding her cloak, she flung it over her shoulders and charged out of her tent, Elyne hot on her heels. When she heard voices outside

Finn's tent, though, she paused. Shoving aside her apprehension, she peered into the tent. The two squires stood at the foot of Finn's bed. Another man leaned over him. Finn managed to curl into a tight ball on his side, clutching his stomach and moaning. His face was bathed in sweat. The foul smell in the tent was enough to turn her stomach. She managed to breathe through her nose, trying not to let it overcome her.

"What's wrong with him?"

The healer waved her away, but, steeling her nerves, Maggie entered the tent anyway. She told herself she could stand it.

"He's quite ill," the healer said. "I'm afraid he'll have to forfeit his match today. Come along, my lady. It's best to leave him be and let it run its course."

"I willna forfeit," Finn grunted from the bed. He tried to shove away the bed covers and sit up. "I intend to ride."

"You'll do no such thing," the healer warned. He shoved him back down. "You're not fit for that."

"What happens if he forfeits?" Maggie asked. The healer didn't answer, so she looked at the two squires, Geoffrey and Fergus, for answers. "Well?" She propped her hands on her hips for emphasis, giving them her best motherly look.

"He loses, my lady," Fergus finally answered.

Crap. But that wasn't the least of her worries, was it? What if *this* was what she was meant to do? What if Finn died right here in the tent and she had to nurse him back to health instead of letting him die? She looked at the healer.

"Do you know what's wrong with him? Will he recover?"

"Aye, my lady, he will recover in due time. Mayhap he had some bad meat," he suggested. "It is better to leave him be and let him rest. Give him water, not ale."

Food poisoning? Or something else? Something like…mandrake? She suspected Lord Vile had something to do with Finn's current condition. That bastard.

"Doctor, do his symptoms match that of someone who has ingested, say, poison?"

The healer blinked with incredulity as he looked at her. "I suppose they could."

"Will he die?" Maggie's voice had an edge of desperation, one she hoped the healer couldn't hear.

"I don't think so, no. His symptoms don't appear to be life-threatening, even if he were poisoned. Do you suspect he was?"

But she wasn't sure how to answer that. Yes, she did. But did she have the evidence to support her claim? All she had was a gut feeling.

"I'm, ah, not sure. When will he be better?"

"Mayhap on the morrow, should he find himself lucky," the healer said. "Good day, my lady."

Maggie put her hand on Finn's forehead. His skin was clammy and hot but not feverish, so it couldn't be something contagious. That was a good sign. If it was nothing more than food poisoning, it would run its course in twenty-four hours. But that was time Finn didn't have if he were going to participate in the joust.

"Fergus, fetch me some water and some rags for Finn. Geoffrey, go talk to the list marshal and tell him what's happening. Ask him to reschedule Finn's matches to the morrow," she ordered, as though she knew what she was doing. Someone had to take charge of things.

The boys, though, stood and stared at her wide-eyed. As though she'd grown a second head.

"If the list marshal won't agree then bring him to me and I'll talk some sense into him," she amended. "Do you want your master to get better or not?"

"Go, lads," Finn croaked from the bed. "Do as she asks."

She shooed them out of the tent and they both scurried away to do her bidding. Maggie spied the chamber pot in the corner and knew it was rank. Her stomach turned at the thought of having to empty it out. Swallowing hard, she covered her mouth and nose with a corner of her cloak and reached for it.

"Maggie, no."

She stopped mid-reach. He had never called her anything but lass. Turning, she peered at him over her shoulder. He had rolled to his back and pushed the bed covers down to this waist. His massive chest was dotted with sweat.

"Leave it."

"I will not," she said behind her cloak, her voice muffled. "It needs to be emptied."

"Have one of the lads do it when he gets back." He sounded out of breath, as though he labored to get the words out. "Leave me."

"No." She stepped to the side of the bed and perched on the

edge. "I won't leave you like this. I want to help."

When he looked at her, his eyes were glassy. Not normally the bright silver they usually were. She could tell he felt wretched.

"Ah, lass. 'Tis kind of ye but I dinna need a nursemaid."

"Oh, yes, you do. If you don't drink enough liquids, you'll be even worse off." She wasn't sure he'd understand he'd be dehydrated. She couldn't do much, but she could make sure he drank enough water.

He gripped her hand, his beefy fingers locking onto her wrist. "The list marshal willna reschedule. I'll be disqualified."

"Not if I have anything to do with it."

A faint smile played upon his lips and he closed his eyes, sinking into the pillow. "I believe that, ye ken."

"Rest, now. I'm going to find Elyne."

He released her wrist and she patted him on the arm, hoping to give him reassurance. When Maggie stepped outside the tent, Elyne stopped pacing.

"Well?"

"Food poisoning, I think," Maggie said. "I wouldn't put it past that Lord Vile, either, to be the culprit. Especially after his threats. Is this what I'm supposed to do? Keep him from dying of food poisoning?"

"I don't know." Elyne shook her head.

"Why not?" Maggie demanded.

"Because this didn't happen before," Elyne explained. "He never got sick. Something has changed and this is a whole new string of events. I don't know what's going to happen now."

"That figures. Can't you do something for him?"

"You know I don't have that kind of magic. I've told you that before."

"A girl can hope, can't she?" Maggie asked.

"My lady, I've spoken to the list marshal." Geoffrey ran up and halted in front of her, sweat rolling down the sides of his face. "He says there's nothing he can do. If Finn doesn't joust, he's disqualified."

"But he's ill," Maggie said. "He can't ride in his condition. Did you tell him that?"

"I did, my lady."

"Ellie, stay with Finn. Geoffrey, take me to the list marshal."

"Just what do you think you're going to do?" Elyne asked,

grabbing her by the arm before she could go.

"I'm going to talk some sense into him, that's what."

"I don't think that's a good idea, Maggie," Elyne warned.

"Why not? I can ask him if I want to."

Before Elyne could stop her, Maggie ushered Geoffrey on to take her to the list marshal. He led her through the pavilion, past rows of tents, and to the tourney field where knights were preparing for their coming jousting matches. When they arrived, Maggie knew immediately why he wouldn't reschedule Finn's matches. Lord Litonshire presided over today's events like a king presiding over his court.

"Lady Margaret, what a pleasant surprise," he greeted when he saw her charging toward him.

He must have known he'd see her by the way he sat there, looking complacent. His stoic face never wavered with any emotion, fueling her anger.

She scowled. "Lord Litonshire, you know why I'm here."

"I can surmise it has something to do with Sir Finian, as his squire has already been to see me." He nodded in Geoffrey's direction. "My decision has been rendered."

"Then I suppose I have my answer," she said.

"I suppose you do."

"Which is that you'll not change your mind," Maggie said, though she needn't have said it aloud. She knew he wouldn't.

"Indeed. So, if your knight wishes to continue to be part of this tournament, he'll arrive at his scheduled time and not one minute later."

Taking a page from Elyne's book, she lifted her chin a little higher. "Fine," she said, through clenched teeth. "I'll make sure he does. Come along, Geoffrey."

Picking up her skirts, she spun on the toe of her shoe and only then she did realize she wore only the cloak and her shift. *Way to go, Mags.* That explained all the sidelong stares she got from those she passed as she headed back to the pavilion.

Back at their tents, Elyne stood outside, waiting for her return. Her forehead had a crease of worry, something Maggie wasn't accustomed to seeing.

"He won't change his mind," Maggie announced. "That despicable Lord Vile says that Finn will forfeit if he doesn't go on."

Maggie looked Geoffrey up and down but the boy was too

small and too inexperienced to sit on a horse with a lance. She paced, chewing her thumbnail. She had to think of something. There had to be some way to compete in the tourney without forfeiting. She only had moments to form a plan and then it would be too late.

"Geoffrey, go back and tell the list marshal Finn will be at his match, ready to joust."

"What?" Elyne snapped, her eyes round and wide.

"But, my lady?"

"Finn will be there and he will not forfeit. Understood? Go now and tell him at once." Maggie waited until Geoffrey dashed away before she clamped a hand on Elyne's arm and dragged her toward the tent. Excitement skittered through her. "Come with me, Ellie."

"Just what do ye think you're doing?" Elyne demanded.

"I have an idea."

She dragged her inside where Finn's armor lay, discarded. Maggie kneeled and picked up the breastplate, holding it in her hands while Finn moaned with his stomach illness.

Could she do it? For all intents and purposes, she could. It was the only way to keep Finn in the tournament. She could ride a horse, certainly, but she had never jousted.

"What are you doing?" Elyne asked in horror. Her eyes were wide, her jaw slack.

"I'm riding in his stead. And you're going to help me."

"Help you?" Elyne repeated. "Have you lost your mind?"

"Yes." Maggie paused and looked at the princess. "You are Fae. You can use your magic to help me."

"No, I can't," Elyne said quickly. She folded her arms over her chest, her jaw set in a stubborn line. "You must have Swiss cheese for a brain because you can't seem to remember. *It doesn't work like that.*"

"It doesn't work like that or you don't *want* it to work like that?" Maggie countered.

Elyne pursed her lips in silence.

"That's what I thought. I can't let Finn forfeit."

"Why not?"

"Because then Lord Vile wins. Don't you see? This is just what he wanted. I think he's the reason Finn is sick right now and I'm not going to let him get away with it that easily. He's going to pay for it and I'm going to make sure he does."

"You *are* mad, woman," Elyne said. "If you let him forfeit, then you don't have to worry about keeping him alive. You can go home, Maggie. Back to your time. To your precious twenty-first century. All you have to do is let him lose and then I'll send you back."

"With the snap of your fingers or the wave of your Faery magic wand? No way. There's more to this than I originally thought, Ellie. There are people here who need me. They need my help."

"People like who? Lady Juliet?"

"Yes, her and—" Maggie snapped her mouth shut. She couldn't tell Elyne she had every intention of getting her and Derron together.

"Her and who?"

"A, ah, certain Lord Brian." She thought quickly to pull Lord Brian into the equation, the man she was certain Lady Juliet was in love with. They'd given each other the doe eyes after all. "And Finn. He needs me, too."

"Lady Juliet is a lost cause, Maggie. She's half dead as it is."

"Exactly why I have to stay and help her. I have to get her away from that awful brother of hers," Maggie said, her voice quivering an octave higher. Frustrated, she dropped to her knees, searching for a pair of breeches she could wear. "I don't have time to stand here and argue with you."

"What do you think you're going to do? Wear his armor and joust? Do you even know how to ride a horse?"

"Ride, yes. Joust, no."

Elyne continued to stare at her, stony faced, while Maggie rummaged through his clothing until she found a pair of his breeches. Snatching them up, she pulled them on. Then she searched through his clothing until she found a suitable tunic. Shimmying out of her shift, she slipped the tunic over her head.

"God's teeth," Elyne muttered. "You can't compete in the tournament. 'Tis too dangerous and you're impersonating a man. Something they don't take too lightly in this time. You'll be arrested and thrown in the stocks if they find out. Or worse, you could be killed."

"Then we'll have to make sure no one finds out."

Maggie tried to figure out how to put on all the armor. None of it made sense. Her hands shook as she held up one of the greaves, wondering which leg it went on. She knew she was insane to even consider jousting in place of Finn. She had no idea how it all worked but she was determined. If Lord Vile was competing in the competition later in the week, she had to make sure Finn would be there to challenge him.

"That armor doesn't even fit you. Let me find someone to take his place," Elyne suggested finally.

"There isn't time for that," Maggie said. "I just need a crash course in jousting and I'll be fine." She hoped.

Elyne sighed, resigned. "If you're determined to go through with it, fine. I can't let you die in the saddle."

"Then you'll help?" Maggie looked up at Elyne, hope rising within her.

"Aye, I'll help." Looking her over, Elyne shook her head. "And that armor won't do. Let me find you armor that is more appropriate."

"Thank you, Ellie."

"Save your thanks for when you don't die," Elyne snarled.

Maggie inhaled a breath to calm her jangled nerves. No second thoughts. She was determined. And she would win.

Her life and Finn's depended on it.

Chapter 9

Maggie had no idea where Elyne conjured up armor that actually fit her. She had disappeared from Finn's tent and moments later returned with the full gear. It took some doing to get Maggie into the armor, but Elyne seemed to know all about it. From the greaves to the bracers, to the gauntlets to the breastplate. Maggie was all suited up and ready to go.

It was amazing, really.

"Does this armor make my butt look big?"

"Very funny." Elyne scowled, unfazed by Maggie's humor.

"But...I'm too small and skinny to look like Finn," Maggie complained, looking at her reflection in the polished steel. She couldn't quite make out what she looked like other than a foggy blob. She wished she had a real mirror.

"Don't worry about that. I can cast a glamour over you. No one will ever know."

"Really? You can do that? I thought only Fae could have a glamour."

"I can cast a Fae glamour over anyone. Only a Fae will be able to see your true form—and mine—while the glamour is up."

"Sir Derron will be able to see my true form, then." Maggie worried about that.

"Aye, but he's not due in the lists today," Elyne replied.

"What about Fergus and Geoffrey? Will they be able to see me as I am or as Finn?"

She huffed her annoyance. "We don't have time for me to explain Fae magic to you."

"Humor me." Fergus already knew Maggie was taking Finn's place. The last thing she needed was for him to know Elyne was of the "fair folk."

"I can make them immune to the magic. They will see you as you are but everyone else will see you as Finn. Now, come on. Let's get you to the lists."

They exited the tent to find Fergus waiting outside, pacing and wringing his hands. "Are ye sure about this, my lady?" he asked. "Sir Finian won't be very happy when he finds out."

"He's not going to find out," Maggie warned. "Because neither you nor Geoffrey will tell him. Now, tell me what I need to know."

Grabbing Fergus by the arm, they headed from the pavilion to the lists. She wanted to arrive before the scheduled time so Lord Vile wouldn't try to disqualify Finn.

"Sit firmly in the saddle, my lady," Fergus explained patiently. "Make sure you keep your feet in the stirrups and use your knees to cling to the horse. Hold the lance upright in your right hand. Keep it upright until the last possible moment, and then lower it at an angle across the horse's neck." He used hand motions to give her a visual.

"Got it. What else?"

"Once you have it lowered, couch it under your right arm, pointing it forward across the tilt barrier. Like this." The boy paused to pick up a stick and showed her what he meant.

Maggie nodded. "Right hand, point across the tilt barrier. Sounds easy enough. Anything else?"

"Aim for the middle of his chest," Fergus said. "And brace yourself for the impact by leaning backward slightly. The only way your opponent can win is if he knocks you off the horse and I promise he'll try to knock you off the horse. And you'd best do something about that hair." He eyed her long, auburn locks hanging down her back.

"Oh, I forgot. Help me, Ellie."

She twisted it into a crude bun on top of her head while Elyne pinned it. With her hair secured to the top of her head, she slipped on the helm. It wasn't completely comfortable with her hair in a knot, but she would have to bear it. For Finn.

"Anything else?"

"Don't die," Elyne said. "I don't want to have to explain that one to Finn."

"I'll do my best not to."

They had arrived at the lists and Maggie's stomach clenched into a tight knot. No one seemed to give her anything but a cursory glance. Whatever glamour Elyne cast, it appeared to be working. The blood pulsed loudly in her ears, drowning out even the sound of the roar of the crowd. Despite the adrenaline rushing through her veins, her heart fluttered. She had a sickening feeling in her throat. Her lungs felt as if they were about to explode.

And, to make matters worse, the armor was heavier than she had even imagined. She was hot. Sweat rolled down the side of her face and down her back. And damn it all, she could barely see out of the slit in the helm. How did men *do* this?

Cheers and roars and laughter filled her ears over the pounding of her throbbing heart. Geoffrey waited with Finn's destrier, which was also covered in armor. He handed her a shield emblazoned with the heraldry of his lineage. The weight of the shield nearly knocked her off her feet but Fergus was there to catch her and hold her upright. She slid the shield on her left arm, the weight of it making her arm ache. After only a few minutes of holding it, her muscles quivered, her elbow drooped to her leg.

With her heart hammering in her chest so hard she thought she could hear it reverberate in her breastplate, she stepped into the stirrup. Geoffrey hoisted her into the saddle with a gentle push. She swung over her other leg, stuck her foot into the stirrup and settled into the saddle, clutching the reins with her left hand. The shield was a problem, though, and tended to get in her way. She was an experienced horsewoman, but sitting in the saddle holding a shield was something altogether different.

Exhaling a shaky breath, she smiled, though no one could see her face.

"Good luck to you," Elyne whispered and patted her armored knee before stepping away.

Confidence swelled inside her as Fergus handed her the lance, which also weighed her down. She hadn't held it long before the muscles in her right arm started to ache. Great. Now both her arms seemed to have turned to Jell-O. Maggie wished she'd spent more time in the gym lifting weights like her trainer wanted her to do. She regretted it now.

Glancing up at the wooden pole, it wiggled in the air, a direct result of her hand and arm muscles shaking from both angst and fatigue. With sweat rolling down her face, she turned her attention once again in front of her.

In the center of the lists near the tilt, the list marshal stood. Lord Litonshire himself, the vile beast. She scowled and stuck out her tongue, knowing no one could see her. It made her feel better.

Litonshire glanced from her to the opponent and back again.

She waited agonizing moments until at last he snapped up the flag, signaling the beginning of the match. The knight three hundred feet away kicked his horse into a full charge.

And then the world seemed to pass into slow motion. Maggie was acutely aware of the knight and his twelve-hundred-pound horse charging forward, aware of the dirt clods his steed kicked up behind him, aware of the loud din of the crowd all around her, and very aware of the sudden sick feeling clenching her stomach. She swallowed the rising bile. She would not throw up. She could do this.

Firmly in the saddle, feet in stirrups, cling to the horse with your knees and for God's sake, don't fall off.

Geoffrey slapped the destrier's rump and bellowed a roar of good luck as the stallion took off at a full gallop. With the lance wobbling in her right hand and the reins gripped so tight her left hand ached, she held her breath as her heart beat a wild tattoo. Her opponent lowered his lance, pointing it directly at her torso. It occurred to her she ought to do the same, but the lance wobbled in her hand. Her muscles refused to cooperate with her.

Grasping it in her hand and biting her lip, she did her best to lower the lance. It trembled in the air, back and forth, as she struggled to keep it steady. She managed to tuck the end under her arm, holding it close to her body. Every muscle tensed and she made sure she clenched her knees around the heavy beast under her. She was so intent on keeping her lance steady that when she looked up, she saw her opponent's pointing lance only a few feet in front of her.

She gasped and squeezed her eyes shut as the lance struck her square in the chest, splintering and raining shards of wood all around her. With the reins gripped in her hands, she snapped backward, holding on for dear life. The horse reared, making his discomfort known and whinnying loudly. The blow was so hard she lost control of her own lance and it fell from her hand, unscathed. A loud cheer went up from the raucous crowd, only adding to the roar in her eardrums.

Gritting her teeth, she forced herself to release the reins, letting them go slack in her hand as the horse slammed his front hooves back on the ground, jarring every bone in her body and rattling her back teeth. She fell forward, panting heavily as fear coursed like acid through her. Leaning against the neck of the horse, she patted his mane, cooing soft words to calm him. What transpired in only a few seconds seemed like a vast eternity to Maggie.

Hearing her own panting, she glanced around to see her lance lying in the dirt. Not shattered like her opponent's, not splintered and broken, but still intact. Turning her head, she peered through the slit in the helm to see the damage. The other knight remained on his horse with nothing left of his lance but a rather short stick.

Elyne and Geoffrey ran toward her. The boy grinned broadly while concern creased Elyne's face. Was he laughing at her? If so, Maggie made a mental note to kick his ass later.

"I suck at this," Maggie said, her voice booming loud inside the helm.

"That was a bad first attempt. Two more rounds and you're done," Elyne said. "Hang in there."

"*Two* more? I have to do this *two* more times? Are you freaking kidding me?" How would she ever survive? She could barely hold the damn lance as it was.

"Unless you can knock him off his horse," Geoffrey said. "Then you win."

"Then that's just what I'm going to have to do this time," Maggie said. She sounded much more confident than she felt.

"You'll have to actually hit him with your lance if you mean to do that," Elyne said dryly.

"No kidding?"

Geoffrey gripped the reins and led the calmed horse back to the starting point to reset. As they set up, the crowd continued to roar, cheering and clapping. The squire handed her a second lance. Her weakened hand tried to grip it but it slipped right through and *thunked* on the ground. What was she thinking? She couldn't do this. She was an imbecile to think she could.

Fergus picked up the lance and gave it to her again. He made sure her fingers were wrapped around it before releasing it. The weapon weighed her down and it took every effort she had to hold it up right. Elyne stood next to her, looking up at her.

"You just have to stay on the horse," she said.

"I know that," Maggie snapped. "Trying to concentrate here."

"Concentrate on lowering the bloody lance," Elyne said. "It has to be in position or I can't help you."

"I'll try."

"No trying. Do it."

Her voice was ragged with rage and something inside Maggie snapped. How could she do something she'd never even done before in her life? Oh, sure. Lower the lance. That sounded *so* easy, didn't it?

"All right," Maggie shouted back.

The list marshal lowered the flag and Geoffrey smacked the rump of her horse. She took off so abruptly, her head snapped back and it took several precious moments to right herself again. She clutched the lance, barreling toward her opponent, and forced her weak muscles to work. After several failed attempts, she got the lance couched under her arm. The end quivered in the air as she tried to position it across her body and, gritting her teeth, she lowered it as best as she could.

Her lance wiggled in the air. Her opponent's lance, however, pointed directly at her and she braced for the impact. Her back stiffened and she squeezed her eyes shut as she sucked in a sharp breath, anticipating contact.

Instead, her opponent's horse stumbled and he lost control of his lance. It tumbled to the ground with a muffled *thud-thud* as he tried to gain control of his horse. He jerked on the reins until finally the beast obeyed.

Maggie, though, had lost all control of her lance. Her weakened hand refused to hold it any longer as her horse came to a screeching halt. Fergus was at her side then, taking the lance from her and leading her back to their position on the other end of the lists.

"What happened?" she asked.

"Horse stumbled on a rock, my lady. You're lucky. He would have surely hit you then."

"Lucky." Maggie had a feeling the rock stumbling had nothing to do with luck and everything to do with Elyne.

Once she was back at the lists, Elyne stood next to her, looking up. "That was a better try."

"Gee, thanks."

"You're still not lowering it, though," Elyne pointed out.

"Yes, I know. I'll try it again."

"All you have to do is get it into position. The rest is up to me."

"That's the problem, Elyne, I can't get it into position. It's too heavy."

Elyne laid her hand over her metal arm. "Yes, you can, Maggie.

You *can* do it."

With those words, Maggie felt a surge of strength swell through her. Almost as though she were invincible. She sat up a little straighter in the saddle. No longer did she feel the ache of holding the lance or the shield. Nor did she feel the weight of the armor she wore. Instead, all she knew was that she had to do one thing—knock that knight off his horse.

Litonshire snapped the third flag, starting the final round of the match. Fergus smacked her horse's rump and off she went, barreling toward her opponent who already had his lance in position.

Maggie lowered her lance, this time without any problems. As though it weighed no more than a feather. She tucked it under her arm, couching it in the proper position, lowered it across her body. She made connection with the opponent, jarring her from her wrist up to her shoulder and back down again.

Opening her eyes, she saw her lance in shards and her opponent flat on his back in the lists.

She'd done it. She managed to stay on her horse, lower the lance, and knock the guy off. Deafening cheers surrounded her and suddenly Geoffrey and Fergus were there. One of them grasped the reins and led the horse back out of the lists. Glancing back, though, she had to see if the man she'd jousted with was okay. His squire knelt at his side, helping him off with his helmet.

Much to her horror, Maggie realized she'd knocked Sir Drake off his horse.

Her shoulders slumped as they rode away and relief washed over her, nearly overwhelming her. With the match over, she was ready to get out of the armor. Elyne fell in step next to the horse and glanced up, squinting against the afternoon sun.

"You did it," Fergus said, sounding surprised. "I confess, I dinna think it would work since you're much smaller than Sir Finian." He shook his head, as if he couldn't believe she'd managed it. "Not even the list marshal seemed to take note."

"I, ah..." Maggie was at a loss. Since Fergus didn't know about Elyne's magic, how could she explain it?

"Of course, no one noticed," Elyne interjected. "All those in the grandstand want to see is someone getting knocked off a horse. She managed that. Now run along with the horses." She shooed Fergus away, then turned to Maggie. "Are you all right?"

"I hurt like hell but, yeah, I think I'm all right," Maggie said.

Now that the adrenaline rush was over, Maggie thought she would collapse at any moment. Every muscle in her body felt as though it had turned to mush. Her hands still shook and her heart still stuttered in her chest. Once they were out of the lists, Geoffrey helped her down from the horse.

Elyne grasped her arm, holding her steady as she limped away from the lists. Her victory was short-lived, though.

"Sir Finian," Lord Litonshire shouted in his nasal voice.

Maggie's heart nearly stopped. Hadn't she had enough fear for one day? She turned to face him as he came running from the lists. "Crap."

"Just what we need," Elyne muttered.

"Can't you use a Jedi mind trick on him?" Maggie asked.

"A what?"

"I suppose not."

"Just don't talk to him. I still have your glamour up."

Before Maggie could ask how she was supposed to do that, Litonshire stopped in front of them. He looked her up and down, as though he didn't believe the sight before his eyes.

"How did you do it?" he demanded.

Elyne placed her hand on Maggie's arm as she shrugged.

"Sir Finian is feeling much better," Elyne said.

The earl's beady eyes swung from Maggie to Elyne and back again. "I thought you were too ill to ride."

"He persevered, my lord," Elyne answered.

"Let him speak for himself."

Maggie balled her fist, tempted to punch him. Litonshire took a step backward.

"He's quite fatigued, my lord," Elyne said, taking Maggie's elbow. "I simply must see him back to the tent."

"If I find there is some trickery here—" Litonshire began.

"How dare you?" Elyne snapped. "When you've been seen skulking through the market buying mandrake."

Litonshire's faced turned to ash and his lips pursed into a very thin line. He left Maggie and Elyne and headed back to the tournament grounds. Maggie blew out a breath as they headed back towards their tents.

"What an ass," Maggie said. "His reaction proves he had something to do with Finn's sickness."

"It would seem that way."

"Ellie, remind me never to do that again."

"As you wish, my lady."

"Would now be the appropriate time to thank you for keeping me alive?"

"Aye, it would."

"I couldn't have done it without you, Ellie. Thanks for not letting me die a painful death."

"I do what I can," Elyne said. "And that will be the last time I use my magic for anything other than sifting the sands of time and sending you home. Are we clear?"

"As a bell, your highness."

Maggie limped back to her tent, Elyne at her side. Once inside, she stripped off the helm and tossed it to the ground, letting her hair cascade down her back and blowing out a hot breath. Elyne helped her out of all the armor and into a more appropriate gown. Maggie fell back on her low bed, shaking.

"That was the most terrifying experience of my life," she said. But what an awesome adventure it had been. "If only I could write it all down."

"Here, then."

Looking up, she saw Elyne holding out a quill, an inkwell, and several scrolls of parchment.

"For your research notes," Elyne said. "It's all I could get. I hope that's all right with you."

"Where did you get this?"

"I managed to pick some up at the market for you."

Touched, Maggie took the items from her. "Thank you, Elyne."

Maggie was used to writing everything on a computer and not by longhand. Her heart skipped a beat, though, at the thought of writing part of her thesis the really old-fashioned way. Who would believe she wrote part of it with quill and ink? She couldn't wait to get started.

"Since you'll be sitting with Finn for the rest of the day, you'll have plenty of time to catch up."

"Finn!"

Maggie sat up quickly, trying to get to her feet, but every inch of her body protested. She groaned. Still determined to get to Finn, she scrambled up and hobbled out of her tent and into his to see him sleeping. Fergus had brought a pail of water and some rags as she'd asked for. She put aside her paper, inkwell and quill and sat down next to Finn. Dipping a rag into the pail, she wrung it out and bathed his face. He didn't even stir.

She settled down next to him, taking up the quill and unrolled one of the scrolls. Where should she begin? She started with the title *How to Become a Jousting Hero by Lady Margaret Ann Chase*. Dropping down a line or two, she began to write.

Fergus came to check on his master, bringing fresh water and dry rags. He even cleaned the foul chamber pot. Maggie was glad it no longer stank in the tent. She wrote nearly a page on the scroll when her hand started to cramp and Finn stirred. Putting aside her writing, she reached for a damp rag, carefully wiping his sweating face. He hadn't moved much since she sat down next to him. Now she reached for the water skin.

His eyes came open and he fixed his silvery stare on her. He blinked several times as though trying to get her into focus before rising up on one elbow. She handed him the water skin. He drank deeply, nearly draining it before handing it back to her.

"I'll have Fergus refill it," she said. "How are you feeling?"

"A mite better, lass."

"Good. I was worried about you, Finn."

"As was I." He lay back down on his back, his breathing heavy as though that little movement had been a great effort. "I dinna feel as though I'm going to die."

"That is an improvement."

"And how are ye feeling, lass?"

"Fine. Why do you ask?"

Her brows knit and suddenly she worried about her previous conversation with Elyne. Had Finn overheard them arguing about her jousting? And if he had, what else did he hear?

"Ye wouldna have gone and done something mad, would ye?" He cracked an eye and pinned her with a molten gaze.

It took all her willpower not to squirm under that one-eyed glare. "I don't know what you mean, Finn. I've been here with you."

"Not since dawn, aye?"

He had her there. She needed to concoct a lie and quickly.

Never one of her strong suits. "No, I…had some errands to run." It sounded ludicrous even to her own ears.

Finn shut his eye. "*Och*, lass. Dinna give me falsehoods. I ken ye were about no good."

"I wasn't." Even though her chest still ached from the lance she took to the breastplate. And her armor was stashed in the sleeping quarters of her tent. She made a mental note to make sure that all was removed immediately.

"I heard ye and wee Elyne earlier."

Crap. There was no getting out of this one. Unless she could convince him he'd been delusional with his sickness.

"Why, Finn, whatever do you mean?"

"Lass…when I get well enough to get out of this bed, I intend to take ye over my knee and thrash ye good for all the lies."

She gulped.

"Tell me the truth now. What did she mean…yere time?"

Crap. He'd heard everything and her secret was out. She couldn't admit it, though. Not yet. Though her paper she'd been writing was incriminating enough. She reached for the scroll and slowly rolled it up, trying not to make much noise with the parchment. Her blood pulsed in her ears, a deafening sound she couldn't seem to get away from these last few hours.

"Oh, Finn. You must have been dreaming."

"I dinna think so. She said she would send ye back to yere twenty-first century. By my calendar, lass, this is the fourteenth century." He turned his head now, looking at her with a cross expression of bemused resignation and anger. "If I dinna forfeit, then who rode in my stead?"

"Fergus," she said quickly. "A very fine squire he is, too."

Finn heaved a heavy sigh. "Fergus 'tis but a boy and not near experienced enough to joust for me. He can barely hold a lance. Out with the truth, now."

Maggie gathered up her parchment, the inkwell, the quill. "It was me, all right? I did it." She jumped to her feet, ready to bolt. "Elyne helped me. I made her. I told her she had to because you couldn't forfeit."

"*You* did it?"

Maggie thought for sure she could hear his breath catch in his throat. She didn't want to stick around for his wrath. Instead, she turned on her toe, took two hurried steps to leave him in his small bed chamber of the tent.

"How?"

He asked it so quietly, she stopped cold. She couldn't very well tell him the truth because he had no idea Elyne was a Faery princess.

"And how is it ye dinna get killed?"

"Lucky, I guess?" She gave him a dismissive shrug.

"Why do ye help me?" An easy smile played at the corners of his mouth.

Why *did* she help him? She could have done what Elyne said, let him lose and be home in her own bed right now. If she had, then what would have happened? Lord Vile could win the tourney, Finn's reputation would never be repaired, and Lady Juliet would die an anorexic. She couldn't allow any of that to happen because, much as she was afraid to admit it, she was attached to these people.

"Lassie? Why do ye help me?"

"Because I think Litonshire poisoned you to take you out of the tourney, Finn, and I intend to see him punished for it."

"Poison?"

"He was rather smug when I talked with him about postponing your match. In fact, he was downright gleeful you wouldn't be there." She turned to face him, saw him sitting up and his face ashen. "Finn, you shouldn't be up yet."

"What are ye writing?" He eyed the scrolls cradled in her arms.

"My memoirs," she snapped. "Does it matter?" The last thing she wanted to do was explain her thesis to him. He would never understand.

He scowled, probably due to her snappish attitude. "Have ye no sense? Ye should stay away from Litonshire."

"I know he's dangerous, Finn. I get it. But I couldn't let you forfeit."

"Why?"

"Because something has to be done about him. And someone needs to get his sister away from him. He shouldn't be hitting her."

"'Tis not for us to interfere in their family, lass."

"But he's killing her."

Finn rose to his full height and Maggie was relieved to see he wore breeches, unlike the last time she'd seen him in bed. He reached for a tunic and pulled it on over his head.

"I ken he is, lass." He sounded so calm. Didn't anyone have a sense of urgency about the poor girl? Was she the only one who cared?

"Is there nothing to be done about it then?" she asked.

"Why do ye want to help so much?" he wanted to know.

"Because it's what I do. I help people. When my only sister was killed by a drunk driver, I didn't break down. Instead, I was there for my parents, helping them through it." She fought the tears that threatened to spill as she paced the length of the tent. Her words tumbled out of her and she was unable to stop the flow. "And when the stress from their deaths caused my mother's cancer to come back, I was there for her and Dad. I was even there when she died, helping Dad through that. I made sure the bills were paid, there was food to eat, all while going to school full time and working part time."

She stopped suddenly, staring at nothing, remembering those horrid eight months of her life not so long ago. Bitterness landed on her tongue. She could taste it there, a vivid acid taste that would never go away. "But who was there for *me*? No one. That's who."

She started to pace, still cradling the scrolls against her chest. "Dad tried but he had enough to worry about without having to coddle me."

The only one she had was Beth, who was always there when she needed her. She helped when her mother died and was her rock when her sister was killed. And that helped but what she really wanted—needed—was someone to take charge. A big, strong man to right the wrongs of her world. To hold her and tell her everything would be all right. Escaping to Scotland had been part of her solace, a way to help her cope. She didn't really need to come here to finish her thesis but she *did* need to come here to find herself.

Instead, she'd found Finn.

A tiny part of her wished Finn could be her someone but she knew better. When all this was over, she would return to her world. He would stay in his. Six hundred years apart.

"I'm sorry." Maggie sniffed and whisked away the tears on her cheeks, turning away from him. "I hate to cry. I try to never do it."

"Dinna be sorry, lass." His hands, warm and strong, landed on her shoulders. Giving her the comfort she so craved. "Ye still look like a bonnie lass to me."

Which made her tears flow even faster. She squeezed her eyes shut, letting them roll down her cheeks in silence. All the fight went out of her and she sagged against him. Using her sleeve, she wiped away the tears, willing them to stop.

"I dinna ken what all that means, lass," he said. "But I dinna think ye should bear it all alone."

"It's my burden to bear." Regaining her composure, she inhaled sharply. "And never you mind about any of that. I want to help Lady Juliet. Finn, you helped her once. Can't you help her again?"

"So ye dinna believe what ye've heard?" he asked, ignoring her plea for help.

"You're not the barbarian that's been rumored." He'd proved it once again with his compassion for her situation, which she knew he could never understand. "I have it on good authority your reputation isn't as tarnished as you think. There are ladies out there who believe you had nothing to do with Lady Juliet's condition."

"Is that so?"

"Yes. I've talked with several of them."

She craned her neck to look up at him. He was big. And brawny. She should be intimidated by the sheer size of him, but she wasn't. She was enamored.

"So, anyway…" She swallowed hard. "I took your place to keep you in the tourney so when you joust Litonshire you can squash him like a bug."

"And no one knew it wasn't me?" He peered at her, askance.

"No one seemed to notice or ask any questions."

She tried to keep her voice steady and sound believable. Her mouth suddenly went bone dry and she swallowed hard. It wasn't quite the truth, as Litonshire confronted her afterward but Finn didn't need to know about that. Hopefully, he would drop it. He still gave her a look that said he didn't quite believe her. And when she thought he would question her more he smiled, the corners of his mouth barely turning up. He turned her to face him. Cupping her face in his hands, he kissed her forehead, making her heart flutter.

"And how did ye do in my place?"

"I managed to stay on the horse." She omitted the part about how Elyne helped her stay on the horse. Mostly because she wasn't sure how Fae magic worked. She wasn't sure if Finn knew Elyne was a Fae princess, much less believed in magic.

"Good. And yere opponent?" He feathered kisses along her hairline. She wanted to sink into a pile of goo.

"Knocked him off," she managed. "You should probably know it was Sir Drake."

He chuckled. "Very good, lass. Mayhap he willna be so cocky in the lists should we meet again. Yere missing banquet."

As if on cue, her stomach rumbled. "I don't care. You should lie back down until you feel back to normal."

"*Och*, lass, most of my parts are feeling back to normal."

He pulled her closer to him, if that were possible, and pressed all the hard planes of his body against hers. His chest pressed against her, the fabric of their clothes the only thing between them. Heat flashed through her, though whether from his close contact or her hormones, she couldn't be sure. He hadn't been lying when he said most of his parts were back to normal.

Instead of obeying her, he tipped her face toward his. Maggie expected another kiss. Finn's gaze took on a hard edge and she tried not to shudder from fear. Finn could look menacing.

"Ye shouldna have done something so dangerous. Ye could have been killed."

"I'm sorry, Finn. You're right. I shouldn't have. But I thought it was the only way."

"Aye, then. 'Tis done and we canna undo it." His face drained of color then. Cradling her papers and ink in one arm, she slipped the other around his thick waist and turned him back toward the bed.

"Rest. You need more rest," she ordered. "I'll stay with you."

"'Tis no' necessary. Go to banquet. I'm sure to be well by morn."

"Well, only if you're certain," she said. "I could sit with you, if you'd like."

He gave her a faint smile. "Go dance with the wee Sir Derron since you fancy him so."

"I don't fancy him at all."

"No? Who then?" Despite his illness, there was a mischievous twinkle in his eye.

"I'm not falling for that trick." When he chuckled, she swiveled quickly, and headed toward the tent. "Good night, Finn."

"Good eve, Mistress Maggie."

She could hear him chuckling as she left the tent.

Chapter 10

Maggie would never know how much she'd helped Finn by taking his place that day. The very thought was unconscionable. Why should she risk her life for him? He knew she hadn't a clue as to how to joust. She was a passable rider but jousting took skills he knew she didn't possess. But she'd thrown all caution—and good sense—to the wind and heartily taken on the task. With that she'd managed to keep him in the tournament and his land out of Litonshire's hands. At least for the moment.

How could he ever repay her?

Finn waited until he was sure Maggie was well on her way to banquet before throwing off the bed clothes and standing up again. He did feel much better—better than he let on. In truth, he felt well enough to seek out Elyne.

He left his tent, weaving his way through the pavilion looking for the blonde-haloed woman with the big blue eyes. He needed to talk to her and find out what she meant by twenty-first century and sending Maggie back to her time. How had she managed to help Maggie live through the jousting match? The two spoke to each other like old friends instead of servant and lady.

Most everyone who attended the tournament—both participants and fans alike—were at banquet this time of night. But there were some who preferred the solitude of their tents. And still others who found enjoyment and danger in the gambling underground of tourney. Indeed, that's where he'd found most of his trouble last tourney. Taking on a game of dice with Lord Litonshire was his worst mistake.

He could sniff out the gambling tents a mile away. His feet took him there before his mind could reason with him and tell him to stop. Wasn't he in enough debt already? Yet he couldn't stop himself from entering, seeing the card games in play and the dice games underway.

Much to his surprise, he found the lovely Elyne sitting at a card table, primly holding a hand of cards, a pile of gold in the center and a neat stack in front of her. Stunned, he stood and watched as she bet against the only other player willing to go the distance. Everyone else had folded.

"I'll see you and raise you two," she said and plunked two more gold coins on the pile.

"Call," the man said across from her, adding yet more coins. He smiled, wolfish. "Let's see them."

She laid her cards on the table in front of her and immediately the man scowled. He flung down his cards and shoved back from the table. "You wench."

"I thank you, good gentles, for your generosity." Elyne giggled as she scooped all the gold toward her and the men rose from the table. "You're all leaving so soon?"

"Ye send us to the poor house, lass," Angus said while the others walked away.

"Suit yourselves," she called after them, still grinning as she put all the gold into a drawstring purse.

"Elyne," Finn said. His voice boomed louder than he intended.

Her head snapped toward him, her eyes wide with surprise. She finished scooping the coins into the heavy purse, tied it, and then stood. "Good eve, Sir Finian. You're looking quite well since this morn."

"Aye, indeed, I am much better." As she walked by him, he snatched her by the arm. "We must talk."

She gave him a sidelong glance. One that said she wasn't interested in talking to him but knew she didn't have a choice. "And to what do I owe the pleasure of this talk?"

"'Tis about Lady Margaret."

Her smile faded. "Mayhap we should take a walk then."

"Aye, we should."

Glad he resisted the urge to participate, he led her out of the gambling tent while other games went on behind them toward a copse of trees on the edge of the pavilion. There they would have some privacy and he could ask her about the conversation she'd had earlier that day with Maggie.

"I think I know what this is about," Elyne said, starting the conversation. "You found out about what Maggie did this afternoon, didn't you?"

"Her taking my place? Aye, and I'm no' too happy about it

either."

"I tried to talk her out of it, but she would have none of it," Elyne said. "She insisted."

"And ye let her?"

"As if I could stop her." Elyne snorted. "She's a bit bull-headed."

Finn could agree with that. Maggie was stubborn and beautiful. A deadly combination. "What did ye do to help her?"

Elyne blinked and appeared taken aback. "Help her?"

Losing patience, Finn growled. "I'll not play this game with ye, too. Tell me how ye helped her."

"Fergus is the one who told her what to do."

"Ye told her to let me lose so you could send her back to her time. Back to the twenty-first century."

"Oh. That. You heard that?" Elyne took a step backward, perhaps to get away from his wrath. She looked ready to bolt.

Finn took a deep breath to calm down. "Aye, I did. What does it mean?"

"You want the truth?"

"From someone, aye."

"Great. And you picked me." Elyne sighed. "Maggie is from the future."

"In truth?"

"Aye, I sent her back in time at your request."

"Mine? That's no' possible. I never met the lass ere a fortnight ago."

"That's only partly true," Elyne said.

"By Saint Mary, yere talking in riddles. I dinna understand."

"It would be easier if I could show you."

"Then show me," he growled.

Nodding, Elyne reached for him and placed her hand on his arm. Her eyes met his. A wave of sickness came over him and he clamped a hand on her wrist. But Elyne shook her head, shoving his hand away.

A moment later, he was seeing tournament as they arrived. Except no Maggie. Then a confrontation with Litonshire about his gambling debts. They'd fought. Litonshire had threatened him. Finn had punched him in the nose. Still no Maggie. The next thing he knew, he was on a horse, ready to joust. He charged after his opponent, shattering his lance on the man's helm.

With horror, he realized his lance had been tipped. But he hadn't done it. He'd been set up. He saw Litonshire smiling, his eyes hooded with menace, and Finn realized he'd accidentally killed the other knight, Sir Derron. Finn knew Litonshire had everything to do with it because he wanted him out of the way so he could quietly take his lands. He'd called for his arrest, sent him to the stocks.

Elyne came to him, her pretty face tear-streaked. *You killed my love*, she'd said. *For that you will pay. I curse you for all eternity.*

Then later Litonshire had come, told him he'd take good care of his castle in Innisborough. When Finn spit in his face, he drew a dagger. Stabbed him in the ribs. Once. Twice. Three times.

He'd died.

Elyne returned to him, told him she'd cursed him to wander his castle. Doomed to live out eternity alone until someone with a noble heart could right his wrongs. But his castle, she'd said, would be invisible to everyone but the one person who would be his savior. Litonshire would not be able to claim the lands after all. His savior had turned out to be Maggie when she'd taken shelter one stormy summer night.

And Elyne had suggested she return him to his time with Maggie.

He jerked his arm away, took two steps backward and stared at Elyne. Disbelief coursed through him, the vision of what could happen again in the near future combined with the memory she'd returned to him slammed into him hard. Like a giant stone in his chest. That was reality, but they'd gone back in time and somehow Maggie had changed everything. Litonshire had been the one to tip his lance. He'd been Derron's murderer. He knew that now.

"Ye are one of the fair folk."

"I am," Elyne said with a nod. "A Fae princess betrothed to Sir Derron, Knight of the Realm and Protector of the Otherworld."

"I dinna kill Sir Derron."

"Aye, you did. I saw you with my own eyes. Your lance hit him in the helm. He died in the lists." Her skin flushed, turning her pale complexion red. Her fists clenched into balls at her side and sparks flashed in her normally calm eyes.

With her fiery anger, her true form shone through. Elyne's dazzling beauty rivaled that of any maid he'd ever seen. Her golden hair shimmered with an ethereal glow. Her blue eyes turned bright, reproachful. But most peculiar of all were the pointed tips of her ears.

"Aye, that much is true, Elyne," he said calmly, eyeing her ears. "But the lance was tipped and I wouldna do that. Murdering a knight in the lists isn't the way of the Code. Or the way of my code."

She took two calming breaths and released her fists. She returned to the way she was before, her hair no longer shimmering. Her eyes returned to their normal cornflower blue. Her ears were no longer pointed.

"If you didn't, then who did?"

"Lord Litonshire," he said. "He wanted me out of the way so he could get Castle McCullough."

"But he never got it."

"No, for upon my death ye cursed me and the castle." He grinned then. "And I should thank ye for keeping it out of the vile man's hands."

"Oh. You're welcome, I suppose. Why does he want it so badly?"

"It sits near the border of Scotland and England. A strategic stronghold. If he gains control of it, he can then invade Scotland."

"Your human battles are of no interest to me," Elyne said, giving him a glance of pure disdain. "I don't care if you kill each other or not."

"But ye do care if your precious knight is alive. Tell me, Elyne, if ye are betrothed, why does he have such an interest in Maggie?"

"She's human. Why else?"

"And the other women?"

She grimaced. "Derron is my problem, not yours."

"He is my problem if he's interested in Maggie. And didn't we have an agreement about her?"

"As I told you before, I'm not a matchmaker," Elyne said, scrunching her perfect angular features into a scowl. "What about all those charms of yours? I don't see you using them to woo her. She's supposed to keep you out of trouble and instead you're letting her run all over tourney trying to fix everyone else's problems."

"I'm no' letting her do anything. She does it and ye help her." For emphasis, he pointed at her with an accusatory index finger.

"Don't point that meaty sausage at me." She shoved his hand

away. "If you want to keep Maggie from wandering off, then I suggest you do something about it."

Elyne didn't wait for him to reply. She strode away with long, purposeful strides, her golden locks swinging down the length of her back. And they shimmered once more.

Finn knew exactly what he could do about it. The very thought sent his heart pumping. Judging by the way they kissed, their tupping would be heart-pounding, too. From now until the end of tourney, he would make sure Lady Margaret would be completely distracted. By him.

There wasn't any sense wasting time. Finn decided to head back to his tent, change his clothes, and meet Maggie at banquet. If Derron was there, he'd need to get her away from him as quickly as possible. The man was a scoundrel. One he didn't want anywhere near his woman.

As he passed the gambling tent, one of his usual gambling partners stopped him. An English knight by the name of Sir William Peckham.

"Sir Finian, come to enjoy a hand or two of cards? Or mayhap dice is more your game," he said.

"I canna play tonight. I'm late for banquet."

With a jaunty wave, he headed through the pavilion and back to his tent. He had better temptations waiting for him than dice.

Maggie had danced with Sir Drake, who was charming beyond words, until her feet hurt. She liked him. He had an engaging smile. He knew how to compliment her without seeming too forward. He made her feel like a real lady to be cherished.

Derron, as it turned out, was intent on getting her to accept his proposal to run away with him to Faery. She had managed so far to keep him at bay. He wouldn't take no for an answer, so insistent was he on taking her away from there. Much to her dismay, she hadn't seen one hair of Elyne since she left Finn alone in his tent.

To avoid Derron, she made sure she kept occupied with Sir Drake and her mead. She finally collapsed in a chair at the table and guzzled her fourth tankard. Her nape was damp with sweat from all the dancing and she couldn't stop smiling.

"You're a fine dancer, Lady Margaret," Drake said.

"You're not so bad yourself," she replied, while waiting for the servant to refill her cup.

"Would you grant me your favor so that I may joust for you on the morrow?" he asked.

Warning bells sounded in her head. Her first instinct was to say yes, but then if Finn learned she'd granted Drake her favor, it could hurt him. Even though they hadn't moved beyond a few kisses. "I…um…"

"Will Sir Finian mind?"

She certainly didn't belong to Finn by any means even though she wanted to belong to him. Heart, mind and soul. To avoid the question, she guzzled another tankard. "This mead is *so good*. I love this stuff."

"Indeed," Drake said, eyeing her with one raised dark brow. She tried to ignore the disappointment on his face.

Blushing, she put the tankard down, resisting the urge to gulp down the rest of it, though there could only be a swallow or two left. She licked her lips, getting as much of the last drop as she could. She grinned at him. "You're handsome, Drake. Did you know that? There has to be another lady here who would allow you to joust for her favors."

Did she slur her words? All she knew was she was suddenly drunk, feeling the effects of the mead punch her, hitting her hard and fast. It was unlike anything she'd had before, sending a warm tingling sensation up and down her body. She glanced around the room, looking for any maid who might do for Sir Drake.

"What about her?" She pointed to a lovely young girl with doe-brown eyes and auburn hair wearing an emerald-green velvet gown.

"I thank you, my lady, but I believe she's spoken for already," he said. "Mayhap it's time I escort you back to your tent. You look a bit flushed."

"Do I?" She pressed her palms into her cheeks. They *did* feel warm. "Maybe you should."

He stood, taking her arm and lifting her. She grabbed the tankard, though, and downed the rest of the mead. How much of this had she drunk? She'd lost count. Though she knew she was on the tipsy side, she also had enough brain power left to realize she didn't care. That was the side effect of being drunk. She lost all her inhibitions.

Drake pried the tankard from her hand and put it back on the table with a thump. She pouted, and then sagged against him, her hands on his shoulders. She giggled and blushed to the roots of her hair.

"Come, my lady."

Drake led her from the castle into the night air. She leaned all her weight on him to steady her footing. She couldn't ignore the way his body pressed against hers. When was the last time she'd been with a man? She couldn't recall. School and family obligations had taken every spare moment of her life for the last eight months. In fact, she'd broken up with her boyfriend long before her mother ever got sick.

The closest she'd gotten to being with a man was when she and Finn kissed. Though he hadn't indicated he was interested in her beyond that. Maybe she was a bad kisser and that's why he hadn't taken it any further. Or maybe Finn didn't think she was pretty enough. Desperate to test out that theory, she stopped and turned to Drake.

"Sir Drake, do you think I'm attractive?"

"My lady?" he asked with questioning eyes.

She staggered a step or two backward, made a half-hearted attempt to spin. "I mean, do you think *Finn* thinks I'm attractive? Because all he's done is kiss me and that's it." She stuck out her bottom lip in a pout. "Do you think he thinks I'm a terrible kisser?"

She didn't know why she was so desperate to find out what he thought about her. It wasn't as if it mattered. She'd be gone from this time in a few days anyway.

"I'm sure I wouldn't know, my lady."

"I've been told I was good at that." She was having a hard time concentrating on the words now as she formed them.

"We best get you to your tent."

"Why? I'm not ready to go home yet." She leaned into him, gazing up at him with her best adoring look.

"Oh, aye, you are."

But this wasn't Drake that answered. Turning, she looked over her shoulder, saw Finn standing there in a fresh tunic and breeches and looking like the Devil. She shuddered. Drake pushed her away, held her at arm's length.

"Finn," she grinned, swaying toward him. "How lovely of you to join us."

"Ye got her drunk?" Finn asked, looking directly at Drake.

"She got herself drunk," Drake corrected. "I had no hand in that."

"That's right, he didn't. All we did was dance. Don't blame him, Ffffinn," Maggie slurred. "That mead was too good."

"I was taking her back to the pavilion," Drake explained.

"Yesh, and he is shuch a gentlemen, that Drake," Maggie said. "Lovely man, really. I was going to let him have a favor."

"Ye willna be doing that," Finn said. Through her hazy drunkenness, she could see him glaring at Drake.

Drake held his hands up as if in surrender as Finn wrapped an arm around her shoulders and tucked her into his big body.

"Oh, Finn." She nudged him with her elbow. "Don't be mad at Sir Drake."

"Come, lass."

Taking her by the hand, he led her back to the tents. Maggie waved at Sir Drake. "Good night, Sir Drake. Thanks for the dances."

Finn pulled her along, making her stumble over her feet. She grunted her discomfort but he ignored her. "Can you slow down, Finn?"

"Ye stay at my pace, lass, or I'll carry ye back."

"You wouldn't."

"Wouldn't I?"

He stopped so fast, she crashed into him as he spun toward her. He gripped her arms to keep her from falling.

"Would ye like to test that, lass?"

Maggie gazed up into his smoky eyes that said he meant every word. Still, she couldn't help but taunt him. She tilted her head back and jutted out her chin.

"Maybe I would."

"As ye wish, my lady." She squealed when he flung her over his shoulder and walked through the pavilion, every step abrupt and jarring.

"Finn, put me down!"

"Nay, lassie."

Their parade through the pavilion garnered curious glances and snickers from other tournament-goers. It also jostled the contents of her belly, making the mead slosh while all the blood rushed into her head. She could swear she saw little pinpricks of light dotting her vision and making her head pound.

When they reached their tents, he set her on her feet. She wobbled, woozy from the sudden change in altitude. Her stomach rolled from all the mead she'd had and she pressed her hand against her rumbling belly to stave off the queasy feeling. It didn't help.

"Good night, lass."

Finn disappeared into his tent, leaving her wobbling in the cool night air. Realizing he'd left her, she flung aside the tent flap and charged inside in time to see him remove his tunic and sit down on the edge of his bed. She stopped short, admiring the wall of muscle in front of her.

"Oh—"

"Something ye need, lass?"

His eyes had darkened, smoldering with a hint of passion. That look of liquid silver made her weak in the knees. Even in her inebriated state, she managed to resist the urge to run her hands over his smooth chest, outlining the washboard abs, the hard pectorals, the shapely shoulders.

She blinked and flushed, snapping out of her trance and propping her hands on her hips. Sure, she saw a lot of things she needed and it started from the neck down. The world seemed to tip on its axis as she stood there, trying to form a coherent thought in her foggy mind.

"You didn't kiss me goodnight." Even in her state of mind, she knew that was a feeble attempt at an excuse.

"Was that a requirement then?"

"It was."

He shook his head. "'Tis no' right to be taking advantage of ye in yere state."

"What state is that? I feel fine." To prove it, she advanced on him, nudging herself between his thick thighs. She placed her hands on his broad shoulders, relishing the warmth of his skin against her palms. "So, do you."

His hands landed on her waist, as if to push her away. "Lady Margaret—"

She leaned down to whisper in his ear. "Maggie," she corrected. "My name is Maggie."

Her breath must have had an effect on him for she could see the rise of gooseflesh along his skin. She smiled, satisfied with his response. To torture him more, she nuzzled his earlobe with the tip of her nose, and then licked his neck. He grunted, his hands sliding from her waist to grasp her buttocks and squeeze.

Heat pumped through her, making all her parts stand up and cheer. Her heart throbbed along with the pulse between her thighs, aching for him to touch her there. But the layers of material between them proved to be an annoying obstacle. She wanted to rip the gown off so she could feel his damp mouth on her skin. Licking, tasting, kissing.

"Finn…"

Her hand slipped down his chest, over the rock-hard abs, and paused above the waistline of his breeches. When he made no move to stop her, she went farther, slipping her hand over his erection and feeling the pulsing of his arousal under her palm.

Perhaps sensing her next move, he grasped her by the waist again and pushed her away.

"Nay, lassie. Ye've been in the bottom of a tankard and are not in yere right mind."

"I'm in a perffect shtate of lucidity." As she looked up at him, he wavered in her line of vision.

"Not like this." He shook his head again, and then took her chin in his hand. His thumb grazed her jawbone, forcing her eyes on his. A slight touch she would have missed had she not been paying attention. "I want ye, lass. But not like this. For when we tup, I want ye in yere right mind so ye remember everything."

The corner of his mouth quirked. At his admission, her body wanted to burst into flame with the desire hiding in those hooded eyes and she knew he meant every word. She wished she were sober now, for she wanted to feel the big hands on her like she had that morning in his bed.

Perhaps it was the heat of arousal snaking through her that made her stomach knot or the mead had turned against her. Whichever the case, sobriety was far from her reach as she pulled out of his grasp, doubled over…and hurled at his feet.

"I dinna know I had such a strong effect on ye."

"I-I'm sorry."

"Let me help ye."

"No. Stay away." She put her hand up to keep him at bay.

Maggie stumbled backward toward the tent flap, mortification replacing desire. She ran to her own tent and dove into bed to hide.

Chapter 11

When she opened her eyes, Maggie was sure a Mack truck had flattened her on asphalt. She felt like one of those cartoon characters with tread marks who had to peel themselves off the pavement. Groaning, she rolled to her side, drawing her knees to her chest to make the sickness go away. Sunlight pressed against her closed eyelids, warning her of the impending afternoon.

Her head hurt so bad it felt as though a drum pounded inside her skull with a rhythmic *bum-ba-bum-ba-bum* sound. When the sound persisted, she realized with some annoyance it wasn't her head at all but someone beating a real drum somewhere in the pavilion of tents. She groaned again.

If she were in her own time, she knew the remedy for a hangover was two Advil and an ice-cold Coca-Cola. The Advil for her aching head, the Coke for her churning stomach. It always worked. But there was no Advil and no Coke in this time, which made her discomfort even more hellish.

Memories from the previous evening played through her mind like an old reel-to-reel movie. She could swear she heard the *clickety-clack* of the projector. Remembering her behavior with Finn made her shrink under the covers. How could she be so stupid? How could she fling herself at him like some wanton hussy on the prowl for a man? He would probably never speak to her again.

There was no sense in cowering in bed all day. She'd have to deal with the hangover—and Finn—eventually. She flung off the bedclothes and sat up, her head objecting. She grunted disapproval.

"Hungover, I see."

Elyne had somehow materialized out of thin air. Maggie jumped at the sound of her voice. "Do you have to sneak up on people?"

"I wasn't sneaking. I've been standing here for the last ten minutes but you were too busy hiding under the blankets to hear me."

Maggie put her head in her hands and massaged her temple.

"Don't yell. It hurts."

"What did you do last night?"

"I danced and drank a lot of mead."

"I thought you didn't like that stuff."

"It's an acquired taste. I seemed to have acquired it."

"And did you do said actions with Finian?"

Maggie snorted. "No. He didn't show up until the after-party to carry my sorry ass home."

"That explains why he's in such a foul mood."

Maggie looked up in time to see Elyne cross her arms across over her chest. "He is?"

"Don't pretend you don't know. What did you do?"

"Nothing." Maggie flushed, remembering her failed attempt at an advance. "He carried me back to the tent and left me."

"And then?"

"And then nothing. I tried to flirt with him but he would have none of it. He told me to go to bed." She left out the part about puking at his feet. It was too humiliating.

"Because you were drunk," Elyne pointed out. "You should try again. This time sober."

It was something Finn had said to her. *I want ye in yere right mind so ye remember everything.* Maybe she hadn't made a giant fool of herself like she thought. Maybe she was overreacting. Remembering his words, the way he looked at her and the way he *looked* period made her mind buzz with all the sexual thoughts she could conjure.

And then she remembered Elyne standing there and flushed. Maggie lowered her eyes to slits. "Why do you care all of a sudden?"

"Does it matter? What matters is you get your arse out of the bed and get dressed. Finn jousts in less than an hour."

Maggie shot to her feet, her head objecting to the sudden movement. "Why didn't you say so?"

"And keep you from wallowing in self-pity?"

Maggie shot her a look full of daggers while she flung gown after gown out of the trunk, looking for something suitable. She chose a crimson one.

"Not that one," Elyne said. "This one. It goes with your eyes."

The one Elyne held was an emerald green that did indeed match her eyes. Maggie looked at her, suspicion rolling through her.

"What's going on?"

"Nothing. This one will look much prettier on you, don't you think?"

Maggie snatched it out of her hands and dressed. She had the distinct feeling something was up with Elyne but she wasn't quite sure what it was. Yet. Once she was dressed, Elyne insisted on fixing her hair and then using some of the rouge she'd managed to procure from the market, or so she'd said. She then lined Maggie's eyes with kohl. If Maggie didn't know any better, it seemed as though the Fae princess was playing matchmaker with her and Finn. Before they left the tent, she gave Maggie the blue silk Finn had bought her in the market.

"You'll want him to wear your favor for the joust," Elyne explained.

"Is that like marking my territory or something?" she joked.

Elyne only gave her a sour look as she ushered her out. She continued to fuss over her as they left the tents and headed for the lists. Finally, Maggie stopped and turned on her, hands on hips.

"Just what is going on with you, Ellie? You never seemed this interested in me and Finn before. Why now? What's going on?"

Elyne huffed out a breath, not even bothering to hide her guilt. That was certainly a change from the day before.

"Finn knows who you are."

Maggie blinked, unsure what she meant. "Huh?"

"Finn knows you're from the future. He knows you came to his castle and I sent you both back in time. He knows everything, Maggie."

"How?"

"He asked. I told him."

Fear and uncertainty swarmed through her. "He knows I'm supposed to keep him from dying?"

"Oh, well, I didn't him tell *that* much," Elyne amended.

"What exactly *did* you tell him?"

"That if he wanted to keep you from wandering off, he should do something about it." She looked her up and down, as if appraising her. "And it's high time, too. You've been giving him the doe eyes for days now and he's been stomping around and punching people out for you."

Maggie waved away the thought. "He just doesn't like Derron, that's why he did that."

"No. He's jealous. Now stop trying to play matchmaker to me and Derron."

Dawning came then. "Ohhh...that's what this is about. You're trying to distract me with Finn so I won't try to get you two together. It won't work. I already told Derron I wouldn't be going to Faery with him and he shouldn't have petitioned the court to cancel your betrothal."

Maggie had no idea a Fae's face could drain of color until she saw Elyne pale. Her normal pink pallor was now a stark white. Her fists clenched. Maggie realized, too late, what she'd said.

"Oh, God. You didn't know. Elyne, I'm so sorry." Maggie reached a comforting hand to her but Elyne snatched her arm away.

"He petitioned the court, did he?"

"Elyne, I—"

"I didn't want to marry the sot anyway." The color had returned to her face and her hair shimmered with a bright glow. Maggie could see the distinct point of the tops of her ears and knew she was on the brink of exploding.

"Elyne—"

"Go. Go to your knight and bed him well." Elyne started off, leaving Maggie in the street.

"Where are you going?"

"To take care of Sir Derron once and for all."

Watching her go, Maggie knew there was nothing she could do to stop her. She'd never seen Elyne so angry, so pink and so shimmery. Her hair and skin glowed with an ethereal golden light, and as she brushed by people on her way to find Derron, she garnered quite a few curious glances. Maggie watched her go, peering at the tips of her ears to see they returned to rounded. Even though Elyne glowed, she seemed to have kept most of her glamour in place. Maggie shuddered to think what would happen if she dropped her glamour completely.

With nothing left to do, Maggie headed to the lists to watch Finn in his next match.

Maggie wound the silk around her hand as she hurried to the lists, hoping to catch Finn before his match started. How could she be so stupid? Why did she tell Elyne that? She loved Derron, even though she was loathed to admit it, and now she'd gone and ruined everything. Any chance of getting those two together was now blown.

She wondered what Elyne planned to do to Derron. Even though he was a bit of a player, she didn't want to see him hurt. She felt horrible for Elyne, knowing she'd crushed the Fae princess's hopes of marrying the knight someday. She'd have to find a way to make it up to her.

But for now, she'd focus all her attention on Juliet and Brian. She needed to find a way to get her away from her horrible brother and get those two together. The song Matchmaker from *Fiddler on the Roof* wafted through her mind and she snorted.

"Some matchmaker I am," she muttered.

When she arrived at the lists, she found Finn about to mount his horse talking with Fergus.

"Finn!"

When he turned to look at her, he pushed up his visor. She could only see part of his face under the helm. His eyebrows drew up in surprise as she unwound the silk and paused in front of him.

"I thought ye would still be drunk, lass."

"No." She shook her head slowly, despite the throbbing pain. "I'm glad I caught you before your match. Will you wear this for me?"

He looked down at the silk in her hand and two heartbeats passed between them before he reached for it and slipped it from her fingers. "I will, lass."

And then, before she could find a seat in the grandstand, he reached up and placed his armored fingertips on her cheek, giving them a gentle brush. His metal fingers were cool against her face, causing a shiver to run up her spine and making her forget all about her hangover. The look on his face told her everything she needed to know—Finn wanted her. She made up her mind then and there she would let him have her tonight after banquet.

He smiled, his eyes wrinkling in the corners before removing his hand and mounting his horse. As he looked down at her, he gave her a wink and then closed his visor. Her feet light and her heart pounding, she made her way to the grandstand and found a seat in front to watch the match.

The list marshal today wasn't Litonshire, which made the fact he was yesterday when Finn was sick all the more suspicious. The two opponents took their positions on either end of the lists and there in the middle, the herald announced both of them, listing their royal lineage. The crowd cheered loudly for each, but there was a definite division in who was cheering for whom.

Maggie watched Finn, the way he sat tall and proud in the saddle. And there, on his left, her silk was tied to his lance and fluttering in the breeze. She smiled.

The list marshal signaled the beginning of the match with the first white flag and off they went without waiting a breath. Maggie bit her thumbnail as she watched Finn charge toward his opponent, lance couched under his arm and pointing forward.

The two collided, both lances making a direct hit on the other and both lances shattering, raining shards of wood down around them. The crowd cheered and Maggie bit her thumbnail harder. Finn trotted back to his end of the lists, handed the broken stick to Fergus and then took a new one from Geoffrey. They stood at the ready, waiting for the list marshal to wave the second flag.

When he did, they both took off again toward each other. Finn seemed more determined this time as he shifted forward in the saddle, his lance pointing forward. This time when the two collided, Finn knocked his opponent off his horse, wood shards raining down around him as his mount galloped away. The crowd cheered and Maggie clapped wildly.

He'd won.

Finn galloped to a halt in front of her, pushed back his visor and gave her a bow from his mount. She blew him a kiss.

"How lucky he fancies you," a lady next to her sighed. "He's so handsome."

"Yes," Maggie agreed. "He is."

And she intended to show him how awesome she thought he was later. Her heart pounded in sweet anticipation.

That night, Maggie went to banquet on Finn's arm. Since Elyne had managed another disappearing act, she'd struggled with her hair and clothes alone. It had taken her awhile but she managed and she was finally pleased with the outcome. She had taken care to look her best, wearing a gown of emerald green, long sleeved and buttons to the elbow. Tonight, she wore a ruffled cap with a transparent veil. Could she feel more like a medieval princess? She already had her knight, after all, and she hoped there was a night of mutual seduction ahead of them. She made a mental note to stay out of the mead so she could keep her wits about her. And if Sir Derron came along to try to ruin their evening, she'd have to put her foot down and tell him to bugger off.

Even though she hated the thought. He *was* her jousting hero, after all. But hadn't her thesis become a lost cause? Did she even care if she finished it or returned to her time?

She could answer with complete certainty she cared nothing about her thesis anymore. Her time in the future seemed like a distant memory now and nothing but a dream. Her world was now here, with Finn, because he was all she cared about now. She wanted to save his life and to spend the rest of hers making him happy.

The realization slammed against her hard, making her reel and her head went a little swimmy. She gripped the edge of the table to steady herself. Moments of pure thoughtless shock prickled her.

Glancing around, she checked to make sure no one else noticed her sudden discomfort. She released her hold on the table and put her hands in her lap.

She would stay here with Finn if he asked, even though she would suffer the loss of her father. Maybe there was some way she could get a letter or a note to him. Maybe Elyne could get him a message to let him know she was okay.

It seemed forever before the evening would end and they could return to the pavilion for the night. Maggie tried to eat but had a hard time finding an appetite. Her stomach was in too much of a knot with nerves and anticipation.

It didn't help Finn continued to distract her by resting his hand on her knee under the table. When she cut him a glance, the smile in his eyes contained a sensuous flame. It caused her heart to stumble and heat to wash over her.

Maggie wasn't immune to the uncomfortable glares Litonshire gave them throughout the meal either. And neither was Finn. She'd spotted the earl staring almost as soon as they walked in together. And next to him, his doe-eyed sister looked more pitiful than ever.

"Finn, isn't there something we can do about Lady Juliet?" Maggie asked.

"I dinna ken," he said, glancing their way.

"I would love to get her away from that overbearing jackass brother of hers."

"Aye," Finn said. "Dinna let it fash ye. 'Tis naught we can do." He laced his fingers with hers, lifted her hand and kissed her knuckles.

Her heart fluttered. Did he know what he did to her? When she looked into those silvery eyes, she could see the desire there.

"I think I'd like to retire now," Maggie said. Which was code for *I'm ready to straddle that fine manly physique of yours and get it on.*

"Aye." He rose, her hand still in his, and led her from the table.

But as they left the great hall and crossed the courtyard and gardens, Sir Derron intercepted them. His nose seemed to be healing from when Finn punched him, but now he sported a fresh left black eye. Maggie wondered if Elyne had done it to get back at him for trying to break their betrothal.

"Ah, the lovely Lady Margaret. Come, let us dance," he said, as if nothing had ever changed between them.

When he reached for her, Finn put a protective arm around her shoulders and pulled her close. She suppressed a grin.

"I'm afraid I'm on my way back to the pavilion, Sir Derron," Maggie said.

"Allow me to escort you then." He stuck out his arm.

"I see I wasn't clear. I'm on my way back to the pavilion *with Sir Finian.*"

Derron glanced at him, and then back at her. "With this oversized ox? How tragic."

Maggie felt Finn's fingers dig into her shoulder as he flexed them and she knew he was ready to pummel the Fae.

"Good night, Sir Derron," Maggie said and started walking again.

"You told Elyne about the betrothal, didn't you?" he shouted to their backs. "Why?"

Maggie paused. Her heart had leapt into her throat. She'd never considered what it would do to Derron and Elyne if she told her. Never considered how Elyne would really feel knowing the truth.

"What's that about, lass?" Finn asked.

She slipped out of his arm and turned back toward Derron, ignoring Finn's question, and stepped toward the Fae knight.

"I didn't mean to. It slipped out."

"Have you any idea what you have done?" Derron asked. And he suddenly sounded angry. Gone was the playfulness from his voice. For the first time, the flamboyant Fae was replaced by this irate new version.

"Oh, like you care," Maggie snapped. "What did you think was going to happen when she found out? And anyway, you have women flinging themselves at you daily *in front of Elyne*, I might add, and you don't even see her. Not to mention the fact you've been pursuing me since the day you saw me."

"It was no reason for you to tell her about me petitioning the court." He puffed out his chest, his skin turning from the dusty pink to a deeper shade of red.

"Maybe I should have told her you asked me to go to Faery with you and live as your consort, eh? How do you think *that* would have gone over?"

She had told Elyne he asked her to go to Faery, but not the part about her being his consort. She really hated when her words came back to haunt her. She hated even more she'd hurt Elyne.

"He wants to take ye to Faery?" Finn asked, and for some reason, it didn't sound strange coming out his mouth. Like he totally accepted the fact Elyne and Derron were Fae and there really was such a place.

But Maggie would ponder on that later. Right now, she had an irate Fae knight on her hands.

"You're so blind, Derron. All you have to do is open your eyes and see what's right in front of you. And now you've blown it. Elyne would have found out about your little stunt anyway. I just sped up the process."

"You had no right to tell her."

"For the love of Pete," she sighed. "When were *you* planning to tell her? When you'd managed to have the betrothal broken?"

"The High Court denied my request," he said, crossing his arms. "Thanks to you. She went to them, told them I was here in the human world jousting. I've been ordered to return to the Otherworld immediately."

"Well, good for her, then."

"I told them she's been using Fae magic here. She was ordered to return, too."

"Wait. What?" Her stomach clenched tight as her pulse raced. Anxiety spurted through her. No. No way. Elyne couldn't go. If she went, then Maggie would never make it back to her time. Okay, sure, she had been considering staying but now that she didn't have a choice about it at all, she panicked. "She can't go."

"She's already there," Derron told her, sounding smug. As if he knew all along what the punch line would be and he wanted to see Maggie's reaction. He confirmed her suspicion by smiling.

"No. She can't be gone. She has to come back. I need her to come back!"

Maggie balled her fists. It was like the two Fae were having a pissing match and Maggie had been caught in the middle. And now she'd lost her only link back to her world. How would she get home? Her dad would be beside himself with grief. He would think something dreadful had happened to her in Scotland. That she could be dead somewhere in a ditch. She pressed her hand against her roiling stomach.

"She's gone. Thanks to you. Looks like you get your Scottish ox after all. Now I have to report to the High Court. Farewell, Lady Margaret."

Maggie watched Derron walk away, the last link to Elyne and her beloved twenty-first century. She'd taken everything for granted and now the loss of it hit her. It took all her strength to stand there and watch him leave. Her knees wanted to buckle. Her stomach threatened to heave the banquet feast.

She only remembered Finn still stood beside her when she felt his hands on her shoulders—big, strong, reassuring hands.

"Come, lass."

But instead of heading back to the pavilion, Maggie turned into Finn, buried her face in his chest, and sobbed.

Thinking of everything she'd lost when Derron walked away shattered Maggie. The thought tore at her insides and shredded what fragile control she had left, leaving nothing but tatters of a life she once had. Raw and primitive grief overwhelmed her as she wept against his tunic, feeling bereft and desolate. Finn hugged her, patted her back, and didn't say a word.

When she finally composed herself, she slipped away from him, whisking tears from her eyes. She didn't want him to see her like this.

"I'll never get back now," she said. "And it's my own fault."

"Is it so terrible to be here with me?" Finn asked. He was behind her, his words in her ears. His hands landed on her shoulders, warm.

She could hear the pang of sorrow in his voice.

"I don't belong here, Finn. I belong in another place and time."

"Aye, I ken. The fair princess told me." He turned her around, cupped her chin and forced her to look up at him. "I canna replace what ye've lost, but I can offer ye shelter and protection."

She smiled. Deep down his medieval instincts of protecting a woman came out. She loved that about him. It was in that moment she knew she had to have him. She leaned toward him, stood on tiptoe and slid her arms around his neck. Even so, he still towered over her. She tried to stretch toward him, tilting her head back. His gaze was dark, hooded with passion.

"Take me away from here, Finn. To your tent. Please."

He wasted no time. Blood surged through her veins, making her feel alive when he took her by the hand and led her from the courtyard of the castle and through the pavilion with a determined look on his face and desire in his step. He spared no one a glance as he went, only had the single-mindedness of getting to their destination.

Maggie's heart banged against her chest in sweet anticipation. Since waking up in Finn's chamber nestled against him that first morning, she'd tried to keep the thoughts of being underneath him at bay. And now, as they headed past tent after tent, her fantasy was coming true. Nothing and no one would be there to interrupt them this time.

And she was terrified, with a gut-wrenching sorrow filling her. She shoved away the sorrow, determined not to let it consume her. Not now. Not yet. She'd worry about it later. Right now, the only thing that mattered was being with this man. She was sober. She was happy. She was going to enjoy this.

Finn shoved aside the flap to his tent and she entered before him. He was behind her suddenly, pulling her to him. His hard chest pressed again her back as one arm went around her waist, holding her steady. He bent to kiss her neck, her head tipping to the side to give him the full access she long desired.

She kicked off her slippers, turned into his arms, her hands on his massive chest. He was warm, inviting and everything a big rock-hard Scotsman should be. She chided herself for wasting so much time chasing Derron in the pages of history and wondered why she had never found a Scotsman to want. Until now. Now Finn was all she needed, all she wanted.

He whisked her into his arms, carried her to the bed. When he placed her gently on the mattress, he took off his tunic. Maggie shook with anticipation, need, nerves. She fumbled for the hem of her gown but he pushed aside her hands. When she gave him a questioning glance, she knew everything in his eyes said, *let me.*

She'd let him. Even as she trembled with the needs to touch him everywhere at once and to feel him touching her everywhere at once. Patience was certainly not her virtue but she waited, her heart a frantic beat as he took his time undressing her. Undressing him.

A whisper of material and then there was nothing left between them when they fell together, their limbs tangling. He kissed her, his mouth fusing to hers as his fingers twined in her hair and her world had been kicked off kilter and she knew without a shadow of a doubt where she belonged.

She was home.

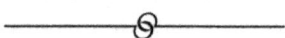

Hours later, they lay still coiled around each other buried under the coverlet and sheet and listening to the night sounds as dawn neared. She never wanted this night to end, never wanted him to release her from his powerful arms.

And yet…yet, she knew the sun would rise and another day of tourney would commence. Another day of worry over whether he would live or die.

"Finn?"

"Hmm?"

"Promise me." She paused as her throat clotted with sudden emotion. "Promise me you'll be careful in the lists." Because she feared that's where he'd died in the previous timeline. She wanted to safeguard him. With Elyne gone, she wasn't sure what would happen now.

He brushed his hand through her hair and chuckled, a low rumble deep in his chest. "Ah, lass. Ye needn't concern yere wee self."

Maggie rolled on top of him to face him, her hands pressed against his stubbled cheeks. "Promise me."

The mirth faded from his eyes as he realized she was serious. He tucked a wayward lock of hair behind her ear.

"Aye, I promise. Ye ken on the morrow, I have another sword match."

"Another one?" She was beginning to dislike tourney.

"Aye."

"Is your opponent Lord Litonshire?"

"I dinna think so. Why?"

She cocked her head to one side, a smile tugging at the corner of her lips. "I'd so love for you to pummel his ass."

He was laughing when he kissed her.

Chapter 12

Maggie spent the night in Finn's tent. She hadn't gotten a lot of sleep, due to a certain horizontal position they tended to continue to get themselves into. It was perfectly fine with her. She enjoyed being with Finn. And when they did sleep, he held her close, as though he would never let her go.

As the night wore on, she drifted in and out of sleep. In some ways, she felt as though the world had been ripped from her, as though a piece of her had been torn from her forever. The loss of her century left a giant hole in her heart. In those desolate moments, she forced back tears of fear and uncertainty, knowing she didn't belong here. Knowing she would never quite fit in.

In other ways, she couldn't stop the quiver of excitement rippling through her. Living here, with Finn, was like a dream come true. Not exactly the dream she'd had when she first left for Scotland, but a different dream. A new dream. A better dream.

It was the chance of a lifetime. How many people wished to go back to a time, a place they were fascinated by? How many people would stop at nothing to get that? Which made her wonder if the Fae still walked among humans in the twenty-first century.

She teetered between feeling as though she'd lost everything to feeling happy to be alive and in Finn's arms. In those desolate moments, she had to force back the tears. She wondered, though, how she would live without Starbucks or iTunes or even toilet paper. She'd never thought of toilet paper as a luxury item until now.

But being with Finn…none of those things seemed to matter as long as she had him.

When she finally woke, she heard the rustle of fabric and knew Finn was up and dressing. She rolled to her side, watching the sinew of muscles work under the bronze skin. He was magnificent and he was quickly becoming her world.

"Where are you off to?" she asked.

"*Och*, lass. I dinna want to wake ye." He pulled his tunic over his head, smoothed it out. "To the practice field for a few runs at the quintain before my next event."

She sat up on one elbow, looking him over with an appreciative gaze. "I'll come with you."

He smiled, one side of his mouth quirking as he leaned toward her. "Rest." He kissed her forehead. "And stay out of trouble, aye?"

"Me? Trouble?" But she couldn't help but giggle. "Surely you jest."

But in the back of her mind, she'd already decided she would seek out Lord Brian and Lady Juliet and start working on getting those two love birds together. She'd start with Lady Juliet and try to find out who attacked her in the stable last tourney. She had seemed open to talking to Maggie that day in the market, so perhaps she could get more information out of her.

"Nay, lass." He gave her a stern look as if to say *I mean it*. "Stay away from Litonshire and his sister."

Maggie made a sour face. How did he know that's what she'd planned to do? Still, he said nothing about Lord Brian. She knew where to find Lady Grace, his sister. She knew she was taking a chance, but she had to go alone.

"Could I visit the market while you're away? Since I have nothing better to do, I may as well get in some shopping." Right after she searched for Lord Brian.

He tossed her a small purse full of coins. "Take Geoffrey with ye, aye? For safety."

She examined the pouch he'd tossed her. It was the softest suede she'd ever felt with a drawstring closure. Near the top, there was a small shield embroidered with fine, delicate thread.

"What's this? Your family shield?" she asked.

"Aye. My mam did that for me before she died."

Maggie traced her finger over it. "It's beautiful. I promise to take good care of it."

"I fight today and then later joust. I'll see ye in the grandstand," he said.

When Finn left, Maggie tossed off the blankets, dressed and went to her tent for some fresh clothes. Finn asked her to take Geoffrey with her, but she didn't need the boy following her around like a puppy. Besides, he would tell Finn what she'd been up to and then he'd be angry with her. She stood there, alone, for a long moment looking at the trunk Elyne had packed. Sorrow nearly overcame her. The Fae princess was gone back to the Otherworld. She repeated the phrase over and over in her head, trying to grasp the idea.

After everything they'd been through, she thought they were finally becoming friends. She actually missed Elyne.

Shrugging out of her gown, she pulled on another one, still deep in thought about everything that'd happened with Elyne and Derron. Remembering the night with Finn and how much she'd enjoyed it. How much she wanted it to last forever.

"There you are."

The voice made her squeal and jump. Maggie spun around, facing Elyne, who stood with her hair shimmering and her eyes burning bright. Her glamour faltered and Maggie could see the tips of her ears changing from rounded to pointed and back again.

"Elyne, you came back." Maggie launched herself at the princess, hugging her tight. "Derron said you'd gone back to the Otherworld."

"Aye, I did. I shouldn't be here now." Elyne struggled free of Maggie's grasp, held her at arm's length. "Where were you last night?"

"With Finn."

"Ah, I thought as much. About time, too."

Maggie flushed hot, feeling the blood rush to the roots of her hair. "What are you doing here?"

"I promised you I'd send you back home. I came back to do that."

"But Derron said you were caught doing Fae magic here. Won't you get in trouble?"

"I managed to slip away. No one knows I'm gone. Let's get you home quick before I'm missed."

Maggie jerked away from her, taking several steps backward. "I'm not going back."

"What do you mean? All this time you've been whining to get home and now you don't want to go?"

"I haven't saved Finn yet," Maggie said, her hackles rising. "I'm not going anywhere."

"You think he needs you here to save him?" Elyne shook her head and laughed. "I told you before, events have been altered.

Things have changed. Nothing is as it was before. Anyway, I only told you that to make you stick close to Finn so he wouldn't kill Derron in the lists."

"I don't understand. You said I had to stay here to save Finn before I could go home. That was a lie?"

Elyne blew out an exasperated breath. "Not all of it. Finn *did* die but he also killed Derron. I needed you here to keep Finn distracted long enough to stop him from killing Derron. But none of that matters now. Derron is back in the Otherworld where he should be so he won't be getting killed here in the lists because he won't be jousting."

"You used me." The realization slammed into her hard, like a fist to the gut.

"Isn't that what you humans do?"

"That's not what *I* do." Maggie had never been cut so deep before. She couldn't believe she had been a pawn in some elaborate game Elyne played to keep her precious knight from dying. And here she thought she and Elyne had become friends. "I'm not going back."

"You have to," Elyne said. "This isn't where you belong."

Again, Maggie's world shifted. Less than a few hours ago she had resigned herself to living here with Finn. Now Elyne handed her the opportunity to return? She didn't like being on this emotional rollercoaster lifting her up and then plunging back down. Somehow, she knew if she accepted, she would regret leaving.

"You brought me here. And whether believe it or not, I'm here for a reason. Maybe you don't agree and you think I'm stupid for staying here, but staying I am. I have to make sure Finn gets through the rest of the tournament alive."

Her eyes narrowed. "You realize I can sift you out of here, don't you? I don't *need* your permission to do so."

"You didn't exactly ask my permission when you brought me here," she spat.

Her lips thinned into a white line. "Fine, then. If you mean to stay and help that waif Lady Juliet, you're crazier than I thought you were."

"I do intend to help her. Lord Brian loves her. I'm sure of it. And I'm going to see to it that she gets away from that awful brother of hers."

Maggie started to stalk out of the tent but Elyne's iron grip snatched her arm, pulling her to a stop. "Maggie, her brother is the one who raped her."

Startled, Maggie stared at her. *Her brother...*Lord Litonshire had raped and beaten Lady Juliet? Disgust raged through her as nausea gripped her. While it was probably true those actions were normal for this time, it revolted her to think he'd done that to his own sister. Maggie's determination to help Juliet surged through her.

"How do you know that? You couldn't know that." Maggie jerked her arm free.

"I do know, Maggie. Litonshire is dangerous. Far more dangerous than you think."

"You told me he was harmless. Not to worry about him. Or was that a lie, too?" Maggie couldn't help but feel as though Elyne had betrayed her.

"I was trying to protect you, but you're so hard-headed you insist on continuing this investigation into who hurt Juliet."

"I'm trying to help her."

"Stay away from him and his sister. There's nothing you can do for her anyway. She's tainted goods now. No man will want her."

"Lord Brian does."

"He won't if he knows she's been touched by her brother."

Maggie fell silent, unable to comprehend what she was saying. Unable to fathom how Juliet's own brother could do such a horrendous thing. She hated him even more for it.

"That's the way things work in this time. Lord Brian doesn't know, I'm sure, or he wouldn't even speak to her," Elyne said.

"Then I have to stay and help her. If I don't, no one will," Maggie told her, more determined than ever. "She's dying and he's killing her."

"And if Finn finds out? He told you to stay away from them."

"Do you know everything?" Maggie scowled.

"Aye." Elyne nodded. "Let me send you back and end this."

"I told you I'm not going and that's final. I'm staying."

The princess folded her arms over her chest. "Then you stay forever."

"So be it." Maggie lifted her chin and looked down her nose, an action Elyne had perfected. Probably millennia ago.

"Fine. Have it your way. But this is the last you'll see of me."

"Fine. Just go then," she said, even though she didn't mean it.

And with that, the Fae princess disappeared.

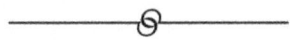

Maggie was so angry by the time she left her tent, she hurried through the pavilion, weaving her way through crowd traffic, determined to find Lord Brian and try to talk him into getting Juliet away. All this walking on eggshells was enough and she was going to make sure he and Juliet would be together. She'd decided on her way she wouldn't mention anything to him about the suspected rapist. She wasn't sure she believed Elyne anyway. How could she know? Was she there? Did she see him?

Maggie wanted proof. Needed proof. It would not only help get Juliet away from her disgusting brother, but also exonerate Finn of the crime. How she could get that proof, though, she didn't know.

She remembered where she had met Lady Grace and found her at her tent, chatting happily with her brother. Her pretty face lit up with a smile when she saw Maggie.

"Lady Margaret, how fare thee? Brian, have you met Lady Margaret?"

"Yes, we met in the market," Maggie said quickly. "I'm well, Lady Grace, thank you. And you?"

"Wondrous well, my lady. I'm wondering how Sir Finian is." She giggled a young girl's giggle and Maggie longed for the days of youthful naiveté. She was beyond having a crush, especially on Finn.

"Lady Grace, your manners," Lord Brian chastised.

She instantly composed herself and dipped a quick curtsey to Maggie. "Apologies, my lady."

"It's quite all right. I was hoping to have a word with you, Lord Brian, about a delicate matter," Maggie said, turning her attention to him. She hoped she could get her point across without actually having to say Lady Juliet's name. Besides that, she wasn't all too sure how much Lady Grace knew about the woman.

He flashed a look at his younger sister that must have translated to *run along* because she immediately excused herself.

"Walk with me, my lady." He gestured toward the open field away from the pavilion and eavesdropping ears. "I assume this delicate matter has to do with Lady Juliet."

"Yes. You're in love with her, aren't you?"

"This is none of your affair, I should think," he said.

A response Maggie hadn't been prepared for. "I'm trying to help her. I know you're in love with her, aren't you?"

"Since the day I saw her," he said without pausing to think about the question. "But I've been denied her hand in marriage by Lord Litonshire."

"Why?"

"I suspect because of his controlling nature. That and he is looking for a more suitable match for his sister. One that will hold a large sum of money for her marriage. A duke, mayhap."

"You're saying he thinks you're not good enough for her," Maggie said.

"Something of the sort." Brian kept his eyes forward but Maggie could hear the disdain in his voice, knew he was disgusted by the man and longed for Juliet.

And how could Maggie blame him? The man *was* disgusting, especially if what Elyne had said was true.

"My lord, Lady Juliet's health is in great danger the longer she stays with her brother. I fear he may kill her if someone doesn't intervene," Maggie said.

"Intervening in those family matters is not for me," Brian said, matter-of-factly. "Litonshire would never allow it. I could never get close to Juliet. Every time he sees us even glance at each other he makes sure to pull us further apart."

"When was the last time you saw her?" Maggie asked. "I mean besides at the market."

"It's been too long."

"Since before the last tourney?"

"Lady Margaret, what is it you wish to know? If I was the one that attacked her in the stable?" He got right to the point.

"Was it you?" Pausing, she put her hands on her hips.

"What sort of monster do you take me for, my lady?" His brows drew together, an angry line between his eyes.

Maggie softened, smiling and placed a gentle hand on his arm. "None at all. I merely wondered if you knew what had happened to her."

"She and I spent a good portion of the last tourney together. It was in Guildford." He looked thoughtful as he remembered. "We were happy. I knew she loved me but I also knew she would never be free to marry me. 'Tis why we had to hide from Litonshire during tourney to be together."

"Did he know?"

"Oh, most certainly. We were to meet that night, after banquet." A slight breeze ruffled his hair as he cleared his throat. "In the stable."

Maggie quickly put the pieces together. If Litonshire knew they were to meet and knew they had been sneaking around behind his back to be together, then what Elyne said *had* to be true. And Litonshire attacked and raped his own sister to keep her from sleeping with Brian and keeping her under his full control. *Bastard.*

"But you never made it," she guessed.

"I was detained. I went back to my tent to change clothes. When I got there, several young men were tampering with my armor. I caught them trying to steal my lances," he said. "We fought. I took them to the guards and had them thrown in the stocks. By the time I reached the stable, Sir Finian was there. He'd wrapped his tartan around Juliet and was carrying her away from the stable."

"You never found out who did it?" she asked.

"No, and Lady Juliet refuses to tell me."

"Mayhap we can get her to tell us. Do you know where she is now?"

"If you intend to intervene, as you call it, I haven't the means. Should I confront Lord Litonshire, I risk losing everything I have," he said.

That may be true, Maggie thought, but if Elyne was right and Litonshire *had* raped his sister then he would be dealt with in a swift manner. One that, Maggie hoped, would lead to Litonshire's ultimate demise. The proof she needed lay with Lady Juliet. She would have to get her to tell the truth about that night, find out what happened while she waited for Lord Brian to arrive. Maggie thought she already knew the answer, but the only way she'd know for sure was if she could get Juliet to tell her.

"But you love her," Maggie insisted. "All you need is love." And suddenly she could hear John Lennon singing in her head. "What I mean is you should get her from Litonshire before it's too late. Before Juliet isn't around anymore *to* love."

He looked Maggie over, a thoughtful expression on his handsome face, considering her words. "Did you have something in mind, then?"

Maggie grinned. "Oh, yeah. I do."

Maggie found Lady Juliet locked in the castle, alone, while Lord Litonshire was off busily running tournament. Lord Brian waited away from the castle walls while Maggie went inside, inquiring of the maids where she could find her. She finally gained the help of one maid, who led her to the frail lady in the tower.

"What are you doing here, Lady Margaret?"

"I've come to take you for a walk, my lady," she said, all too aware the maid in the room eavesdropped. "I think the fresh air will do you good."

"I'm not sure it will, Lady Margaret, but thank you for the offer."

"Ah, but there's a certain young lord who wishes to see you," Maggie said, hoping that would get her attention.

Lady Juliet's eyes lit up. "Indeed. I'd be happy to go for a walk."

When they made it out of the castle and away from listening ears, Maggie told her of the plan. A few hours later, she blinked tears from her eyes, pleased with her success. Her friend Beth would say, *don't break your arm patting yourself on the back, Mags.* Still, she couldn't believe she'd been a witness to such a happy occasion. She'd smiled so much her cheeks hurt.

The priest blessed the newlyweds with a final prayer after the quick impromptu ceremony in a small copse of trees far from the tournament field. Maggie had lured the priest from the chapel with five gold pieces, asking him to keep the ceremony private and away from prying eyes because the bride was quite ill. She figured it was a better way to spend the money Finn had given her instead of on useless items in the market.

Lord Brian held Lady Juliet's hand in his, kissed her knuckles, and they each looked at each other with so much adoration and love it made Maggie's heart melt into a giant puddle.

After the ceremony, Lord Brian approached her.

"Lady Juliet and I will be leaving England at once," he said. "I can't risk her life when Litonshire finds out what's happened."

"I understand, of course," Maggie said. "Where will you go?"

"I have family estates in the Highlands. I plan to take her there."

"I wish you both well."

"I've asked her to write a letter to the king, explaining the circumstances in detail. I understand his majesty is due here by tournament's end. I've left instructions with my squire to make sure he gets that letter."

"What will happen to Litonshire?" Maggie asked.

"With any luck, he'll be drawn and quartered." His words were bitter as he glanced at Juliet still speaking softly with the priest. "She thinks I know only that Litonshire beat her, not what other monstrosities he did to her."

"And you love her anyway."

"Aye, I do."

Juliet still looked emaciated and exhausted but Maggie knew with Brian's love and support, she would make a full recovery. Lady Juliet joined them, then, her cheeks rosy and her eyes sparkling with life.

"I can't thank you enough for what you've done for us, Lady Margaret," Juliet said. She beamed. A positive improvement over the listless way she'd looked at the previous banquets.

"It was my pleasure," Maggie said, "I'm very happy for you both."

Juliet hugged her tightly and Maggie swore she could feel every bone in her body.

"Brian can never know the truth," Juliet whispered.

The words sent a cold chill up Maggie's spine. It pained her to think what the poor woman had been through with her brother. When she pulled away, Maggie smiled and gave her a quick nod as if to say *I know exactly what you're talking about and mum's the word. I swear.*

Maggie bid the couple farewell, knowing it would be the last time she would see them. She hoped Brian really was able to get that letter to the king. Even so, she was never one to walk away from a fight and she surely wouldn't allow Litonshire to get away with raping his sister.

He would certainly pay. With his life if Maggie had anything to do with it.

Maggie felt rather proud of herself as she walked from the secret wedding back to the pavilion. She remembered on her way that Finn was fighting that afternoon and picked up the pace to head toward the tourney field. It took her some time to find where the event was held.

As she headed toward the arena, two men approached her. At first, she thought they were heading past her but the closer they got, the more she realized they were looking directly at her. They were big, too. Topping out at over six feet tall. The one on the left had a long, scraggly beard and unkempt hair. His teeth were yellow stumps and he had a menacing glint in his eyes. One that sent a shiver up her spine. The other had a smirk on his scarred face. His lecherous gaze raked her up and down and she realized with some horror they intended to do her harm.

Penance, she realized, for wandering around alone.

Maggie quickly glanced around but no one seemed to be paying her any attention. Which meant she was now in a precarious position. They probably wanted nothing more than the heavy purse of gold she carried. She would gladly give it to them if they'd go away.

"Lady Margaret," the one with the scraggly beard said, and tipped his head to her in greeting.

"Do I know you?"

"Nay. But there be someone wantin' ter know you." He smiled, showing off those yellow stumps. He, too, gave her a look that said he'd like to see her without her shift.

She swallowed hard, a lump of bile rising in her throat. There was no Elyne or Derron or even Finn to get her out of this one.

"Who?" she asked.

"Now I can't be tellin' you that, can I?"

The second man had moved around behind her, sandwiching her between them. Not good. What was she going to do? She had no weapon.

"If it's gold you want, I have some. You can have it." She held up the purse of gold and sent a silent apology to Finn. She hated the thought of losing the purse his mother had embroidered.

She felt a hand land on her shoulder and, glancing down, she saw it belonged to the other man. His fingernails were caked with dirt, his hands calloused and hard. It took all her willpower not to squirm under his grasp.

"Tryin' to pay me off, eh?" He chuckled. "Nice try but not gonna work." He looked at his partner then and gave him a nod.

"Do your thing, Ox."

Ox? The guy behind her was named *Ox*? She tried to turn and look at him. Before she could move, he pressed against her, wrapping one thick arm around her and pulling her close. She tried to scream and was greeted with a rag in the mouth. He picked her up around the torso and Maggie kicked, aiming for scraggly beard guy but missing since Ox was moving away from him. He was taking her somewhere away from the pavilions.

She fought against him, struggling until her muscles were weak.

"You best stop it," Beard said. "You'll just make it worse for yourself."

When she refused to stop struggling, he shrugged.

"Fine then." His gaze landed on Ox, who stopped long enough to put her back on her feet. "I don't want to be doing this, but you give me no choice."

She saw the hilt of the dagger before she felt it. He smacked her hard on the head. Pain exploded in a flash of light behind her eyes and before another thought could filter through her brain, she mercifully passed out.

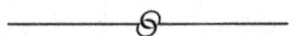

When Maggie finally came to, the first thing she was aware of was the blinding pain. Her head throbbed where the bearded guy hit her with the hilt of his dagger. She knew without feeling there was a lump there. The second thing she realized was her hands and ankles were bound by rope and she still had the disgusting rag in her mouth. It tasted terrible and she didn't even want to *think* about what might be on it.

With some effort, she managed to work the material from between her teeth and spit it out, coughing and gagging on the rancid aftertaste.

She lay on her side, trying to get her bearings. It took a few minutes for her eyes to adjust to the darkness. She was in a dimly lit room with a stone floor and walls. It felt damp and cold and she couldn't tell if she were in some sort of dungeon or what. She supposed the men had brought her someplace away from the tournament field, but how far and where exactly she didn't know. How long had she been out?

Finn would wonder where she was and when he couldn't find

her, she could only imagine the rage he'd be in. Did the men have anything to do with Litonshire? Was it retribution for her arranging his sister marrying Lord Brian? How could he already know that?

Unless he'd been watching her and had her followed. Then he would know. What would happen to Brian and Juliet then? Would the earl be so enraged, he'd kill them both? She hoped not. She dragged her lower lip through her teeth.

She remembered then the purse full of coins. Doing a quick mental inspection, she discovered it was missing. The men had taken it anyway, even though Beard said he didn't want her money. Could this be a simple robbery? But, if so, why kidnap her? What would they hope to gain?

Unless they planned to do other things to her. She shook her head. No, she wouldn't think that way. She had to remain positive. Finn would find her. He would murder both those thugs with his bare hands when he found them. He would save her.

She hoped.

She could hear footsteps somewhere in the distance, the scrape of boot on stone. She tried to turn to see who was there, but she couldn't even roll to a sitting position. Perhaps it was best to stay where she was and not move. Maybe they'd think she was still unconscious and leave her.

The footsteps got closer. She could hear the clink of a key in a lock, the groan of hinges on an ancient metal door.

She wished then she'd taken Elyne up on her offer to send her home. She'd be there right now.

"Awake, I see."

She knew that thin, nasal voice. Maggie rolled to her side. Using her hands still tied in front of her, she struggled to a sitting position. He laughed, grabbed her by the hair and jerked her upward. The roots of her hair pulled hard, making tears spring to her eyes. He yanked her to a sitting position and looked down at her.

"I tire of your meddling, my lady," Litonshire said.

"What do you want?" Maggie's voice wasn't as strong as she would have liked. In fact, she croaked the words because her throat was dry from having the rag in her mouth for who knew how long.

"I want you out of the way," he said. "That's what I want. You're ruining all my plans."

"What plans?"

He released her hair, shoving her head forward. She tried not to show the pain in her face. Her head still throbbed from the hit and now she had other problems. It looked as if she might not be getting out of there alive.

"You think I'll tell you that?" He shook his head. "You'll stay here until you rot, for all I care."

"Where's Finn?"

Litonshire scowled. "Your precious knight won't be saving you, either."

Fear coursed through her like acid. What had he done to Finn? What if the earl managed to kill him in the lists while she wasn't there to stop it? Even though Elyne had said she'd only been using her, Maggie was still determined to save him. It had gone beyond her obligations now. Now she had feelings for him, she wanted him to live. She *needed* him to live.

"What have you done to him?" she demanded.

The earl offered no more information as he turned and left the cell. He banged the door closed behind him, keeping his gaze pinned on her as he locked the door. Frustrated with his silence, she blurted the next thing that came to mind.

"Did you kill him?" Her voice pitched high and she realized she sounded almost hysterical.

"He's alive. For now."

"You're the one that attacked Lady Juliet in the stable last tourney, aren't you?"

Maggie couldn't help it. She had to know. Now that a set of bars separated the two of them, she felt she could ask him without his backlash.

He stood so still she wasn't sure he continued to breathe. He hadn't moved until he blinked once, his eyes turning to obsidian orbs. "What makes you think so?"

Elyne had been right. He *was* the one who did it and he was far more dangerous than Maggie had accounted for. She had been a fool to think she could handle the man. What had she done marrying Juliet off to Brian? What would happen to them when Litonshire found out? He would be furious. Murderous, even. Maggie wouldn't put it past him.

"You did it," Maggie accused, so sure. "I know you did. I plan to prove it."

His faced darkened with a dangerous glint. "Try. And I'll kill you." Then he laughed, baring his teeth in a feral smile. "Of course, you'll have to get out of here first."

He left her there, the echo of his insane laughter bouncing off the stone walls. To rot, he'd said. That meant he hadn't planned on coming back to give her food or water. She really *would* die here.

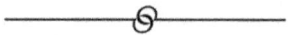

Finn sat astride his destrier and scanned the crowd in the grandstand. He hadn't seen Maggie all day and didn't see her now. It was odd, really. He thought she'd be there for his sword match, but she never arrived. When he checked her tent, she wasn't there either. He'd told the lass to take Geoffrey with her wherever she went, but the boy hadn't seen her all day.

When he couldn't find Maggie in the tent, he went looking for her in the market. None of the merchants had seen her. He was ready to rip the entire market apart looking for her when Fergus gently reminded him, he was due in the lists. What if Elyne had come back and Maggie had begged to return home? And Elyne had granted that wish?

He wasn't even dressed in his jousting armor yet. He had to hurry to get ready and then head to the lists where he now sat perched atop his horse.

"Any sign of her, laddie?" he asked Fergus.

"None, my lord. But Geoffrey is still looking," Fergus said. As if that would make him feel better. Geoffrey didn't know his head from his arse at times.

"Dinna stop looking until ye've found her," Finn ordered. "Someone has surely seen her."

"Aye, my lord."

He charged toward his opponent in the lists, lance at the ready, but Maggie never left his mind and it caused him to miss. His opponent managed to shatter his lance on Finn's breastplate. He, however, hadn't even broken the tip, which garnered a few well-deserved boos.

He trotted back to his squire who handed him another lance. "Try this one."

Finn said nothing as he took the lance, holding it upright. What if Elyne was missing because she'd sent Maggie back to her time? What if Maggie had requested the Fae princess send her back, deserting him? Had their tupping been that bad that she'd run all the way back to her century?

The thought pained him, stabbed him to the core. He had gotten used to her being with him every day and now she was gone?

"My lord?"

Fergus' voice snapped him back to the present and he realized the list marshal had signaled the start of the second round. He charged ahead, lowering his lance far too late. It barely nicked his opponent in the shoulder, while he took another full-on hit in the chest. He wobbled in the saddle, nearly toppling out. He could hear the collective gasp of the crowd, followed immediately by a mixture of cheers and boos.

He really needed to get his head into the game or he'd lose this match, endangering his loss of the tourney, which in turn would risk losing his lands to Litonshire.

Pressing his lips together in annoyance, he snatched the lance Fergus offered as Geoffrey came running up, his face flushed. Hope and expectancy swelled within him.

"Well?"

"No sign of her, my lord," Geoffrey said.

"Keep looking," Finn said. "Dinna come back until ye find the lass."

He charged toward the opponent, anger and fear coursing through him. He directed it through his lance as he couched it under his arm. How could she leave him without saying farewell? When he got his hands on that wench, he'd—

His lance slammed hard into his opponent, knocking him from his mount. The knight crashed to the ground, his squire running into the lists to keep the galloping horse from trampling his lord. Finn turned his horse around and headed back to his squires, to the rabid cheers of the crowd.

He'd managed to win that one. He needed to find Maggie and soon. And if he couldn't find her, then he had to find Elyne. He thought he knew where to start looking.

Chapter 13

With his adrenaline still high from this match, Finn made his way to the gambling tents after changing out of his jousting armor. He had no intent of going to banquet until he found Maggie or Elyne. He didn't want to think about the possibility that Maggie could have left him to return to her home. It pained him too much.

He'd been tempted by the gambling tents once and was unable to resist. He'd come away from that game of Hazard the winner. Luck had been on his side. That and he only bet what he could afford to lose. The second time he came, he'd found Elyne playing a hand of cards and winning. He'd resisted the lure of the game then since he'd been more intent on finding out who Maggie was.

When he arrived, he scanned the usual crowd, looking for the fair-haired princess. She was nowhere to be found. Instead, he saw one of his card buddies, William Peckham, playing a game with two other men he didn't know. One of the strangers was a big man with a long, scraggly beard and a squinty left eye. He had a pile of gold coins in front of him, an empty pouch sat at his left elbow. It looked familiar enough to want to join the game.

Finn remembered then he'd given Maggie the pouch of gold coins earlier that day to shop in the market. He'd made most of the money in that pouch from his earlier dice games. He only had a handful on him now, but he knew it would be enough to buy into the table and play a few hands.

"Finn, come join us, old man." This from Sir William.

Which was exactly what he intended to do.

Finn took a seat across from the scraggly bearded man, eyeing the gold coins in front of him. "You're doing well, good sir." He nodded toward the money he'd made.

"Aye. Seems to be on a winning streak, I am." He looked Finn over with a curious eye. "You goin' to be buyin' in?"

"Moose has been winning all night," Sir William said with a laugh. "Have a seat, Finn."

Finn looked at Sir William, whose winnings were paltry compared to Moose's. He knew what his friend was trying to say. Sit down and clean the beggar out.

Finn tossed two of his six coins on the table. "I'm in."

"Four players it is, then," the dealer said. "Here are the rules. A two-coin minimum wager upon the card you wish to bet. Any or all cards may be bet. Any cards matching dealer's of the same rank double your money. Any cards matching same rank and suit, triple. Clear?"

There were nods all around. Finn knew this game and wasn't fond of it. It was a game of pure chance and no skill. He would need luck on his side.

The dealer reached for another deck of cards, shuffled them with the two he already had, and then dealt thirteen cards to each man, face up. Finn glanced at his hand, rearranged them to group the same suits together and then in order from lowest to high. He had a four and eight of spades. A two, nine, king and ace of clubs. A six, eight and ace of diamonds. And a two, four, three and six of hearts.

"Place your bets," the dealer said.

Finn fingered the four coins he had in his hand. It would be a total luck of the draw for him to win. He placed two coins on the three of hearts. The other three men at the table placed their bets and Finn kept an eye on the man across from him. He placed a bet on four of his cards—a two of diamonds, a six of spades, a nine of spades, and a king of hearts. Two red, two black.

The dealer waved off more bets, then drew one card from the bottom of the deck and turned it over. Three of diamonds.

"All threes win," the dealer said.

No one had an exact match of rank and suit. Finn was the only one with a matching three and doubled his money. Moose, however, lost all four of his bets.

Satisfaction oozed through Finn when Moose scowled as he watched the dealer move the money from him to pay out Finn's winnings.

Once the dealer had paid out the winnings, he said, "Place your bets."

Finn moved his four coins to the king of clubs. Moose put ten coins each on his seven of spades, his three of spades, and his queen of hearts.

The dealer waved off bets and drew from the bottom of the deck. King of clubs. Finn had won again. Moose pounded his fist against the table when the dealer scraped back all his money.

And so, it went. Over and over. Until Finn had methodically placed his bets on different cards and won, he watched Moose continuously lose his money, hand after hand.

As Finn scooped his winnings towards him, he was pleased to see he'd cleaned out Moose, whose pouch now lay empty. Moose picked it up and tossed it at Finn, a scowl on his ugly face as he pushed back from the table and stood. Finn picked up the pouch, examined it closely and saw his mam's embroidery.

He scooped the coins into the pouch, quickly drawing the string closed, and stood. Moose had already left the table and sauntered through the gambling tents to seek out other games he could play. Finn had only left the man with the same amount of coins he, himself, had brought. He went after him, determination running through his blood.

He knew then Maggie hadn't left him at all. Moose had something to do with her disappearance and he intended to find out where she was, even if he had to beat the answers out of him. When he caught up to the man, he slowed his stride to his.

"Where did ye get this?" he asked, holding it up for Moose to see.

He shrugged. "Found it."

"Found it *where*?" Finn asked. "And dinna tell me falsehoods or yere nose will be meeting my fist."

Moose looked down at Finn's hand, as if assessing what damage his knuckles would do.

"'T'aint no business of yours where I found it. I just did."

Finn snatched him by the neck of his tunic, picking him up bodily and shoving him outside the tent. He dropped the pouch at his feet and drew his dagger, holding it at the man's throat.

"Did ye get this from a bonnie lass in the market?"

"Not in the market," Moose said, his eyes wide with fear now. "She weren't in no market."

"Where was she then?"

"Coming from the copse of trees on the other side of the tourney field."

God's teeth. What was she doing there? She said she was going to shop in the market but, clearly, she'd lied and gone elsewhere. He suspected it had something to do with Lady Juliet and Lord Brian. The woman was bent on getting those two together.

"Who was with her?" he demanded. His mellow baritone was edged with control. He pushed the blade into the man's throat, dangerously close to breaking the skin.

"No one. She was alone."

He growled. The lass was daft, wandering around alone. "There was no one else with her?"

"Nay."

Maggie went alone? To do what? "Who hired ye? The truth."

"A man… I don't know his name, I swear. He had a hawk nose and he dressed in fine clothes. Me an' Ox, though, we needed the coin. He gave us a lot to take away the girl."

Lord Litonshire, that boil upon humanity, had hired these men to take her somewhere. Maggie was in danger now and he couldn't waste any more time with this despot.

"Away where?" Finn's voice has lowered into a deep, almost feral, growl. He pressed the blade harder into his skin, drawing a dot of blood.

"We took her to the edge of the tournament field. He put her in a cart and drove off with her."

Fear trickled through Finn. Was she even still alive? Had he killed her? If he did, he would rip Litonshire apart with his bare hands.

"Does she live?"

"Aye, she lived when he took her. By God's death, I tell you true."

Finn removed the blade and sheathed it, blowing out a breath. Maggie was alive. But he wasn't going to let Moose get away without at least some punishment.

"Don't kill me."

"Aye, I willna kill ye."

No, he wouldn't kill the man this time. He grabbed the man by the tunic and landed his fist in his face. Moose staggered backward a few steps, covering his bloodied nose.

"But should I see ye near the lady again, I will," Finn amended.

Finn pummeled him again with another hit to the face, this one so hard Moose fell to the ground, unconscious.

Now he had to find Maggie before it was too late.

Anger buzzed around Finn's skull as he headed back from the gambling tents to the pavilion, his pouch safely tucked away. The winnings he'd walked away with were the money he'd given Maggie, the money Moose had stolen. Worry gnawed at him. Where was she? Would she still be alive when he found her? He needed to find Litonshire.

Knowing Maggie hadn't gone to the market as she had said she would, Finn started his search by finding the last person she would have talked to—Lord Brian. When he arrived at the man's tent, though, the only person he found was his young sister, Lady Grace.

"Sir Finian," she greeted and curtsied. "Good eve."

"Where is yere brother?" he asked, getting right to the point.

She blinked in surprise at his gruff response. "I'm not sure, sir. I haven't seen him all day. Not since early this morning when Lady Margaret came to speak with him."

"Lady Margaret was here?"

"Aye, this morning, as I said. She asked to speak to him about a private matter."

"Where did they go?"

"They left the pavilion, heading away from the tournament field. I'm not sure where they went—"

Before she could finish, Finn dashed away, heading for the castle. He could hear Lady Grace calling him, but he ran like the devil was on his heels. He needed to find Lady Juliet.

As he headed toward the castle, though, he blinked when he saw Elyne. *God's teeth, the fair lass came back.* Mayhap she knew Maggie was in a spot of trouble and returned from the Otherworld. Whatever the case, relief flooded him when he saw her. He'd never been so glad to see one of the fair folk.

She walked with a purposeful stride toward him, her blue eyes blazing, her blonde hair shimmering. She had with her a big man, her hand clamped around his wrist as she dragged him along. How the princess managed to tow him behind her was something Finn puzzled over. He noticed, then, the man had two black eyes and blood running down one side of his face as though he'd been hit with something. He blinked in surprise.

"Where's Maggie?" he asked before she could even draw a breath. He sounded panicked even to his own ears.

"Mayhap Ox will tell *you*, because he wouldn't tell *me*." She nodded at the man next to her who winced with pain. "It took some doing, but I finally found him. Even so, he won't talk to me."

Finn grabbed him by his tunic and jerked him forward. "Ye helped kidnap her," he growled. "Where is she?"

He stared at Finn, wide-eyed and silent. When he refused to answer, Finn clamped a hand around his throat. "Tell me."

"He didn't want to tell me either because he truly didn't know. But I did," Elyne said. Her mouth turned in a mischievous smile. "I made him tell me how they kidnapped her. Go on. Tell him."

"A man paid us," he croaked, "to take her away."

"Aye, I ken that already. Where is she now?" This last question he directed to Elyne.

"Lord Litonshire tossed her in the dungeon of Middleham Castle," Elyne said.

Finn directed his gaze back to Ox and squeezed his throat harder. "Alive?"

"Aye." He gasped for breath. "She was…when we left her."

Finn shoved Ox roughly away, his hands clenched. "Be gone. Before I kill ye."

But he continued to stand there, clutching his throat and trying to catch his breath, not moving.

"I'd suggest you do what the man says," Elyne said. "Before he decides to bloody your face even more."

Ox glanced between the two of them, stumbled a few steps backward before he got his footing and ran away.

"I'm verra glad to see ye, princess."

"I couldn't sit idly by without helping Maggie. That's why I came back."

"I thought ye sent her back to her time," Finn confessed, watching the distance expand between them and Ox.

"I offered but she refused. She wanted to stay here with you."

"I need to get to her now." He grabbed her by the arms. It took all his self-control not to shake her.

"Finn…" she said slowly, calmly, her voice barely above a whisper. She shrugged off his grip and reached for him, putting a soft hand on his arm. "If he's locked her up in the dungeon of the castle, there are guards posted outside."

"I can get in."

Elyne put a hand on his chest to stop him. "They have orders to kill you on sight. You'll never get past them. Let me go."

"Ye go, princess?" He shook his head. "I canna allow ye to do something so dangerous."

She gave him a bland half-smile, propping one hand on her slender hip and then looking down her nose at him. "Did you forget? I can sift. I'll be in and out. No one will even see us."

"I dinna like it."

"Finn, you have to return to the tournament field and continue or else you'll forfeit. Litonshire knows this. He's using Maggie as a distraction to keep you from the games. Go back. Let me handle it," she said.

She was right, of course. Litonshire wanted him to forfeit so he would lose his lands to him in payment of his debt. He wouldn't— couldn't—allow that to happen.

"Go," she urged. "I'll bring her to you as soon as I have her."

"Aye, then. Bring her back to me safe."

"I will."

"I thank ye for your help, princess."

The tips of her ears, he noticed, turned pink, as well as her cheeks. "You two are starting to grow on me."

"Is that why ye came back?"

"I suppose. Besides, Derron really doesn't want to marry me," she said. "I never thought I'd actually *like* humans but you two are okay."

Finn chuckled then and put a hand on her shoulder. "Bring Maggie back to me, aye?"

"Aye, Finn. I will."

Maggie wasn't sure how much time had passed. There was no window, nothing to mark the passage of time. As soon as Litonshire had disappeared, she'd started working on the ropes around her wrists. As disgusted as she was by it, she even tried to use her teeth to untie the knots. But it was useless. Her wrists were raw and bleeding from the continuous rope burn.

She'd given up and now sat against the stone wall staring into the space ahead. Her eyes had gotten used to the dim light. Her stomach had growled so much she was sure it was ready to digest itself. She waited for Litonshire to return with that menacing look on his face. What was stopping him from killing her? Or worse, raping her, and then killing her?

No one knew where she'd gone. Elyne was long gone. She'd made it perfectly clear to Maggie her offer was for a limited time only. And Maggie had refused. She snorted. How stupid she'd been. She closed her eyes, whispering Elyne's name in the hopes the Fae princess would miraculously hear her and swoop in to help. Deep down, Maggie knew it was useless.

The only other person who knew to look for her was Finian. Since he hadn't made an appearance yet, that could only mean he'd given up on her. He was probably dancing with some other maid right now at the banquet. Maybe even Lady Grace. She would laugh and look up at him adoringly. He would sweep her off her feet and carry her back to his tent and—

"Stop it, Mags."

She couldn't think about that right now. Finn was the least of her worries. She had to get out of here. If she did, where would she go? Would Finn even want her anymore? He knew she was from the future, so for all she knew he'd given up on her, thought she'd returned to her time after their night together. Maybe he thought that was all she wanted before going home.

She hiccupped a sob, swallowed it and forced away the thoughts. The last thing she wanted to do was hurt him. It gave her renewed desperation to get out of here.

The first thing she'd do is go to him, tell him what had happened. That Litonshire had locked her up. He would be furious. He would seek vengeance. Knowing Litonshire would suffer at Finn's hands made her happy, but she couldn't help the worry that followed. What would be the consequences of him attacking the earl?

She twisted the ropes again around her wrists, trying to loosen them. Her brain was numb to the burning, stinging. Or was it her fingers that were numb? She wiggled them, feeling the pinpricks of a thousand needles stabbing the tips. Even her feet had lost feeling long ago.

"What good will it do?" she asked no one in particular. "It's not like I can walk out of here."

Wherever "here" was. She had no idea. She'd been knocked unconscious before even leaving the tournament field and she had no idea how long she'd been out. Could it have been hours or days? She shuddered.

"Can't be days," she muttered.

Yet her stomach rumbled an objection to that.

"Oh, shut up," she told it. "I will *not* die here."

She jerked her hands apart, trying to make the ropes give. They wouldn't, and her only reward was a hot, searing pain ripping through her.

"I hate my life."

Great. She'd resorted to talking to herself. Maybe being in solitary confinement was making her lose her mind. Maybe she would go crazy and then when someone *did* find her, she'd be nothing more than a babbling idiot who drooled out of the corner of her mouth. They would lock her up in the nearest sanitarium.

"*In*-sanitarium is more like it," she said and giggled at her own joke.

The only response was her echo in the dank cell.

"This is a fine situation you've gotten yourself into, isn't it?" Elyne's voice asked.

Maggie looked up at the Fae princess, her hair shimmering in the light, the pointed tips of her ears clearly visible. She had never been so happy or so relieved to see Elyne before in her life. Tears of joy flooded her eyes, blurring her vision.

"Ellie. Thank God. You came."

"Do you know what I've risked to get here?" Elyne asked. "I had to sneak away from court again. You should have accepted my offer to go home when I gave it to you. But no. You had to be stubborn, didn't you?"

"Did you come to chastise me or get me out of here?"

Elyne waved her hand and the cell door opened with a groan of ancient hinges. She knelt down next to Maggie, looking her over. Maggie could see the horror in her gaze and knew what she must look like. She'd lost her shoes and had terrible rope burns on her wrists from fighting with the bindings.

"Oh, Mags," Elyne whispered. "You struggled."

"I had to get out of here, Ellie." She made a note the princess had called her Mags. Something only her very close friends called her.

Elyne untied her wrists, then her ankles. "Finn has been looking for you. He thought I sent you home."

"I wondered if he'd think that." Elyne put one of her arms

around her shoulders, helping her to her feet. "How long have I been here?"

"Almost twelve hours."

Twelve hours? That was it? It felt like an eternity. No wonder she was nearly delirious. No wonder she felt so weak. She'd just about given up hope anyone would ever find her. No one had come. Not even Litonshire had returned, nor the two brutes who kidnapped her in the first place.

"You need water and food," Elyne said.

Once they were out of the hated cell, she put Maggie on a nearby stool and handed her a water skin. Maggie clutched it between her shaking hands and guzzled the water. She'd never been so happy to taste something so cold and wet.

"Where is Finn now? And where is here?" she asked when she'd gotten her fill.

"Finn had to stay at tourney and finish," Elyne said. "I told him I would come get you. And here is the dungeon of the castle."

"I don't like this place. I'd like to go home now."

"Home?" she repeated.

Perhaps Elyne was wondering if by home she meant back to her time. But what Elyne couldn't know was that she had stopped thinking of that as home. No, instead, home was wherever Finn was. Whether here at tourney or his castle in Scotland.

"Yes." Maggie stood on weak legs. "Take me home to Finn."

Before Maggie could question Elyne on how she was going to get them out of there, the Fae princess had grasped her by the arm and in a quick flash returned her to her tent. Maggie blinked, her head spinning a bit as she realized she was no longer in the dank cell but instead in her softly lit bed chamber surrounded by canvas. She stumbled, trying to get her bearings, but Elyne held tight.

"Thank you," she said.

Elyne eased her down to the bed, then handed her the water skin. Maggie took another long draw before handing it to Elyne. She lay back, happy to be resting against the down bed. She placed gentle fingertips against the bump on her head. She could tell the skin was broken and there was dried blood surrounding the wound. Scraggly beard guy must have hit her harder than she realized.

"You need a healer," Elyne said. "Your head doesn't look good and your wrists are raw."

Maggie knew what her wrists looked like. It was the damage

she'd caused trying to escape her bonds. She had stopped feeling the throbbing pain long ago. But glancing down at them now made her stomach turn. They looked like raw ground meat.

"You shouldn't have struggled so much," Elyne reprimanded.

"You're right. I probably shouldn't have. But he left me there to die. And I sure wasn't going to die there."

"Aye, I know, he did. That fecking bastard. And you would have if Finn hadn't searched high and low for you."

Maggie's heart swelled. He had missed her. Gone looking for her. And she'd had visions of him forgetting her. How could she doubt him? He really was her knight in shining armor. She would never leave him without telling him goodbye. She couldn't. And the very idea of leaving him at all sent her into a near anxiety attack. She wasn't so sure she could let him go so easily.

"Would you do something for me?" Maggie asked, and when Elyne nodded she continued. "My father will be worried sick about me. He's been through so much already. If I wrote him a letter, could you take it to him?"

Knowing the princess could sift the sands of time, she hoped Elyne would agree. It would be difficult for Dad to accept, but at least he would know she was still alive.

"Aye, I will. If you really intend to stay here, I'll make sure he gets your letter."

"Oh, thank you, Elyne."

Guilt swarmed her then as she thought of the mess she'd made between Elyne and Derron. She would have to figure out a way to make it up to her. And she would start with an apology.

"Elyne, I'm really sorry I told you about Derron breaking the betrothal. I really thought you knew already. You're the last person I wanted to hurt."

Elyne's porcelain face looked chiseled from stone as she stared at Maggie, holding perfectly still. Then, as quickly as she stilled, she waved it away. "It's not your fault, Maggie. Derron can't help who he is. And I knew he was that way. I should just...accept it." She smiled faintly, as though she didn't really believe it.

"Why did you come back?"

"Someone had to rescue your arse. No one knows I'm here. Not even Derron. And if my mother finds out..." She shuddered. "Well, let's just say I won't be visiting your world again anytime soon."

"You'll be grounded?" Maggie asked and Elyne laughed.

"Something like that. I'll get you some food and bring the healer. You rest and I'll be back." She handed her the water skin. "And keep drinking water."

When the princess left, she could hear voices outside her tent. One Maggie recognized as the deep timbre of Finn. Her heart sped up in anticipation, waiting for him to make an appearance. When she saw his broad body enter, hot tears sprang to her eyes. She had never been so happy to see him.

He paused to look her over, his gaze landing first on the cut on her head, then on her wrists. He took in her dirty gown, her bare feet and her damaged ankles. They'd fared better than her wrists. He knelt down next to her bed and stoked hair away from her face.

"*Och*, lass. Ye put the fear of God into me with yere disappearance." He sounded so relieved to see her. His dark eyebrows slanted into a frown, replacing his normal brooding expression.

Maggie sniffed, trying to quell the tears. "I should have listened to you in the first place, Finn. I shouldn't have been wandering around alone and I shouldn't have gone after Lord Brian, but I thought—"

"Shh. Yere safe now. 'Tis all that matters, aye?"

She nodded. His face went from smooth, soft lines to hard ones as his forehead creased in concern, and then he gave her a dark look that told Maggie she was about to be in big trouble.

"Why did ye go see Lord Brian? I ken ye didna go to the market, so dinna even give me falsehoods about that."

He really had searched high and low for her and she'd been caught. She hated telling him the truth, that she'd deliberately lied to him to help Brian and Juliet. She kept her gaze away from his, pinned on the canvas ceiling above her.

"I'll tell you but you have to promise not to be angry."

He hesitated only a moment before finally nodding. "Aye, I give ye my word."

"I know you told me to stay away from Lady Juliet and Lord Brian—"

"*Och*, lass. Aye, I did." The words exploded from him, cutting her off.

She refused to be derailed as she pressed on. "But I couldn't let Lord Vile keep abusing her. He's the one who raped her, Finn."

He stilled and stared at her with such disbelief, she thought he would tell her she was crazy for thinking so. But Elyne had told her the truth and she knew from Juliet's semi-confession and swearing her to secrecy—even from her new husband—that it was true.

"The night you found Lady Juliet in the stable alone, he'd just left her before you found her. Maybe he was trying to set you up or something. I don't know yet," she continued.

"Yet?" he repeated. "Nay, lass, ye stay away from the lot of them."

Maggie ignored him and continued. "When I found out it was true, I went to Brian. He loves her, Finn. So much, he's willing to risk everything for her. I took him to her, found a priest, and the two married in secret in the copse of trees on the edge of the tournament field."

"Ye…did…what…?"

"I arranged their marriage," she said, sounding pleased and proud.

It had been nothing short of a small feat to get the two together and married. She had begged the priest not to breathe a word to another soul of their secret wedding.

"Lady Juliet is safe now. Away from her horrid brother."

"Do ye realize what ye've done, lass?" he asked. "When Litonshire finds out—"

"He'll spew his venom and wrath all over tourney. I know." She sighed. "But he can't touch her now. Lord Brian said he was taking her out of England. It had to be done, Finn. Don't you think?"

She looked at him, then, finally meeting his silvery gaze. She didn't see anger and annoyance. She saw compassion and tenderness. He'd only looked at her like that one other time and, as it had then, it shredded her heart now.

He nodded slowly. "Aye, lass. I ken it." He laced his fingers with hers. "Ye did a good thing for her, though it was mighty daft of ye to be running off alone. Ye should have come to me."

"Like you needed any more distractions."

She smiled, placing her free hand on his cheek, his burning skin warming her frigid fingertips. She hadn't realized how cold she was until that moment and she shivered. He pulled the coverlet up to her chin, tucked it around her.

"After I left them, I headed back to the tournament field. I intended to come to your match. That's when I ran into that scraggly bearded man and his sidekick. They knocked me out and I woke up in a cell. Litonshire told me he intended to leave me there to rot."

His free hand fisted by his side as she said the last words and she knew he had visions of killing the man. She'd kill him herself if she could.

"And he'll pay for that."

"I knew you'd say that. Lord Litonshire plans to kill you."

"Dinna worry yere bonnie head about him, lass. I can handle him."

"I'm not so sure, Finn. I'm afraid for you."

"'Tis no reason to be. Tourney only has two more days left and I'm in the lead. If I win the next two jousting matches, I win."

And that's what Maggie feared the most. If he was on the verge of winning, what would Litonshire do to stop it?

"Why does Litonshire want you dead so badly?" His body tensed and stiffened and his face closed, as though guarding a secret. A muscle ticked in his jaw as he clenched it. When he seemed as though he wasn't going to answer, she took his hand in hers and squeezed. "You know the truth about me. Now I want to know your truth."

He sucked in a breath and then blew it out, long and hard. "I made the mistake of gambling with the man at last tourney. He cleaned me out of money and when I had no more, I was foolish enough to bet my estates. Castle McCullough. My family lands."

"Oh, Finn…"

"If I dinna come up with the money I owe him, then he'll take my lands and my castle. 'Tis why I must win the tourney."

Dread filled her. She'd have to come clean about the henchman stealing the pouch of gold coins from her. All the blood drained from her head. She felt positively sick to her stomach and pressed a hand against her abdomen.

"Oh, God…the gold…that man stole it from me."

"'Tis safe." He held up the pouch for her to see. "I found it on the mongrel that kidnapped ye."

"And all the money was there?"

"Nay…no' exactly. I found him in the gambling tents playing a wee card game with all my coin. I had to win it back from him."

"Then you can pay Litonshire off."

"'Tis no' enough, lass."

Good God. How much did he owe? But the question remained unasked and by the look on Finn's face, she could tell it was a warning not to ask. He wouldn't tell her, anyway, if she knew him. He was stubborn like that.

"I'm so sorry. I never meant for any of this to happen."

"*Och*, 'tis no' your fault." He waved it away, as though it meant nothing.

But to Maggie, it was a very big thing and something had dawned abundantly clear. Finn had a gambling problem. It explained some of those disappearances of his and why he had such a wealth of coin. She had to stay now, for Finn. She knew, suddenly, why she was here. It really *was* to keep Finn alive. And that's what she was going to do.

"I won't leave you," she said, watching him. "I'm staying here with you."

His smoldering gaze, full of desire and need and want, met hers. As soon as it did, the world shifted. As if they were the only two who lived and breathed. The only two who would ever matter in the entire universe. He leaned down to her, his lips brushing hers in a soft kiss.

"Ye dinna need to decide that now, lass," he said.

"But—"

He put a finger over her lips to hush her. "Decide after tourney, should I live through it."

"You'd better. Because if you die, I'll kill you."

Finn laughed as he kissed her. Maggie couldn't help herself as she deepened the kiss, capturing his mouth with hers and taking it over. She pulled him closer, slipping her arms around his neck and trying desperately to ignore the pain throbbing in her wrists. But he knew she was in pain and gently grasped her arms and moved them away.

"Dinna hurt yereself," he said, his voice barely above a whisper. "There will be time for more of that later."

Maggie was about to object when Elyne returned with a cloth-covered tray and the healer in tow. She whipped off the cover to reveal a loaf of crusty bread, some cheese, and fruit. Maggie's mouth immediately watered.

"Here's your patient," she said, pointing to Maggie as Finn stepped out of the way.

The interruption was timely, as always with the Fae princess.

Maggie didn't like it but at least they didn't catch them in a compromising situation. She had Finn to thank for that.

The healer checked over her shredded wrists and ankles, cleaned them and put a bandage around each one. Then he checked out the wound on her head. All the while, Maggie kept an eye on the tray Elyne held. Seeing her salivate, Elyne handed her an apple.

"It's a nice-sized bump, that's for sure," he said as he cleaned and dressed the wound. "Do you have a headache?"

"Yes, though I think that's from lack of food and water and not just the head wound," Maggie said around a mouthful of apple.

"Probably so. Eat, drink, rest. You'll feel better on the morrow."

"Thank you, healer."

Once he'd gone, Elyne broke off chunks of bread for her and wrapped it around the cheese. "You, eat. And you," she turned to Finn, "back to your own tent." She shooed him away.

Maggie took the bread and the cheese and nibbled, trying to keep herself in check and not cram it all in her mouth at once. Her stomach rumbled loudly, appreciative of the food.

"Nay," Finn said with a shake of his head. "I'll no' leave her alone."

"I'll be here with her," Elyne said.

"Dinna think I'll leave her after what's happened to her," Finn said, his voice hard and sure. "Ye can stay if ye like, fair princess, but I'm no' leaving her."

Maggie grinned, loving that he wanted to protect her.

Elyne propped her hands on her hips. "Because the only one that can protect her is you?"

"Aye," he said and folded his arms across his chest.

"It's probably just as well. I have to return to the Otherworld before I'm missed." Elyne puffed out a breath, and then peered at Maggie. "But don't think you've gotten rid of me so easily. I'll be back to make sure you stay out of trouble."

"I dinna think the lass can stay out of trouble."

Maggie giggled as Elyne left them alone. She half expected the Fae to sift out and be gone within the blink of an eye but she didn't. She left on her own two feet. Finn stretched out on the ground next to her low bed, folding his hands behind his head.

"What are you doing?"

"Bedding down for the night, lass."

"Down there?" She shook her head, and then scooted to the other side of the bed, patting the mattress next to her. "There's plenty of room. Don't sleep on the ground, Finn."

He eyed the bed where she'd patted it before getting up and slipping in between the covers next to her. When she rolled to her side, he spooned her, pulling her into him and curling around her. She fit, his chin above her head. It was as if it was always meant to be. As if she was his missing half and he hers.

She drifted off to sleep smiling as he stroked her hair.

Sometime during the night, Maggie came out of pleasant sleep and warm dreams to a hand sliding up and down her body. Finn had managed to work his hand under her shift, feeling her every curve. She rolled to her back, allowing him more access to her.

Maggie sat up straight then, looking down at him, and realized he'd shed every stitch of clothing. She really ought to blush at that, but she was too busy enjoying the idea of him sleeping naked next to her. It sent delicious heat swarming through her, pulsating down to the very place where they were connected. It made her feel scandalous.

No longer able to stand the material separating the two of them, she struggled out of the shift and tossed it away with a rustle of fabric. His mouth curved with tenderness as his hands slid between them, caressing. Her decision to stay with Finn, she knew, was the right decision. She couldn't live without him. Her thesis forgotten and dismissed, all that mattered now was being with him, loving him.

As Maggie's body shuddered in response, he lifted up, pulled her to him. His mouth reclaimed her lips, crushing her to him. Her soft curves seemed to fit perfectly against his hard, chiseled ones. As though they were missing links to each other. His mouth moved down, kissing the pulsing hollow at the base of her throat, sending chills exploding through her.

Finn rolled her over, his hands exploring the soft lines of her. All the while his mouth followed and whispered love for each part of her body. Tender, soft kisses sent her mind reeling.

He took his time, as though restraining his movements to

prolong the inevitable. As though making sure she knew exactly what he was doing and where. At last, his body moved to partially cover hers, imprisoning her against him as he took her. When she moved beneath him, he groaned his approval. Unable to hold off any longer, her body burst with the searing need as Finn fulfilled it. Passion and a feeling a such love and tenderness spiraled through her, she was too emotion-filled to speak.

Maggie savored the feeling of satisfaction Finn left with her. She relished it as they rolled together, him pulling her close to his chest and spooning his big body against hers once again. Her life had changed and she had accepted it. This was her world now. Now until the day she died.

Chapter 14

Finn had remained by her side the entire night, never letting her go. As if he were afraid she would disappear if he didn't hold on tight. Maggie came to realize as the night wore on that she quite liked him hugging her close and keeping her safe. No one could touch her now.

As soon as dawn broke, Finn stirred and left the cozy bed. She couldn't help but feel cold and alone once he was up, pulling on his trousers and his tunic.

"Leaving already?" she asked around a yawn.

"I'm off to the practice field." He kissed her forehead, his hand on her cheek. "Stay. Sleep."

She started to rise, pushing the blankets aside. "I'll come with you."

"*Och*, nay, lass." He gave her a gentle nudge back to the bed. "Ye dinna need to come. Rest."

"You joust today?"

"Aye, in the afternoon."

"I'll be in the grandstand cheering you on."

"Aye, ye best be." The beginning of a smile tipped the corners of his mouth.

Once Finn left, Maggie got up, dressed, and headed to the great hall to break her fast. She stuffed herself with a thick porridge, eating until she couldn't eat any more. She decided to head back to the pavilion, change her dress, and find Finn. She'd never really stopped thinking about him since she woke that morning. And it continued as she stood combing out her long hair, remembering all the wonderful things she'd done with him. She couldn't get enough of him and she loved being crushed under the weight of his solid body.

"What's the dreamy look for? As if I didn't know."

Elyne appeared inside the bed chamber of her tent, interrupting her thoughts about Finn. At the sound of her voice, Maggie jumped, her senses on high alert.

"Stop scaring me. Why do you always sneak up on people?"

"I wasn't sneaking. I've been here for around ten minutes but you wouldn't know because you've been standing there with that faraway look on your face."

Maggie tossed the comb and picked up her skirts, giving her a sour look. "I'm going to the lists to see Finn joust."

She headed through the curtained partition, Elyne on her heels.

"You're in love with him, aren't you?"

Maggie stopped in her tracks, her heart doing a flip-flop in her chest, her stomach dropping to her toes. Yes, she was in love with him. Madly. Passionately. Can't-live-without-him kind of love and it hurt. It was painful. What if he died in the lists? What if he didn't love her back?

Nothing mattered anymore. Not her thesis, or her father, or anything. All that mattered was that Finn loved her back. He'd never uttered the words. Maybe he never would.

"Aye, you are," Elyne answered for her. "I knew it."

"What am I going to do?" She turned to face her, the blood pounding in her head so loud she thought for sure Elyne could hear it. "What if he doesn't love me back?"

"I think, dear Maggie, that's the least of your worries."

"What do you mean?"

"I mean, Lord Litonshire knows about his sister marrying Lord Brian in secret. He found the priest you paid off and apparently tortured him until he spilled his guts about who hired him," Elyne said. "He intends to protest the wedding to the church to try to have it annulled. It'll be a bit difficult since no one can find Lord Brian and his new bride."

"Oh, dear." If Maggie's stomach hadn't already been in her shoes, it certainly would be hearing those words. Now her stomach twisted in a knot and a fist closed around it, squeezing. She was glad the newlyweds had fled England.

"Oh, dear is right."

"And the priest...?" She swallowed hard, fearful of the answer.

"Dead."

"My God..." Maggie sank to the edge of the bed. "Someone in the castle must have seen me leave with her. Maybe even followed us. I didn't think about that. I'm sure when Litonshire couldn't find his sister, they no doubt told him."

"No doubt," Elyne agreed with a crisp nod.

"Will he stop at nothing?"

"No," Elyne said. "And next he'll be after you and Finn."

"What do you think he'll do?"

"I don't know," Elyne said. "But if I'm caught doing any more magic here, I'll never get out of the Otherworld."

"Finn could be in danger," Maggie said. "I need to warn him."

"I'm coming with you."

Maggie did a quick check in Finn's tent but found it empty and all his lances gone. He was already headed to his next match. Elyne followed her through the pavilion toward the practice field and the lists.

She spotted him then, outside the practice field in a confrontation with the irate earl.

"That woman married off my sister without my consent," he shouted.

Geoffrey and Fergus stood back, eyes wide, while Lord Litonshire's face was beet red from anger. Finn stared at the man with an impassive look on his face, as though he wasn't even rattled by the earl.

"Aye, she did," he said. "And 'tis a good thing, too, from what she tells me about ye."

"You can't prove anything." He pointed an accusatory finger at Finn. "My sister doesn't know what's good for her. I do."

Finn ignored him, shaking his head, and started to step around the man to head for the practice arena. But the earl put a hand on his chest and shoved. Maggie sucked in a sharp breath. Finn was a big man and the earl...not so much. The shove the earl managed was like shoving a brick wall. Nothing happened.

Until Finn wrapped his fingers around Litonshire's wrist and jerked his hand away. He winced with the pain.

"Be gone with ye," Finn said, his voice dangerously low and quiet. Maggie had never heard him talk so softly and knew he must be holding back his rage.

When he released Litonshire, the man stumbled back a few steps as Finn went about his way. Litonshire pulled his sword, then.

"Finn," Maggie shouted.

Finn turned in time to see Litonshire pull his sword and jump backward, missing the point as Litonshire swept it across him, trying to slice him open.

"Have ye gone mad?" Finn asked.

"This is not over yet between us, Sir Finian," Litonshire said.

"Oh, aye, it is."

"No. I refuse to stand here and be insulted by the likes of you and…*her.*" He pointed at Maggie. "I challenged you to a duel before and now it's time we get to it."

Maggie's heart pounded so hard, she thought it might burst through her chest. Finn took a step toward the earl, his eyes narrowed and the silver glinting hot.

"'Tis over, Litonshire. Why can ye not see that? Lady Juliet is gone and married off. She's no more concern of yeres."

"Oh, aye, she is. The king will hear of this injustice."

"Aye, I'm sure he will. And he'll also hear of the injustice ye did to the lady ye call sister. So be gone with ye. I'm due in the lists."

"Ah, yes. You are, aren't you? Best of luck to you, sir." His smile was oily, his voice dripping with disdain. Litonshire put his sword away and sauntered off.

Once he was gone, Maggie ran to Finn, flinging herself into his arms. "I came to warn you. But I was too late."

He held her closer and she could hear the beat of his heart under his tunic. "Ye did the right thing, lass, getting Lady Juliet from that mongrel."

She stepped back, looking up at him. "Finn, I'm afraid of what he might do."

He smiled down at her, the corners of his eyes crinkling in the way she loved so much. He put his hand under her chin. "I wouldn't be. I'm not."

But Maggie wasn't so sure about that.

"Sir Finian, we must make haste." It was Geoffrey who interrupted. "Yere match."

"Aye, 'tis time. I'll see you in the grandstand," he said to Maggie.

"Be careful, Finn. I couldn't bear it if anything happened to you."

He paused, his gaze fixed on Maggie and then he pulled her into his arms, holding her close and pressing his mouth against hers. It wasn't just a regular farewell kiss. His mouth overtook hers, his tongue touched hers and they kissed as if it would be the last time. It scared Maggie, shaking her to the core. She refused to release him, deepening the kiss and nipping his bottom lip.

"We'll finish this later." He spoke with cool authority, yet the dark notes of his voice shuddered through her.

Maggie watched him walk away, past the practice field and toward the lists with Fergus and Geoffrey in tow, carrying his lances and jousting armor.

"Come on," Elyne said, wrapping her delicate hand around Maggie's arm. "Let's go find a seat in the grandstand."

"I'm afraid for him, Ellie," she confessed.

"I know you are."

Maggie and Elyne both knew what was left unsaid. That should Finn die, Maggie would go back home to her twenty-first century. She would live forever without the man she loved and it would hurt her until the day she died.

"We'll worry about it when the time comes," Elyne said, as though she'd heard her thoughts.

And perhaps she did, Maggie thought. She'd never really stopped to consider the Fae princess could possibly read minds. Or maybe she could just read expressions. Maggie had often been accused of wearing her feelings on her sleeve.

The two of them found a seat in the grandstand down toward the railing where they both had a good view. The last match with Sir Drake wrapped up as they sat. The heralds announced the next round, which was Sir Finian and his opponent, a knight neither Maggie nor Elyne knew. The list marshal waved the first flag and off they went. The two of them charged toward each other, lances at the ready.

When they collided, both lances shattered. Wooden pieces rained down around them. Finn galloped back to his side of the list under Maggie's watchful gaze. He appeared to be unscathed. The other knight had made it back to his own side as well, equally unscathed.

The list marshal signaled for the second round and off they went again. For a second time, both shattered their lances and both managed to stay upright in the saddle. They were equally matched, neither one willing to yield to the other. Each had managed a point and now would come the tie breaker to the loud cheers of the crowd.

Maggie watched Finn take his third lance and nod at something Fergus said. Perhaps a word of encouragement for if Finn knocked the knight off his horse, he would win everything—his horse, his armor, his gold.

The third and final flag went up and the two knights galloped toward each other. Finn readied his lance, crossing it over his body and sitting rigid in the saddle. He made contact with his opponent, the lance shattering and shoving the knight off his horse. He landed with a clatter of armor on the ground, his horse galloping dangerously close to him until one of his squires ran up and led it away.

But the knight wasn't moving. A shriek from the grandstand and Maggie saw it then—a large pool of blood spreading under the fallen knight. The entire crowd was on their feet now, bending and stretching to see what had happened to him, if he even still lived.

"He's not moving," Maggie said, her voice a raspy whisper. "Is he still alive? I can't see. What's happening?"

She leaned over the railing in time to see one of the squires roll him over and strip off his helm. And then Elyne screamed and hurdled the railing before Maggie could stop her.

There, lying in a pool of blood, was Sir Derron.

Maggie's first thought was how? How did he come back here after he'd been ordered back to the Otherworld? He must have defied the orders, like Elyne, and returned. Sir Derron loved to joust and loved the competition.

She looked at Finn, then, who was off his horse and heading toward Sir Derron. But he couldn't know it was him beneath the armor, could he? Could Finn have done it on purpose?

She shook her head. No way. Finn wasn't like that. She dismissed the thought as quickly as it entered her head.

"He's tipped his lance," the list marshal said, loud enough for all those in attendance to hear.

A loud boo resounded through the lists and suddenly there were guards on Finn, pulling him away. Maggie remembered then the apothecary's wife telling her Litonshire had purchased lances in the weaponry. With fear pounding through her, she hurdled the railing, running toward Finn. She'd see about Sir Derron after. Right now, she had to get to Finn and find out what was going on.

"I dinna do it," he shouted, struggling against the guards. But he was still in full jousting armor and couldn't move as freely.

Lord Litonshire had come down from his perch in the higher grandstand, leaving behind his cushioned seat to stand in front of Finn, looking smug.

"Arrest him," Litonshire ordered.

"Sir Finian wouldn't do such a thing," Maggie said, skittering to a halt in front the earl. "I know he wouldn't."

"Your word means nothing to me." Litonshire looked her up and down, as though the very sight of her disgusted him. "Throw him in the stocks."

"No," Maggie shrieked and ran to Finn. She shoved her way through the guards to stand in front of him.

Maggie suspected the earl had something to do with Finn injuring Derron. He'd left his tent unattended last night, after all, to stay with her. She wouldn't put it past the earl to switch the lances with the tipped ones.

"You have the wrong man," she said. "Finn wouldn't do this."

"Remove yourself, woman, or I'll have you removed," Litonshire said.

"'Tis all right, lass," Finn said, his voice soft behind her. "Nothing can be done."

Maggie spun around, facing him, and put her hands on his armored chest. "I'll find out the truth, Finn. I swear it."

"Take him away."

The guards shoved her out of the way, taking Finn away to the stocks. Maggie whirled on Litonshire then.

"You did this," she said, pointing an accusatory finger at him. "And I plan to prove it."

"Do what you like, Lady Margaret," Litonshire said, his nasal voice grating on her nerves. "But Sir Finian will never joust again. I intend to see to that as well as to his lands in Scotland. I've already dispatched my men to take over his castle."

"You son of a bitch. How dare you."

"You dare speak to me like that? Seize her." Two men grabbed her, holding her in place while he advanced on her. "I should kill you for that. In fact, if you ever speak to me in such an insolent tone again, I will." He straightened, aware he had an audience. "Now you can tell your master that his gambling debt has been paid in full to me." He smiled, his mouth thin-lipped.

Maggie balled her fists. He'd taken her life away and all she could think to do was scratch his eyes out. She bit her tongue to keep from spewing another acid retort. The last thing she needed was to get herself killed.

How could she prove he had switched Finn's lances with the

tipped ones? As her mind raced for answers, Litonshire signaled his men to let her go and stepped closer to her. So close she could smell his rancid breath. He slid a hand around her waist, pulled her to him. His warm body pressed against hers and she was suddenly assaulted by his bad hygiene. She gagged, trying to get out of his slimy grasp but he held fast.

"Know this, Lady Margaret. I know you took my sister from me. Our quarrel is not over yet."

With that, he released her and walked away, leaving Maggie shivering in the warm sunshine. He'd already tried to kill her once. What would he do a second time?

She shoved away the thought as she ran back to the lists to see about Sir Derron. When she arrived, he had been loaded onto a crude stretcher. Two squires carried him away to the hospital tent. Elyne followed and Maggie hurried to catch up to her.

"Is he all right?" Maggie asked.

"It's bad, Maggie. I don't know if he'll make it." Once they were out of the lists, she turned to Maggie and grasped her by her hands, squeezing. "If he dies…"

"Shh," Maggie said. "He won't. We have to think positive."

"Finn?"

"They've taken him to the stocks," Maggie said and tried hard to hide her own fear and worry.

Elyne hugged her then, something that was completely uncharacteristic of the high-and-mighty Fae princess. Maggie was so surprised by it she was momentarily taken aback.

"Finn didn't do this," Elyne said, her voice a coarse whisper in her ear before pulling back. "He wouldn't. Despite the fact he and Derron dislike each other, Finn would never willingly hurt another knight during a joust."

"I know," Maggie said, somewhat relieved Elyne understood that. "What am I going to do?"

Before Elyne could answer, a puff of pinkish-blue smoke suddenly exploded next to them. Maggie squealed and ducked but Elyne stood still, not moving. She didn't even blink. When Maggie recovered, she peered through the strange fog into the face of the most beautiful woman she had ever seen.

She was tall, lithe, with long golden hair that shimmered in the sunlight and pale-blue eyes. Her skin was like porcelain, her cheekbones high and chiseled. Her face looked as though it had been carved from the finest marble by the best sculptor. She had a dimple in her chin and a scowl on her lovely face. She wore a layered gossamer gown of pale blue and white that seemed to float around her.

"Mother," Elyne greeted, though she gritted it out between clenched teeth.

This woman was her *mother*? Maggie gaped at the woman who could only be Queen of the Otherworld. Maggie glanced between the two. She could definitely see the resemblance though they looked more like sisters than mother and daughter.

"You are to return with me immediately," she said. "By my command."

"I'm not going anywhere with you, Queen Maeve."

"You dare defy me?" Maeve snapped, her head tilted up and back much like Maggie had seen Elyne do. It must have been where the princess had learned the trait. "You've wasted far too much time with these useless humans. You are to return with me at once and stop this silly fascination."

"And go back to what?" Elyne snapped. "A kingdom that isn't mine yet? Frittering away my life in a boorish court? I have no use there and you know it."

"You've caused enough problems as it is. Altering time is a criminal offense. I should strip you of your title and reduce you to nothing but a common peasant."

It must have been a complete insult because Elyne didn't react at all. She maintained her stone-face expression.

"As I said, I'm not leaving. Derron has been injured—"

"Injured? Where?" The queen suddenly changed her tune.

"He's no concern of yours anymore, Mother. You broke our betrothal, remember? You bowed to the pressure of the High Court to give him what he wanted and now he's returned to compete again in the tournament. He could die. He most likely *will* die."

"Take me to him at once."

"No."

"You dare tell me no?"

"Since when do you care about Derron?" Elyne demanded.

"I *will* find him with or without your help. Or have you forgotten, daughter, I am the Queen of the Otherworld?"

"I haven't forgotten anything. Go back to the Otherworld,

Mother, and concern yourself with your court." Elyne waved her off, as though shooing her.

The queen's eyes narrowed to slits. "Since you love the humans so much, I should banish you here to remain with them."

And with that, the queen disappeared in another puff of smoke. Maggie had watched the entire exchange between Elyne and her mother with a wide-eyed stare. She blinked, thankful she wasn't in the princess' shoes.

Elyne inhaled and exhaled a long, slow breath. "She doesn't mean it."

"Really? Because she sounded pretty serious to me."

"She likes to threaten, but I'm her only daughter. She won't *really* banish me. Come on. Let's go see to Derron." She started toward the hospital tent and Maggie fell in step beside her.

Guilt swarmed through Maggie at the thought of the broken bond between Elyne and Derron. She felt responsible for that. Perhaps if Derron saw Elyne by his side now, though, he would change his mind.

"Elyne, are you in trouble for sending me back in time?" Maggie asked. When the princess didn't stop, Maggie grasped her by the arm. "Are you?"

"Aye."

"What's going to happen to you?"

"I don't know yet. I left before being sentenced. None of that matters. All that matters now is getting to Derron."

At the hospital tent, Derron was with the surgeon. The guards wouldn't let them inside until he was done sewing up the Fae knight. Elyne found the healer who had tended Maggie earlier to grill him relentlessly.

"Will he live?" Elyne asked.

"His injuries were severe," he said. "'Tis hard to know at this point."

"I want to see him," she demanded.

"As soon as the surgeon is finished with him," the healer said and glanced up to see the man exiting the small chamber that Derron was in. "Ah, here he is. You may go in now."

Elyne rushed past him but Maggie held back, both she and the healer watching the princess go to him.

"I do hope they hang the man responsible for that knight's injuries," the healer said quietly to Maggie. "I'm afraid he'll not live until morning."

Maggie prayed the healer was wrong. Because she would do everything in her power to keep Finn from hanging.

In the hospital tent, Elyne sat by Derron's side, watching him sleep. The coverlet had been pulled to his chin but she could see the curve of bare shoulders under the edge. She couldn't recall a time she had ever been able to get so close to him. She examined his perfect chiseled features, the way his dark hair curled over his forehead, and she wondered where everything had gone so wrong.

She was crown princess of the Otherworld. She should be able to choose any Fae she wanted to marry. Instead, she had been stuck with Derron and a whole lot of regret. She wondered if, when he had professed his love for her long ago and she hadn't rejected him, if things would be different now. They had been at odds since that fateful day. He had never spoken to her again until the day her mother announced their betrothal. Why couldn't he stay in the Otherworld where he belonged? He insisted on coming to the human realm to joust and put his life at risk. It was a fascination of his, one he couldn't let go, and now it could cost him his life. Again.

Their betrothal had been an advantageous match, according to her mother. One that, when Elyne ascended the throne, would ensure her safety as Queen of the Otherworld. Marriage to Knight of the Realm and Protector of the Otherworld was a good match, according to her mother. Elyne had resented it from the beginning. Derron, of all Fae, had to be the one chosen for her. She knew he had resented it, too. But even so, her feelings for him developed as she spent time with him at court and she had regretted that fateful day she'd shunned his profession of love. She'd hurt him deeply. Once their betrothal was announced, the more she saw of Derron, the more she couldn't deny she had feelings for him. He never looked at her like he did some of the ladies at tourney, nor had he expressed any feelings for her other than that of resigned friendship. Could he love her again? Would he?

When she noticed he would slip off for days at a time, she finally decided to follow him. She came to the human realm, saw him jousting. She had tried to warn him then about the dangers, but he waved her off.

And then the worst thing that could happen did. He died in the joust with Finn. It seemed everything she did to avoid that failed. Perhaps the past—or the future—couldn't be changed. Destiny wasn't something one messed with and Elyne had done her fair share of toying.

Now she was in love with Derron, Finn was wrongly accused, and she had befriended a human. And that was only the beginning. Her mother had tracked her down and, knowing her mother, she wouldn't let that go.

"Damn fool," she muttered, though she wasn't sure if she was talking more to herself or him.

She had been foolish, too. She should have never allowed herself to fall in love with the stubborn knight when it was clear he had killed his feelings for her. But sometimes the heart was stronger than the mind and one couldn't really help who one fell in love with.

"I may be a damn fool..." Derron said, his eyes still closed and his voice soft, "but you're the one sitting here with me."

"I thought you were sleeping." Irritation immediately crawled through her.

He blinked his eyes open and looked at her—really looked—for perhaps the first time in a long while. His gaze was compelling, magnetic yet dark and unfathomable as he paused on her face. It was as though he stripped her bare, studying her with a curious intensity she'd not seen before. Her heart did an audible *ka-thud* and it took all her self-control not to squirm.

"You don't have to stay here, Elyne. I'll be fine."

"You will not. That surgeon said he's not sure if you'll live through the night." That's what she feared, too. He would die and she would lose him again.

"Don't sound too happy about that." He closed his eyes, as if speaking took effort. The injury had taken a lot out of him.

"Oh, shut it," she snapped. "You know why I'm here."

"Do I?"

"Aye, of course. I have to protect the Otherworld's interest."

"The betrothal is broken, Elyne. There is no interest to protect. Unless you're here for another reason." He cracked one eye open and wiggled his eyebrows.

As if she would ever admit to that. "No. Not at all." She gave him a thin-lipped smile. "Why did you come back?"

"I don't know. I guess I really wanted to win the tournament." He grinned widely then, showing off his dimples.

"You're crazy. Why do you insist on trying to kill yourself in tournament?"

"Why do you insist on meddling in human affairs?"

She didn't answer because she didn't know the answer.

"Elyne, I'm sorry if I hurt you," he said, changing subjects so abruptly it made her head spin. "I never intended to. I hope you know that."

She wasn't sure how to respond, so instead she remained silent, wondering where he was going with his apology. He reached for her hand then, slipped his cold fingers into hers.

"I hope we can at least be friends? Let bygones be bygones?"

She looked down at their intertwined fingers. In the years since their rift and then their betrothal, he hadn't touched her. He had always dismissed her and had always had eyes for the fair maidens at tourney.

"Aye, we can," she heard herself say. And did she mean it? Deep down, she thought she did. There was still a glimmer of hope that someday he would change his mind.

"Good, I'm glad." He smiled, released her hand and closed his eyes.

"I'll let you rest."

She rose to leave and as she turned toward the door of the tent, she startled. Her mother stood with a fierce look on her face and a gentle-looking man behind her.

"Move aside, daughter."

Before Elyne could move, Maeve brushed by her in a plume of jasmine and a fluff of silk. She leaned over to Derron, looking at his ashen face, and then pulled back the coverlet. He was bare-chested except for the extraordinarily large bandage across his mid-section. Elyne could see blood oozing through the dressing.

"Hello, Maeve," Derron said without opening his eyes. "Nice of you to join us."

"No thanks to my daughter," she said.

"Don't be so hard on Elyne," Derron said. "She means well."

Elyne couldn't help the beginning of a smile that tipped the corners of her mouth. For the first time, Derron had defended her.

Maeve glanced at Elyne, giving her a look that said *I'll deal with you later* and Elyne's smile faded. "I've brought my healer, Seamus," she said, turning back to Derron. "You won't survive in this barbaric time with the primitive medical advisors they have."

"Very kind of you, your majesty."

"Don't *your majesty* me. You could have died. *Again.* And then where would we be? There would be no heir for your father. No one to take over duties as a Guardian of the Four Treasures. No more Protector of the Otherworld or Knight of the Realm. I told you to stay in the Otherworld but do you listen? No. You come back here and put your life at risk and for what?"

"A jolly good time," he said weakly.

She ignored him, though, and continued. "And as for you..." She swiveled back toward Elyne. "You broke one of the first rules of Fae magic by intentionally bringing a human back in time to change the course of history."

It took a lot of self-control for Elyne to remain calm. She balled her fists. "Derron was dead," Elyne said. "I had to do something, Mother."

"Aye, well, what's done is done and there's no changing it now. You've already messed with history enough, dear daughter. Any more meddling and we'll have a real mess on our hands." Maeve sighed, exasperated. "You should have never sent that woman back in time."

"And I should have never cursed an innocent man to live as a ghost," Elyne snapped back. "Finn was innocent of killing Derron even then and I was too hot-headed to realize it. I sent him back— and Maggie, her name is Maggie—to right that wrong. To keep Derron alive."

"You didn't know what you were doing," Maeve said.

"I had to come back, Mother," Elyne said, tilting her head back and looking down her nose. "But *you* wouldn't understand that."

She thought of Maggie and wondered how she could explain it to her mother. She would never comprehend helping the humans, nor did she approve of Elyne's use of magic in the human realm. She'd altered time, after all. And if Maeve knew she'd use a glamour spell to hide Maggie's true identity while she jousted, there would be all kinds of hell to pay.

"You went back in time for me?" Derron's voice was quiet, unbelieving, as he blinked owlish eyes at Elyne.

Her heart pattered quickly. Aye, she'd changed history for him.

She would move heaven and earth for him. She'd used Maggie to save him. And only now did he realize it. Her cheeks heated.

"For more than six hundred years, you were dead," Elyne explained. "When Finn killed you in the lists I… Well, I cursed him for it."

Time moved differently in the Otherworld than it did in the human realm. Six hundred plus years to a human was more like the beat of a heart to a Fae. She felt her face flush, the roots of her hair tingle. And she knew her glamour was failing. She could never keep it intact when consumed with such fiery emotion.

"Aye, and that's another thing we'll be talking about," Maeve scolded, giving her a stern-faced expression. "You using curses when you've no idea how to use them. Not to mention leaving the Otherworld when I specifically told you not to. Not once, but twice. And using Fae magic *on humans*." She blew out another hasty breath and then slanted her sharp gaze at Derron. "Lucky for us you didn't die in the lists a second time. I suppose that's the one good thing that came out of all this. I need you in the Otherworld. Our problems there are real."

"Hold on a minute, will you?" Derron's gaze never left Elyne's as he pressed his hand against his side where he'd been wounded. It took shear strength of will for her to stand still and not fidget under his stare. "I'm still trying to get past the whole 'Elyne cursed Finn because I died' thing."

Seamus cleared his throat, wringing his hands, his face lined with worry. He obviously wanted to interrupt but was too afraid of his queen's wrath to do so.

"As soon as you're healed, I need your help as Protector of the Otherworld. A few Fae nobles have disappeared and I want to know why."

"Fae nobles? Who has disappeared?" Elyne asked, alarm in her voice.

"That doesn't concern you, daughter."

Derron's response was a groan.

"Your majesty?" Seamus pleaded.

"Quite right. We'll discuss it later. Now, Seamus, see to Derron before the poor man dies." She snapped her fingers and the healer got to work.

"That's how you expect everyone to respond, isn't it, Mother?" Elyne asked. "You snap your fingers and everyone jumps to do your bidding."

"I've had just about enough of your insolence, Elyne."

"Ladies, please," Seamus said. "I cannot do good work with you two bickering."

"My apologies, Seamus. Please carry on," Maeve said but she gave Elyne a glare that spoke volumes.

There will be consequences.

It put an end to their discussion but not for long, Elyne knew. Maeve would never let it go, nor would Elyne. The very fact her mother told her that it "didn't concern" her bothered her greatly. She was crown princess, due to inherit the throne of the Otherworld. What wouldn't concern her?

She shoved away the disturbing thoughts of her kingdom and her mother and watched as Seamus sat on the bed next to Derron. He peeled away the crude bandage to reveal the jagged wound that went across his chest. It was ugly, red, and already festering. Infection had set in and quickly. Probably because he was Fae and the tools the surgeon used hadn't been sterilized.

The Fae body would never be able to sustain this type of injury. It wasn't built for that, nor would sewing him up save his life. He would die within the hour and every Fae in the tent knew that. Even Derron. That's why he'd tried to make peace with her. To ease his conscience.

Seamus placed his hands on Derron's wound and closed his eyes, lifted his head toward the heavens. A shimmering blue-white light glowed under his palms and Derron grunted. The light grew in intensity before it finally exploded with a blinding brightness and then disappeared. When Seamus removed his hands, the wound on Derron's chest was completely gone. Not even a faint tell-tale pink line was there.

Elyne exhaled a breath of relief.

"I trust you will stay out of the lists now, Sir Derron," Maeve said. "That's not a request."

"Aye, your majesty."

"I want to see you back at the Otherworld." She turned on Elyne. "And you, too."

Queen Maeve and her healer were gone in the blink of an eye. Elyne glanced at Derron, who sat up on his elbows, staring at the space the queen vacated.

"Are you going?" he asked.

Elyne mulled over the question for a long moment, already knowing what the answer would be. If she defied her mother's orders again, she really would banish her.

"No."

Derron laughed and stood, the coverlets falling away to reveal his brawny torso and the thin breeches he wore that hugged every curve and muscle. She looked away.

"Me, either. Now, let's go find who tried to kill me."

Chapter 15

Maggie left the hospital tent to go to Finn. She knew he'd been thrown in the stocks, but where was a mystery. After asking questions, she learned he was in the center of the market, on display for all to see.

She hurried through the square, pushing past people, trying desperately not to inhale the scent of unwashed bodies in close proximity. There he was, in the middle of the square, his hands and head in the stocks while people threw rotten vegetables at him. Infuriated, she hurried to him, stood in front of him.

"Stop it. All of you!"

"Maggie?"

She bent down to him, grasped his hand and squeezed. "I'll get you out of here, Finn."

"Ye shouldna be here," he said. "Get back to the pavilion, where it's safe."

"No, Finn. I'm not leaving you."

Something cold and slimy crashed into the side of her head. She flinched, reached up and touched dampness in her hair. When she glanced down at the ground, she saw the remains of a spoiled peach. She turned back to the crowd surrounding the stocks. A small boy looked up at her, smiled sweetly, and then chunked another rotten peach at her. It hit her square in the chest and splattered at her feet.

"Enough." She put her hands up in surrender. "This man isn't the one you should be angry with. Sir Finian would never have tipped his lances."

"He tried to kill that knight," someone shouted.

The crowed agreed with a hearty cheer.

"He should be hanged."

"His lances were tipped. It's against the Code."

"That knight is already dead."

A boisterous roar of anger burst through the crowd. Maggie

scanned the faces, trying to see who said it. She wouldn't be surprised if it was Litonshire himself or one of his hired henchmen. The crowd surged forward, demanding blood for blood. She stood in front of Finn, her heart pounding wildly, wondering what to do. She would be trampled if they had their way.

"Go, lass." She heard Finn, his voice quiet and weak from behind her. "Get out of here while ye still can."

"No, Finn. I'll not leave you." She said it over her shoulder, hoping he could hear her over the din.

"'Tis too late for me," he said. "Go."

But Maggie refused and was about to object once again when the crowd suddenly stilled. And parted. And there, standing in the middle of them all was Sir Derron, holding a sword by his side, wearing clean clothes and looking healthy as a horse. Elyne stood behind him, her arms crossed over her chest. Maggie wondered if she had anything to do with Derron's miraculous recovery.

"This man is no criminal," Sir Derron said.

He looked and sounded different. Maggie couldn't quite put her finger on the change. It was as though the flighty knight of the Otherworld she knew before was gone and instead in his place was a serious man. One who knew what he wanted and how to get it. He walked toward the stocks, his piercing gaze on the two guards on either side of Finn.

"Release him," Derron ordered.

"Only Lord Litonshire can order the prisoner's release," one of the guards said.

"Lord Litonshire is responsible for McCullough's tipped lances," Derron said. As soon as the words were out of his mouth, a collective gasp echoed through the crowd. "Now, release him."

When neither guard moved, Derron held up his sword, pointed it at his throat. "I do not wish to spill your blood, but I will if pressed."

Maggie grinned from ear to ear. Elyne's expression remained impassive as she looked on.

The guard reached for his keys and unlocked the stocks. As soon as Finn was free, Maggie reached for him. He faltered when he tried to take a step. She slipped an arm around his waist, helped him to stand.

"Are you all right?" she asked.

"Bloody bastards," Finn muttered but nodded in answer to her question.

"He's injured," she said to Elyne and Derron.

"Let's get him back to the tent," Elyne said and turned on the toe of her silk slipper.

The crowd remained parted as they headed through it, leaving the stocks and the guards behind. But Maggie knew Litonshire would discover Finn had been released and come after him again.

Derron moved to the other side of Finn and helped Maggie shoulder his weight.

"I don't understand," Maggie said, puffing with the exertion. "I thought Derron's injuries were life-threatening."

"They were," Derron answered.

"My mother came with her healer," Elyne said, and she sounded sour.

"How do ye know Litonshire tipped the lances?" Finn asked.

"We don't," Elyne said. "At least, not for certain. We don't have proof but I have suspicion."

"We can get proof," Maggie said. "He hired those strong-arms to kidnap me. He must have hired someone to switch the lances, too. Maybe the same guys."

"Ye are to stay away from him," Finn said to Maggie. "And 'twould be wise if you all did."

"Not a chance," Maggie said. "He tried to kill you. And when that didn't work, he tried to have you arrested for something you didn't do. Not to mention he kidnapped me."

"'Tis why I want ye to stay away from the lout."

They reached Finn's tent in the pavilion. With some relief, Maggie released Finn and let him sink onto his bed. She pulled up his tunic to see black and purple bruises on his ribcage. She was alarmed at the swelling.

"He needs the healer," Maggie said. "Where's Geoffrey or Fergus?"

"Worthless squires," Finn grumbled. "Likely they're off in the gambling tents or drinking away their silver."

Maggie turned to Elyne. "Can't your mother help Finn?"

She snorted. "Clearly, you don't know my mother. She's not into helping humans."

"I'll find the healer," Derron said.

He gave Elyne a passing glance before leaving the tent. Maggie caught it and wondered what it all meant. She couldn't dwell on that now, though, she had other problems.

"Elyne and I are going to see if we can get some evidence on Litonshire and his cronies."

Finn reached for her, grasped her by the wrist. "Dinna tempt fate, lass. He's caused us enough trouble already. As soon as I can get back on my feet, I plan to finish the tournament."

Maggie kept her eyes on Finn, unwilling to look at Elyne for fear her reaction would give her away. How could she break the news to Finn that he'd been disqualified from the tournament and Litonshire had already sent men to his lands in Scotland? That he'd already lost everything.

"Why do ye look at me like that, lass? As though I'm on my deathbed."

"Tell him, Maggie. He needs to know," Elyne said.

Maggie swallowed the bile that rose in her throat. Her gut burned.

Finn glanced from Elyne back to her. "Maggie?"

"Finn, you've been banned from the rest of the tournament."

She braced herself for his explosion but it never came. He stared at her for a long horrid moment before releasing her wrist, closing his eyes and leaning back into the pillow. He seemed utterly defeated. It hurt Maggie to see him that way. That wasn't Finn. He was her big, strong knight. He was the one that could make everything right. It hurt her even more to tell him the next bit.

"There's more. Before the end of the last match, Litonshire dispatched his men to your lands in Scotland to take them as payment for your gambling debts."

"The bastard will steal my lands no matter what we do," Finn said. His hands fisted.

"That only proves he intended to have you arrested in the lists," Maggie said. "He'd already sent his men before your match even started. He *knew* your lances were tipped and he didn't care who he killed to get you out of the way. I intend to make him pay for what he's done to you."

Finn smiled faintly. "Ah, lass...ye are tenacious, indeed."

"And I'm going to help her," Elyne said.

Maggie's head snapped to the Fae princess. She sounded as serious as she looked. "Really?"

"Aye, really. As soon as Derron returns with the healer, we'll find that vile Litonshire and take care of him once and for all."

It was the best news Maggie had heard all day.

"I'm coming with ye," Finn said. He rose and winced with the pain.

"No, Finn. You need to stay here and recover." Maggie put a hand on his chest and tried to shove him back down.

"She's right. If Litonshire sees you, it'll only add fuel to his already inflamed fire," Elyne pointed out. "Maggie and I can handle this."

Finn gave them both a dubious look. "I canna allow two ladies to go alone. Especially after what happened to ye, lassie."

"We won't be alone," Maggie said cheerfully. "Sir Derron will be with us."

"As I said, I canna allow ye two to go alone. Especially with that overly friendly Faery." This time Finn got to his feet, stripped off his dirty tunic and glanced around for a clean one.

"Derron has been ordered back to Faery," Elyne said. "As have I. This time for good. Once we have this mess cleared up with the earl, we're leaving."

"Why do ye tell me this?"

"Because Derron is no threat to your Maggie," Elyne said.

There was such a deafening silence in the tent, Maggie was sure she could hear a pin drop. If in fact there was a pin to be dropped. She stopped breathing as she glanced at Finn, who looked at her with that smoldering gaze. It made the roots of her hair tingle and the pit of her stomach twist in sweet anticipation.

He wanted her.

She loved him.

It was that simple.

"Aye, then. I'll stay for now." He never took his gaze off her as he spoke. "But if that bastard harms her, I'll kill him."

"And he would deserve that," Elyne said with a nod. "We start at dawn."

As Finn prepared for bed, he heard Sir Derron calling for him outside his tent. He stepped out into the cool evening air and greeted the Fae knight.

"Lord Litonshire knows you live and you've escaped," Derron said. "He intends to kill you."

"Does he? Not if I get to him first," Finn said. "What's stopping him from coming after me?"

Derron gave a half shrug. "He wishes to duel you. Litonshire likes to flaunt his power. He'll undoubtedly make sure there's a nice crowd there. It would be wise of you to leave tournament tonight before he can find you."

"Nay," Finn said. "I havna run from a fight. I willna start now. I will fight him."

"I thought you might say that," Derron said with a nod. "And I expected it. Allow me to help."

"Why should I be taking help from ye?" As he looked at the Fae knight, suspicion crawled through him. He had never been on good terms with Derron from the first time they jousted and he'd beaten him. He didn't want to start now.

"Because I can allow you to live," Derron said.

Finn raised an eyebrow. "Aye? With that hocus-pocus magic of yeres?" He shook his head. "I'll be passing on that."

"Don't be foolish, Finn," Derron said. "It's the very 'hocus-pocus' that got you here in the first place. If it hadn't been for Elyne bringing you and Maggie back, you wouldn't be alive."

Sir Derron had a point with which Finn hated to agree. Maggie had truly saved his life over the last few days. She had stood by his side, refused to believe the rumors and was determined to uncover the truth. If it hadn't been for her, he would still be stuck in ghostland, roaming the ruins of his castle.

"Aye, then. What did ye have in mind?"

Derron pulled green herbs tied in a bunch from his pocket. "Sprinkle this in your ale and drink an entire tankard."

"What is it?"

"Just a little herb to help you live should you become mortally wounded. It'll speed your recovery."

"Does it work then?"

Derron smiled. "You'll have to trust me, Finn."

He held the herbs in the palm of his hand, examining them. They looked strangely like a bunch of four-leaf clovers with sprigs of something that smelled like rosemary. "I dinna ken how this will help me and I shouldna be trusting the likes of ye." He looked at Derron then, who still smiled somewhat smugly. "But I suppose I have no choice, aye?"

"If you want to live through the duel with Litonshire, aye. You have no choice."

It was against his better judgment, but Finn decided he'd rather err on the side of caution than take his chances. "All right, then. I'll take yere herbs, faery."

"Good luck, Finn. Maggie is a good woman," he said. "Even though I don't think you deserve her, she loves you and she's willing to stay with you."

"How do ye ken this?"

Derron laughed. "Are you so blind that you can't see that for yourself?"

He wasn't. But he also wasn't willing to accept that she wanted to stay with him, in his time. He had prepared himself for their eventual separation. That she would go home to her twenty-first century and he would never see her again. Even though it pained him to see her go, he would let her if that's what she wished.

"It's up to the lassie to decide if she wants to stay here. I canna and willna ask her."

"Pity," Derron said, shaking his head, then clapped him on the shoulder. "Good luck on the morrow."

Finn clasped the herbs in his hand and watched the Fae walk away, then glanced at Maggie's tent across from his. He imagined her sleeping, wanted to go to her. He resisted and went in search of a tankard of ale.

Maggie's sleep had been restless. She had tossed most of the night in her tent across from Finn's, worrying about him. But Elyne insisted she not stay with him. And Finn thought it best, too, in light of everything that had happened over the last few days. So, with much objection, she had returned to her own tent with Elyne.

It didn't mean she had to like it.

She was still awake at the first twitter of morning birds. Still awake even when first light started to pierce the cloth of the tent. She could no longer lie there and sat up, shoving aside the bedclothes and dressed quickly. She peered into the other small chamber of the tent and saw Elyne still sleeping. Odd, Maggie thought. She'd never seen the Fae princess sleep. Or eat for that matter. She had assumed Elyne did all that elsewhere. Or not at all. She wasn't sure how the Fae managed and neither of them had exactly shared that.

As she waited for the sun to rise a little higher, she picked up the quill and parchment Elyne had given her. She glanced over the research notes she had started and smiled. Her words seemed so silly and naïve now as she read over them. She'd learned so much being with Finn. And she wondered vaguely what the history books would say since Derron hadn't died in the tournament after all.

She made a mental note to ask Elyne how all this change would affect that.

Picking up the quill, she dipped it in the inkwell and selected a clean piece of parchment. Since she'd already made up her mind to stay here with Finn—and she sincerely hoped he'd have her—she composed the letter to her father.

She told him the truth about where she was, though she managed to leave out a few parts he probably wouldn't understand. He would still worry about her and wonder if she was all right. All she could do was hope he would forgive her for never coming home again. She hoped he would understand.

She folded the letter, wishing she had some wax to seal it. She tucked it safely in her skirt pocket, intending to give it to Elyne later when all this was over. While she waited for Elyne to rise, Maggie tiptoed past her across to Finn's tent to check on him and make sure he was all right.

As she stepped into the tent, she saw Geoffrey there, fiddling with the lances. She thought it peculiar the way he hunched over them. He lined up three in front of him. She noticed then three behind him and how they were slightly different from the others. They looked well-worn while the other three, the ones he so carefully aligned, looked to be newer.

"Geoffrey?"

At the sound of her voice, he jumped. Immediately, his face turned bright red as he shot to his feet, wringing his hands in front of him.

"I was—I was just…" He panted and sweat appeared on his brow. "Are ye going to tell Sir Finian, my lady?"

Maggie's brow wrinkled. "Tell him what?"

"I shouldna have done it, my lady." His breath hitched and she thought he might burst into tears. "But the earl said if I didn't do it, he'd kill my mam and da."

"Do what?" Her heart fluttered and a fist clenched her stomach into a knot. "Lord Litonshire made you do what, Geoffrey?"

He swallowed so hard, his Adam's apple bobbed in his throat. "He made me switch 'em."

The admission hit her hard. The invisible fist clenching her stomach squeezed and she pressed her hand there. "Oh, Geoffrey."

Tears went down his youthful face, then, streaking his pale skin. "I had to do it. He told me he'd kill them."

All Maggie could do was wrap the young boy in her arms and pat him on the back. "It's all right. We'll get it sorted out. Tell me exactly when this happened."

"Before his last match. The earl came to me, told me his men had taken over the laird's castle and lands. My mam works in the kitchens and my da in the stables. He said if I dinna do what he told me he would kill them both. He already had the lances and told me to switch them," Geoffrey explained. "I dinna want Sir Finian to ken."

"Why?" Maggie asked. "He'll understand why you did it."

"Nay. I betrayed him." Geoffrey pulled away. "He'll punish me for it."

"I willna punish ye, laddie."

Maggie wondered how long Finn had been standing there, eavesdropping. He must have heard every word for he was dressed in a fresh tunic and breeches, a sword in one hand.

"'Tis time to take care of the earl once and for all," Finn said.

"Where are you going?" Maggie demanded.

"To find him," he said. "And when I do, it will be the end of him and I'm getting my land back."

"Then I'm coming with you," Maggie said. "Because I know I can't talk you out of it."

"And I'm going, too." Elyne had joined the party, standing just inside the tent.

"As am I." Derron appeared, seemingly out of nowhere, brandishing his own sword.

The beginnings of a smile quirked the corners of Finn's mouth. "Aye, then, we'll all go. Geoffrey, yere coming, too. For when we find the magistrate, I want ye to explain to him what Litonshire made ye do."

As they left the tent and headed through the pavilion, Maggie couldn't help but feel as if they were the angry townspeople headed after the monster preying on innocents. All they lacked were pitchforks and torches.

It didn't take long to find Lord Litonshire. He sat on a cushion in the grandstand overseeing the day's jousting matches in the lists. They arrived as one round finished up with Sir Drake. Finn, holding his sword, walked to the middle of the lists and turned to the earl. The normally rowdy crowd quieted and the earl and Finn stared each other down.

"Ah, so you do live," Litonshire said at last.

Maggie scanned the crowd, watched as Sir Drake dismounted from his horse. The lists were full of dirty-faced commoners and pious nobles all cheering for their favored knight.

"Aye, I live," Finn said.

"'Tis a shame," Litonshire replied, glancing over his cuticles. "You should have hanged after killing that innocent knight in the lists yesterday."

"I dinna kill him," Finn said and Maggie was so glad he sounded smug.

Litonshire laughed, nasally. "Sir Finian, everyone here saw it happen with their own eyes."

"He lives," Finn replied and glanced toward Derron with an imperceptible nod.

"Aye, indeed I do." He walked into the lists, stood next to Finn.

Through the crowd, Maggie could hear the collective murmurs of those wondering if it really was the same knight who had jousted against Finn the day before or not. Some gasped. Some clapped.

"And ye've taken something that is rightfully mine. I want it back."

Litonshire jumped to his feet, pointing at Finn. "*You* have taken something of mine. My sister was dear to me and you destroyed all that she was."

Maggie balled her fists. "You are a filthy liar, Litonshire."

"Maggie, stay out of this," Finn warned.

"Aye, Sir Finian, tell your *bitch* to stay out of it. This is a discussion between men."

The color warmed Finn's face and he pursed his lips. But anger boiled under Maggie's skin and she took a step forward. That was as far as she got when Elyne grabbed her arms and held her in place.

"I challenged you once to a duel. Now I insist upon it," Litonshire said. "To avenge my sister and restore her good name."

"I accept," Finn said without hesitation. "Should I win, my debt to ye will be forgiven and my lands returned to me. If your men have harmed any one of my people, then ye will pay dearly for that."

"And should I win?" Litonshire asked, looking down his nose at the Scottish knight.

"Then you keep my lands," Finn said.

A wave of apprehension swept through Maggie. Was he so certain he could win against Litonshire?

"And you give me Lady Margaret."

Apprehension turned to sickness in the blink of an eye. Bile rose in her throat at those words. There was no way in hell she would willingly go with that vile man. She couldn't bear to lose Finn if Litonshire didn't fight fair.

"Finn, no," Maggie said. "Don't do it."

"Do we have an accord?" Litonshire asked, ignoring her outburst.

"We do," Finn said without hesitation.

Maggie stared at him, dumbstruck. She couldn't believe he had agreed to such terms. His gaze locked with hers, then, and she could read the pain, the determination, and the hatred of Litonshire in that one glance.

"Then let us proceed to the fighting arena. No armor, to make things more interesting. Bring my sword." He barked the last to his squire who hovered nearby.

Litonshire left his perch in the grandstand. Sir Drake hurried to Finn, his armor clinking and glinting in the morning light as he fell in step with him.

"Finn, are you mad, man?" he asked. "He'll kill you."

"Aye, he'll try. He's taken enough, Drake," Finn said. "And I'll no' let him take any more." He looked at Maggie again.

Her heart pounded so hard she could hear the beats in her ears. He meant every word. She knew it as she knew he wouldn't fail her. He wouldn't die and let her go to Litonshire.

Finn paused in front of her, looking down at her with such tenderness it made her turn to mush and melt. He took her chin in his hand, his gaze never leaving hers.

"This will all be over soon, lass," he said. "And when it is, I intend to take ye back to my castle."

She trembled and wondered if he felt the vibration in his hand.

She found she didn't care so much if he did. Desire and intent filled that molten silver gaze of his and she thought she could dive in, swim in those silver pools until eternity.

"I love you, Finn." She hadn't intended to blurt the words.

He didn't respond. Instead, he bent, kissed her as though it were the last time. His mouth felt warm and soft on hers, his tongue tasting her and she leaned into him, letting her body curve into his. She slipped her arms around his neck, held on to him, never wanting to let him go. He slid his arms around her waist, pulled her close, his hands pressing into the small of her back.

"Please don't die," she said when they broke.

He chuckled. "I'll no' die, lass. Ye can count on that."

Releasing her, he walked with a purposeful stride toward the arena. Maggie, Sir Drake, Derron and Elyne all fell in step behind him, a small entourage following him to his duel. Maggie preferred to think of them as his personal cheering section. A crowd had already gathered there, Maggie noticed, some taking bets on who would win.

Finn stepped into the area. Litonshire was already there, wearing a white linen tunic and breeches and holding a short sword. Ready to fight. The arena master stood between them, a barrier to their rage.

"Sword at the ready," he said, holding the white flag shoulder high. "Begin."

He dropped the flag and vaulted over the railings to get out of their way in a hurry. Finn and Litonshire circled each other, each one waiting for the other to make the first move. Maggie could see he took his time, waiting for Litonshire's first swing. Finn practiced patience, watching him carefully so when he did finally swing, he anticipated the first move.

Their swords clashed with a resounding clang and Maggie winced. Finn, however, didn't flinch. He didn't as much as blink. When Litonshire pulled his sword back in a great, slow arc, Finn was prepared. Afternoon sun glinted off the steel of Finn's blade as metal met metal with a *clank* in a musical cadence. Finn threw all his weight forward, lunging into Litonshire and shoving him back several steps until he came up against the railing.

The crowd rooting for Finn cheered.

"This is maddening," Maggie said to Elyne. "Can't you do something to help?"

"I can't interfere," Elyne said. "If I do, I'll have my mother's wrath on me again."

"It's against Fae law to interfere," Derron put in. He leaned around Maggie and looked at Elyne, his eyes glinting with some humor. "But you've already broken that law."

"As though you have any place to talk," Elyne snapped. "You who play in jousting tournaments…"

Maggie tuned them both out, never taking her gaze off the duel in front of her.

Litonshire shoved Finn off him and regained his footing, thrusting forward and swinging once again in a wide arc. Finn anticipated that again and matched his movements. The earl's blade never even came close to Finn. Maggie could see the annoyance on Litonshire's face as he tried hard to get to Finn. The burly Scotsman clearly had the advantage against the thin earl.

Litonshire paused, taking a step back, his chest heaving with the exertion. Finn looked as though he hadn't even broken a sweat.

"Still want to fight me?" Finn asked.

"You're still alive, aren't you?"

Litonshire lurched forward but it seemed as though he moved in slow motion. Finn cut his sword toward him, making direct contact with him on his wrist. The earl shrieked with the pain as he dropped his sword in the dirt and Finn took advantage of the man's hesitation. He swiped his sword in a wide arc the earl managed to miss by jumping backward. But he lost his footing and down he went.

With Litonshire on the ground, unable to move, Finn stood over him and pointed his sword in his face, planting his foot on his chest. The earl's sword had fallen out of reach and he lay there, defenseless.

"Do ye yield?"

"Never," Litonshire said, blood trickling out of the corner of his mouth.

"Ye lost, Litonshire," Finn said. "Why can ye no' see that?"

"I haven't lost yet," he spat. "You're still breathing, aren't you?"

Finn glared down at him for a long moment, removed his foot and then stepped back. "Ye aren't worth the blood on my sword."

One of his squires entered the ring to help him up as Litonshire laughed. "You weak fool. You show mercy to me?"

He snatched his short sword from his squire, who scurried out of the way, and attacked Finn. But Finn had good reflexes and while Maggie cringed, they locked blades again. She held her breath, watching the stand-off. She caught a glint of something in his other hand and saw the flash of the blade before she could shout out a warning.

Litonshire stabbed Finn in the side under his armpit, a sickening grin on his pinched face. Finn released his hold on his sword and stumbled back a few steps. Maggie shouted his name as she charged the railing. Elyne and Derron held her back, though, keeping her from vaulting over. The crowd inhaled a collective gasp and Litonshire held the dagger dripping Finn's blood.

Hot tears trickled down her cheeks. She watched Finn on his knees, holding his side and blood seeping through his fingers. Fergus charged through the crowd, entering the arena to help his laird.

"It appears, Sir Finian, your woman and your lands are now mine. I daresay I'm more interested in your woman than your lands."

He cut his gaze to her then with such lust in his eyes, she shuddered in the heat. Cold dread pressed against her as he walked toward her, dropping both the dagger and the sword in the sand. When he reached her, he took her face in his hands, his palms clammy against her tear-streaked cheeks.

"Now, my dear, give me a kiss to seal the deal."

When he leaned in, Maggie leaned back and slapped him, her hand leaving a red print on his face. She hadn't even realized Derron and Elyne had released her and now she wondered where the two Fae had disappeared. She knew they weren't by her any longer, nor was the crowd pressing around her. They were giving her and the earl a wide berth.

Litonshire scowled and she could see the vein popping out in his forehead that told her she'd gone too far. He reached for her in a lightning-fast move, grabbed her by the upper arms and jerked her toward him so hard she hit her hip bones against the railing and winced.

"Bitch." His rancid breath wafted over her face. "You will learn to do as I command."

"I would rather fall on a sword," she said, her voice quivering, "than be with you."

His jaw clenched, his grip tightened and he pulled her closer, coming in for the kiss he was determined to get. She squeezed her eyes shut, swallowed the heated bile that rose in her throat but the kiss never came. His grip on her arms loosened.

When she opened her eyes, she watched Litonshire slink to the ground, a dagger at the base of his neck and, standing behind him, blood staining his tunic, was Finn.

Chapter 16

Maggie stared at Lord Litonshire's lifeless body. He was dead. It was over. Finn was free and, most importantly, he was alive. A hush had settled over the crowd as she looked from the earl to Finn and back again. How was Finn still alive? Litonshire had *stabbed* him in the side. She saw it happen. He still had the tear in his tunic, the blood staining the linen and the dagger in his hand. He looked fit and well. Not pasty-faced with a sickly pallor like she expected.

"Finn?"

"Aye, lass, 'tis all over now." He dropped the dagger in the dirt and it landed with a muffled thud.

"I see you've killed the Earl of Litonshire."

Finn immediately bowed low and she noticed then the rest of the crowd that had remained so silent were also bowing or curtsying. She realized why when she turned to see the tall, astute-looking man with the piercing dark eyes, a nose shaped like a ski slope, and a chin and mouth covered in a silvery beard and mustache.

King Edward.

He wore a long velvet tunic in deep scarlet, belted at the waist with long sleeves and gold thread embroidered at the hem and the end of the sleeves. Over this, he had a fur-lined cloak of the softest gray Maggie had ever seen fastened with a large gold brooch. He had a sword strapped to his side, dark hose and pointed-toe shoes. He looked every bit the part of king as compared to the nobles she'd seen wandering through the tournament.

Trying to hide her surprise, she curtsied low. But she still managed to take note of the two men flanking either side of him. Elyne and Derron stood nearby, too, and Maggie had to wonder if the two Fae had anything to do with King Edward's sudden appearance. She wouldn't put anything past those two.

"Your majesty," Finn greeted.

Maggie flashed Elyne a questioning glance. She smiled, her eyes sparkling with mischief.

"Lord Neville tells me Lord Litonshire has been quite the problem during this tournament," King Edward said, nodding toward the tall man standing next to him.

Lord Neville wasn't exactly an attractive man, but he wasn't ugly either. His face was rather common, Maggie thought. His black eyes matched his black hair. His clothes were of the same finery as King Edward's, though not nearly as pristine-looking. His tunic looked woolen instead of velvet and was a rich brown. He, too, sported the beard and mustache combo like the king.

"He's been impossible to control, your majesty," Lord Neville said in a pinched tone. "I've heard numerous complaints. I daresay it was a mistake to allow him to run the tournament."

King Edward's gaze flickered from Finn to the dead earl and back again. Maggie's heart stuttered, fear coursing through her. What would the king do? Would he have Finn arrested for murder and tossed back into the stocks? Or worse…put through some horrid medieval torture?

"Indeed, I believe you are correct." Edward sighed then, sounding resigned. "And I had hoped to see at least some of the tournament before returning to France."

"It was my fault, your majesty. I allowed him to get out of hand," Neville said. "I take full responsibility for the havoc he's caused."

"Nonsense, Lord Neville. The man was a menace and quite a pain in my arse, to be sure." Edward's gaze had never left Finn and now he stepped closer to him so they were a mere twenty feet apart. "I understand, Sir Finian, you owed him a large debt?"

"Aye, 'tis true," Finn admitted.

"And you lost your estates to him in a game of Hazard?" Edward asked.

Finn nodded. "Aye, your majesty."

The king snorted, something Maggie thought she'd never hear a king do, and nearly burst out laughing. She bit the inside of her cheek to maintain control.

"Only a drunkard could lose to the earl," Edward said. "I understand, Sir Finian, you are the best at Hazard."

He swallowed so hard Maggie could see his throat working. What could the king be up to? It didn't sound like anything good.

"I'm a fair player," Finn replied.

"Aye, then, mayhap someday I'll play against you." Edward's laugh was deep and hearty in his chest as he slapped Finn on the back. Maggie could almost be certain she heard the collective exhalation from the crowd around them. "I received a letter from Lady Juliet delivered to me by one of Lord Brian's squires. It detailed the monstrosities the man inflicted on the lady. I know what a knave and a lout he was."

Maggie's head whipped around to Elyne, who stood with her arms crossed over her chest, looking smug. The Fae never ceased to amaze her. How did she manage to pull *that* off? She must have intercepted the squire to help speed things along.

"Lord Neville, what do you propose we do with Sir Finian here? He's a Scot, after all. Should we throw him in the stocks?"

"He should be a decorated hero for ridding the land of that plague-sore boil," Lord Neville replied, his snootiness apparent in his tone.

"Aye, quite right." Edward nodded in agreement, apparently dismissing the stocks idea. "He saved me from a lengthy investigation which would undoubtedly have resulted in Litonshire's death nonetheless. You have my hearty thanks, sir knight."

Finn blinked and glanced at Maggie. She gave him a wide smile and a thumbs-up. One corner of his mouth tipped up as he looked back at the king.

"I've dispatched a garrison to your family lands and ordered Litonshire's men removed. Your debt has been forgiven, Sir Finian, and your lands restored."

King Edward pinned her with a dark, sultry gaze. One of curiosity mixed with question and admiration. "I understand, my lady, you are the one who arranged the secret marriage of Lord Brian and Lady Juliet."

"I did, your majesty." Maggie dipped a quick curtsy. Cold tendrils of fear slipped through her as she nodded. She wasn't sure if she would face the king's wrath or approval.

"Quite a bold move, my lady. One that could have surely gotten you killed. Yet you risked your life to save hers. I find that most intriguing."

She expelled a silent breath, the fear subsiding with relief as it rushed through her. "It was nothing, your majesty. Anyone with two eyes could see Lady Juliet needed to get away from her brother."

"Aye, well, at any rate, I should be quite angry about it but I find I can't muster up the strength. It was a fine thing you did. Now, let's go and enjoy the rest of tourney, shall we?"

"We have the finals, your majesty," Lord Neville said. "Allow me to show you to the castle. The last match will be on the morrow." He turned to one of his men, pointing at Litonshire's body. "And have that removed, will you?"

Maggie pressed her hand against her stomach, still tied in knots, as the king, Lord Neville and their remaining entourage headed off to the lists. Lords and kings made her nervous.

"Thank goodness that's over," Elyne exclaimed. "I thought the king would never leave."

"You're the one who brought him," Derron chided.

Maggie ignored them both and turned her attention to Finn. "I don't understand what happened, Finn." She peeled back the edge of his tunic to see the stab wound that should have been there wasn't there at all. "How is it you've healed?"

"*Och*, lass, 'tis not for ye to fash yere bonnie head about." He grasped her fingers in hers, moving her hand away from the wound that wasn't there.

When she looked at up at him, he was smiling. Finn rarely smiled. But he looked as though a weight had been lifted off his shoulders and it probably had now that he didn't have Litonshire's gambling debt hanging over his head and his lands had been restored.

"Did Elyne have anything to do with that?" She reeled toward the Fae princess. "You told me you couldn't heal humans." She tried not to sound accusatory but it didn't work.

"That's right, I can't," Elyne said with a nod. "And I didn't."

"She had nothing to do with it," Finn said.

"Then how did you manage it?" she asked. "I know you're not immortal."

"Nay, he's not," Derron interjected. "But he did drink the herbs I gave him."

"You didn't." Elyne propped her hands on her slender hips and glared at Derron. "You interfered."

"Oh, as if you haven't, *your highness*. Look at the mess you created." Derron swept his hands around the tournament field. "If it hadn't been for you, none of this would have happened."

"If it hadn't been for Elyne, Finn would still be dead, I'd be lost in Scotland in the future, and I'd have never met him," Maggie said.

Derron raised a brow. "I see."

"And, as I recall, you'd be dead too, wouldn't you, Sir Derron?" Maggie asked.

"You have a point, my lady," he said, bowing with a flourish. "I believe we have a tournament to attend. I don't want to miss the finals tomorrow, nor do I wish to miss banquet tonight." He turned his attention to Maggie, grasping her hand and kissing her fingertips. "Lady Margaret, it's been a delight."

"I'm sure it has," Finn said, putting his large frame between her and Derron.

The Fae knight grinned, waved, and headed off toward the pavilion.

"Not so fast. I have a bone to pick with you," Elyne said, falling in step with him.

Once they were gone, Finn slid his arm around Maggie. "Now, lass, there's something we need to discuss. Alone. In my tent."

Maggie's heart fluttered as he gave her a sly smile, desire sparking in the depths of his eyes. "After you, sir."

He swept her up into his arms, walking toward the pavilion as joy bubbled in her laugh and her heart sang with delight. When he reached his tent, neither wasted another moment as they shed their clothes. She was beneath him, contentment and peace flowing between them. She abandoned herself to the high tide of passion raging through her as he kissed her, sighed her name. And when it was all over, he gathered her close. His hands were in her hair while she lay on his chest, her eyelids heavy and threatening sleep.

"Ah, lass, I canna live without ye. I love ye."

She smiled as she drifted into bliss.

On Friday and by order of the king, the tournament finished with the jousting finals. Finn had been disqualified, and even though the king had offered to reinstate him, Finn declined. He'd had enough stress and anxiety through this tournament to want to finish it off. Maggie didn't do a very good job of hiding her relief, either.

Elyne had chastised Derron for his involvement in the tournament, so he sat out. The foursome took a seat in the grandstand to watch Sir Drake try to claim the title as tournament champion.

On the other end of the lists was Sir William Peckham. According to Finn, he was one of his old gambling buddies. Maggie watched as the Englishman put on his helm and reached for his lance. Sir Drake was ready and waiting in the saddle as the heralds announced the two opponents.

King Edward and company sat on the highest seat in the grandstand. Maggie thought they mostly looked bored as they had seemed to have impassive looks on their royal faces. She was just glad Finn was alive and well and sitting next to her.

On the other side of her were Elyne and Derron. They seemed different. As though they had somehow reconciled their differences. Though, according to Elyne, their betrothal was still off. It made Maggie a little sad. She'd tried so hard to get the two together, but she supposed it wasn't to be. The universe, it seemed, had other plans for the Fae princess and knight-errant.

"Now that tournament is over, Maggie, I have to ask you. Am I sending you back to your time or not?" Elyne leaned toward her, her voice low so only Maggie could hear. "I would have asked you yesterday but with all the excitement, it slipped my mind."

"Dinna stay for me, lass," Finn said before she could respond. Apparently, Elyne hadn't kept her voice low enough. "I ken ye had a life there before me. And that's where ye belong. I would understand if ye wanted to go back."

She knew he said it to make it easier on her if she decided to go. When he thought she was sleeping, he had confessed that he loved her and couldn't live without her.

"No, Finn." Maggie shook her head, snuggling closer to him. "Where I belong is here with you. This is my home now. I can't leave you."

His features softened, the smile pulling at the corners of his mouth. That silvery gaze melted as he put his arm around her, pulled her close. "Ah, lass, 'tis good to hear it." He swept a hand through her hair. "I hoped ye'd say that. And that ye'll be coming back to my home with me."

"I'll go anywhere you go, Finn. I love you."

"And I ye, lassie." He rested his hand on the side of her neck, leaned down close until his lips brushed hers.

His mouth overtook hers in a kiss that sealed their love for each other. A kiss Maggie would never forget for the rest of her days. He was hers and she was his and no matter what hardships faced them, they would face them together.

"From the moment ye woke in my arms in my bed," he said when they broke.

She flushed hot, remembering that fateful morning when she realized she wasn't in some strange medieval re-enactment and instead Elyne had sent her back in time to save Finn. That she'd been determined to finish research on her jousting hero, Sir Derron. Who could have foreseen he was actually a knight from the Otherworld? And that Finn really didn't need saving after all?

Now none of that mattered and Sir Derron wasn't anything like the history books reported or what she'd expected. Things were quite different here after all, and she was elated she had decided to stay.

"I intend to marry ye."

"As you should." Maggie grinned.

"Well, I guess that's settled then," Elyne said.

"And the queen will be happy you aren't using any more of your magic tricks," Derron put in, wagging an accusing finger at her.

"Oh, you *had* to bring my mother into this, didn't you?" Elyne's expression was taut and derisive followed quickly by her lips twisting into a cynical smile. "Can we watch the joust now?"

Maggie removed the letter to her father out of her pocket and slipped it to Elyne who nodded, understanding. She would take the letter to her dad and leave it for him so he wouldn't worry about her. It gave Maggie the peace of mind she needed.

She turned back to lists and watched Sir Drake ride toward his opponent for the final time, his lance shattering on the knight's shoulder and knocking him out of the saddle. He claimed his victory and Finn cheered for his friend. Sir Drake won the tournament and would be named champion at the night's banquet.

Maggie smiled, content with the sun on her face, and the bright future ahead. And maybe, just maybe, there would be a royal Fae wedding in it.

Realm of Honor Cast of Characters

The Humans
Sir Finian "Finn" McCullough: Scottish knight
Maggie Chase McCullough: Finn's wife
Sir Drake Attenborough: English knight and jousting hero
Henry Chase: Maggie's father

The Fae
Princess Elyne: crown princess of the Fae Otherworld
Lord Derron: Knight of the Realm, Protector of the Otherworld
Queen Maeve: ruler of the Otherworld and the Seelie Court
Lord Roderick: member of the High Council
Lord Aldun: member of the High Council
Lord Vaughan: member of the High Council
Seamus: healer for the Fae
King Adhamh: the queen's husband who was murdered
Morrigan: Goddess of War
Lord/Dark King Kieran: dark elf bent on human and Otherworld domination
Lord Gawaine: Queen Maeve's high councilor
Dark King Fergus mac Delbaith: dark king of the Unseelie court
Lord Pwyll: Guardian of the Stone of Destiny
Lord Malcolm: Guardian of the Sword of Light and Derron's father
Lord Llewelyn: Guardian of the Club of Dagda
Lord Udrich: Guardian of the Spear of Lugh

The Elves

King Urdithane emar'Rudul: ruler of the Wood Elves

Andahar emar'Rudul: crown prince of the Woodlands Elven throne

Leopold: Wood Elves royal advisor

Eldrin emar'Rudul: brother to Andahar, Elven ranger

Allanna emar'Rudul: sister to Andahar and Elven Princess

Lord Navin emar'Rudul: brother to Andahar, Woodlands Gatekeeper

Lord-Regent Marath: Wood Elves liege lord

Lord Randir: Fire Elf and Laerwen's betrothed

Laerwen emer'Aranhil Bloodfire: Fire Elf and Princess of the Hin'dar Rhule

Hiram: Laerwen's royal advisor

Lady Talaiel: ruler of the Skye Elves

Turin: healer for the Skye Elves

Brom: healer for the Wood Elves

Lord Malack: one of the noble Wood Elves

Queen Lucinda and King Aleron: ruler of the Fire Elves

The Fomorians

Cormac: Fomorian mage forced to help Kieran

Lorcann: Fomorian mage

The Dragons

Ambrielle: the emerald dragon

Aura: the azure dragon

Luna: the silver dragon

Nero: the black dragon

Moon dragons: silver dragons of the Skye Elves

The Realms

Fae Otherworld: home of the Fae, includes Seelie and Unseelie Courts

Woodlands: a humid forest region and home of the Wood Elves
Hin'dar Rhule: dry, arid volcanic region and home of the Fire Elves
Skye Realm in the clouds: home of the Skye Elves and the moon dragons

Human Realm: home for Maggie and Finn

Underworld: where Morrigan was banished

The Races

The Fae: also known as Faeries, a race of magical beings who can alter time and travel from their realm to the human realm.

Fire Elves: Elves who live in the volcanic realm known as the Hin'dar Rhule. Their bodies can withstand the hottest heat of the fires, but the lava is still deadly to them. They seek help from the Wood Elves when the Fomorians destroy their home.

Fomorians: an ancient race of vile creatures who wreak havoc. They were banished to a watery prison but one powerful Fomorian mage managed to break out and free his people so they could rampage once more.

Skye Elves: a reclusive Elven race living among the clouds with their moon dragons. The legend of the Skye Elves says one is as strong as ten men and they are undefeatable in battle.

Wood Elves: Elves who live in the trees of the Woodlands and who had a long-standing Treaty of Separation with the Fae, dividing the two races. The Treaty has since been abolished, uniting the two and allowing them to work together to defeat the evil in the realm.

Sign up and get your free book!

I love interacting with readers and the best way to do that is through email. Sign up for my VIP Reader's List and get a free book, notifications of upcoming releases, join the review team and much, much more. It's a great way for me to connect with you!

You can get the free book by signing up at:
https://www.subscribepage.com/ VIP

Your privacy is important to me. I will never sell or share your email address.

Did you enjoy this book? You can make a difference!

Reviews are an indie author's most powerful marketing tool. Honest reviews help us get noticed by other readers and increase vis- ibility in the marketplace. It's the best way for indie authors like me to be discovered by fabulous readers like you.

If you enjoyed this book, I would be ever so grateful if you could spend a few minutes leaving a review at your favorite e-retailer. It can be as short as you like. And if you're interested in joining my re- view team, email me a note to let me know! I personally answer every email I receive.

Thank you very much!

ALSO BY MICHELLE MILES

Dream Walker
Call of the Dark

Age of Wizards
In the Tower of the Wizard King
On the Hunt for the Wizard King

A Ransom & Fortune Adventure
Highland Fling, Vol 1
Dead of Winter, Vol 2
The Citadel, Vol 3
Lord of the Underworld, Vol 4

Dragon Protectors
Desiring the Dragon Lord
Seducing the Dragon Knight
Tempting Her Dragon Bodyguard

Guardians of Atlantis
Tempting Eden
Seducing Eve
Ravishing Helene
Guardians of Atlantis Box Set

Realm of Honor
One Knight Only
Only for a Knight
A Knight to Remember
A Knight Like No Other
Shadows of the Knight

Coffee House Chronicles
Talk Dirty to Me
Nice Girls Do
Have Yourself a Merry Little Latte
Take Me I'm Yours
Sex, Lust & Martinis

Forever Yours
A Little Taste of Heaven

Shorts and Anthologies
A Dance Among the Faeries, Short Story
Eorwulf, Short Story
The Soul of Sharah, Short Story
Sinfully Sweet, Short Story
Flights of Fantasy: A Collection of Short Stories

Watch for more at www.michellemiles.net

Did you love *One Knight Only?*

Pick up the second book in the Realm of Honor series, *Only for a Knight,* on sale now at your favorite retailer.

After saving her love from certain death, Princess Elyne returns to the Otherworld by order of her mother, Queen Maeve. But it's not the homecoming she expects. The queen is furious she has been meddling with humans and imprisons her, stripping away her magic. The only way Elyne can get her powers back is to perform one selfless act.

When Queen Maeve sends Sir Derron to find the Guardian of the ancient Sword of Light, one of the Four Treasures of the Otherworld, he can't leave without releasing Elyne. After all, she altered time to save his life in the human world. But freeing the princess comes with a steep price—he must take her with him on this dangerous quest.

Their search becomes much more than a pursuit for the missing Guardian. Dark Elf, Lord Kieran, rises to dominate the Unseelie court. He will stop at nothing to gain control of both the Otherworld and the human realm—he's murdering Guardians and stealing the sacred Treasures of the Fae. Even with the help of Elves, dragons, and their human friends, the odds are stacked against Derron and Elyne.

Can they stop Lord Kieran before he slays the queen and tears down the walls of the Otherworld?

Read more at www.michellemiles.net

About the Author

Michelle Miles believes in fairy tales, true love and magic. She is the award-winning author of the epic fantasy, IN THE TOWER OF THE WIZARD KING, as well as the fantasy romance series, REALM OF HONOR, featuring knights and their ladies fair, and the paranormal dragon-shifter romance series, DRAGON PROTECTORS.

In her spare time, she enjoys listening to music, reading, cross-stitching and watching movies. Even though she's a native Texan, she loves castles, dragons, fairies and elves and is an avid Game of Thrones fan. She can be found online at Facebook, Twitter, Instagram, Pinterest, and Goodreads.